T

H

E

N

E

W

M

A

N

The New Man

By

Jerry Cimisi

Dedicated
to the thousands of victims of September 11, 2001 and to the uncounted people who risked their lives to save others and, in those efforts, often lost their own.

THE NEW MAN

People are strange when you're a stranger

—Jim Morrison

THE NEW MAN

Tuesday, September 11, 2001

1. *Hajj*

His life was saved by the chance of being ten floors below his office at One World Trade Center when the plane struck in the bright morning. He had descended those ten floors to retrieve a co-worker's papers. Wilson had called from elsewhere in the vast office, said with resigned annoyance he was in a meeting, that he had left his attaché case at a certain company elsewhere in the building when making a business call before leaving work yesterday, and added with quick apology he needed the papers in it right away; this meeting might go on all morning; he couldn't leave. After the brief descent in the elevator, receiving the attaché case (in truth a battered old black leather bag) at a desk from someone whose face he quickly forgot, came the explosion from above.

Though there was chaos and fear enough in stomping madly down those innumerable steps, endless steps, in a flight that felt more absurd than terrifying, the survivor was unhurt, emerging in the debris and ash-strewn light and on the street—still clutching Wilson's bag—when he saw the other tower fall. In those first moments he could not—as the rest of us—quite believe the deliberate intent behind the tragedy, but abruptly, like an explosion inside himself, his psyche sensed a terrible end to something long held, and as he fled from the monoliths being consumed, chance again, in the nature of a sudden revelation, allowed him the certainty that he could entirely lose his old life and begin existence as another person, another man altogether. As the city just beyond him filled with billowing smoke and ash, and thousands of workers instantly transformed into refugees, the survivor would disappear among the inexactly counted dead.

He found himself at the edge of the Hudson, following a crowd, filled with the buzz and direction of fear. The fury and focus of the borderland between conscious intent and unconscious need had brought him to water. Soon, among the frightened, displaced hordes, the businessmen and businesswomen who had expected no more than the monotony and safe challenges of the workday, the survivor was abruptly packed in a small ferry, some vessel of succor that had miraculously appeared, to take whomever it could across the brief waters to New Jersey. This might have been his first true step of transformation.

The human cargo of the almost damned could not help but look at the great black roiling smoke of the place they had escaped, and voices cried out or cursed the surreal fate that had struck the World Trade Center and themselves and just like that had whipped itself into the marrow of a nation.

He was on a bus, going somewhere in New Jersey, sitting next to a black woman of about sixty. She had a wide face, thick black framed glasses and was dressed too warmly for the late summer's day. Vaguely, he smelled her sweat—though it was almost a subtle scent, overpowered by the smell of burning, of destruction he realized he himself carried.

The woman reminded him of the comedienne Moms Mabley, who, at the end of an unrecognized life, had been in vogue in the late '60s, her caustic ageing countenance peering from the television at millions of white people. The woman squinted, like everyone else it seemed, at the smoke of the destroyed Towers. The smoke was at once ethereal and corrupt. The black, weaving remnants of the explosions coiled on the woman's glasses, like omens in a fortuneteller's crystal. Within whatever horizon the terrible aftermath could be viewed, eyes were glued to it.

The bus was filled with radios, from boom boxes to smaller receivers of the electronic ether, magic black devices tuned to conflicting stations giving a babble of news. Scattered passengers shouted into cell phones or listened to them numbly. The word "terrorism" shot back and forth across the bus, like an old chant rediscovered. Like a prayer to herself, the woman muttered something about the "evil" God would conquer. As if in a spasm, she gestured stiffly to the sky. The survivor muttered something back to her, something he couldn't recall even as he said it, to be polite, to show that he was as upended and as suffering as anyone. But he was fleeing to freedom. On his lap, pressed against his chest, was Wilson's bag, the worn possession Wilson sardonically called his attaché case. It had the soft, giving feel of having been handled for years, and its own sweaty smell. Perhaps it was the survivor's own sweat; he had clutched it so fiercely. Its weight felt good against his body, like the protective barrier of a disguise. It had saved his life.

At the front end of the bus a disheveled man with wild hair, stubble-faced and in ragged clothes—a cliché of the homeless?—was bent over the bus driver and literally shouting:

"They're killing New York! They're killing New York!"

The driver bellowed at him to sit back down. The man, obviously affronted, cursed, grumbled but complied, plopping himself in one of the front seats, while a much more clean cut man edged away from him.

The survivor noted this as it a meaningless event in a dream. He fell into a momentary reverie, looking at the smoke of the Towers. They were distant enough now to tinge the awful spectacle of their destruction with a surreal quality. Dreams, reverie, the surreal—perhaps this was life at the moment, even more than the madness of the day.

He got off the bus in a town he did not know on a street with a common name—there was the thought that there must be a thousand streets, ten thousand streets in America with this name—and he began to walk. Perhaps he was thinking of a useless fact in order to steady his nerves. But is anything useless the psyche wishes to receive, to insert into thought? Whatever inner turmoil he bore and flight he suffered, he seemed to walk without anxiety now. He moved past the music of the clamor of the horrified voices of the city. The sweat on his back and under his arms had dried. He felt light in his stride. He felt he could move endlessly. He felt he had already shed the past.

The man at the counter in the motel was obviously Middle Eastern, with dark hair plastered over half a head of baldness. Behind him and elevated to the height where the wall met the ceiling, the TV was replaying—like the highlights of a sporting event—the plane slamming into the second tower and the collapse of each of the Towers. And then there was the gaping, smoking side of the Pentagon. The man made a little sound, as if nurturing an agony he made an effort to control.

It was from these scenes he turned to look at the entrance of the survivor. The two men, foreigners to each other, looked at one another—then, as if both needing to be relieved of the other's image, turned to the safety of those scenes on the TV.

When they faced each other again, the survivor said, simply, "I just got out of the city. I need a room."

The man behind the desk seemed dismayed and leery, the instinct of race warning him of the enmity he, being of a certain flesh, might confront. Though he did consider the man who signed the register should have seemed more shocked—at the incredible attack on his country, at the near miraculous fact of his own survival.

The truth was that the awesomeness of these once-in-a lifetime-events was less to the survivor than the astonishing fact of his freedom, even if they had been the source of it. He did not think of how many had died to "free" him. But the quiet joy liberation gave him made him kind, or rather he said kind words, at least spoke kindly to the man who covered his baldness so poorly, making remarks to the effect that the perpetrators of these acts were a breed of beings apart from any person either of them could have known.

"You just can't understand, how anyone could—"

"No, no," said the man at the desk. "To kill all those—"

It was a lie of course—who could deny that the randomness of life might bring one into contact with a serial killer, or terrorist? —but the man behind the counter was grateful to hear it. He blinked his dark eyes in a sort of relief at his appropriate exchange. The survivor even added, in the euphoria of his sudden confidence, a little more detail of how that he had "gotten out of New York. Someone from my company dropped me off—before they closed down the city. I have to wait...until—" He was saved from compounding his own lie by another replay on TV of the president, grave and earnest.

Both men of course watched this, silently.

After the President's voice and image disappeared and the screen was filled with workers from various agencies combing a field in Pennsylvania where the fourth hijacked plane had gone down, the motelkeeper asked the survivor if he had contacted his family.

"Yeah, though I had to wait until I crossed the river to do it." He added he hoped the phones, at least some phones, were still working in New Jersey, though he wanted the opposite to be the case.

"Terrible, terrible," said the man, looking back to the TV, which now showed the view down a long street, at whose dark end smoke ascended. Ash-smeared people fled or stumbled toward the camera, like creatures emerging from a malfeasant creation.

"Is there anything I can do for you?" said the motelkeeper, looking at the register. "Anything you need—Mr...Newman?"

He had signed his name: Theodore Newman. *The*odore *Newman*: The New Man. It was an ironic appellation that had suddenly come to him, like the revelation he could escape his old life. The last name was almost a cliché; and he had almost put the initials "H.E." in between the first and last names to link with the first initial of "Theodore," then, with a cleverness that made him blandly pleased, noted the first letters of that name made it unnecessary....

"I'm all right. I'm fine."

The motelkeeper had to believe anything a survivor of the disaster might tell him. The New Man left this foreigner's solicitations, the kaleidoscope of the TV, and went to his room.

The expression on his face might have been a smile were it not even more mysterious as he switched on the TV. For the moment it seemed the scenes it presented were for his eyes alone. Calmly he watched the patchwork, frenetic coverage of the disaster. President Bush. Bin Laden. A priest in the labyrinth of a hospital, gesturing to some unseen body; the priest's arm seemed to float with a weightless sorrow. A fireman in the street rubbing his eyes. The New Man understood what sights the man's fists were covering. An ash-cloaked man on an ash-layered stone bench next to an ash-cloaked tree: man and bench and tree seemed roughly carved.

The New Man sipped at some water. The plastic glass was frail in his hand; the water was a cool, deep weight. He was realizing a terrible thirst.

He stripped off his bedraggled clothes and showered. He laid himself on the bed in his underwear and slept, in the warm afternoon of September 11, 2001, as the TV went on and the images of "America Under Attack" (the networks' new and immediate consummate cry) might have been out of his own dreams, but his immediate inner life was now so strangely calm and even serenely apart from the awful world that had recreated him.

2. A Suburban Heart Considers

He awoke toward the end of the afternoon. What remained of the summer allowed enough light to give the feeling the day was long.

And had this not been one of the longest days of his life? For the hours of the beginning of metamorphosis may seem infinite.

The TV was off. He did not recall groping for the remote in his sleep, but the intimacy of the device had become so habitual to the human species; to manipulate the small rectangle in the midst of sleep or half sleep was akin to turning over during the common journey of slumber.

But now he reactivated the TV with the consciousness of one about to receive a challenge. He surfed through the flood of images, the pundits, the rescue workers, distressed family members and settled—out of guilt? fraternity?—on a collage of interviews with commuters who had been stranded in the city, and some who had not been able to get into work this apocalyptic morning; an apocalypse that was belied by the cliché of one man saying, "You just don't expect anything like this."

No, indeed, one doesn't. In bars, on the streets or in pizza parlors run by Turks or Asians the commuters expressed shock, lamented being marooned on the besieged island (for couldn't another attack be expected?). A woman in Penn Station, wearing fashionable office clothes sticking to her in the heat, questioned: "Should I stay here—and a bomb collapses the ceiling in on me?" It also seemed an accusation, directed at...*someone*, who should not have let this happen.

While on the greater island that stretched seaward toward Europe, the long island that fitted its name, the commuters who had been saved by later working schedules or simply being late (on this day the God of Procrastination would be given its due) muttered drably or agitatedly the platitudes of grief, outrage and amazement. "My God, if I had caught my regular train," said a man tugging at his loose collar, like a Rodney Dangerfield intimating that chance at least, at last, had given him some respect.

These commuters who had not gotten to the apocalypse were also in bars and eateries, caught midway between the great suburban outposts of Babylon and Huntington and Port Jefferson and the vast, wounded metropolis. With train service severed until who knew when, they awaited wives and husbands to come and pick them up, return them to their suburban sprawl, their cookie cutter developments, their McMansions, their bright lawns worked by enterprising Hispanics: the neighborhoods of malls, the commercial strips of Sunrise Highway and Route 110—where Walt Whitman, the singular poet of "multitudes," had, ironically, a giant clogged roadway and mall named after him.

These were the kin of the survivor, of The New Man.

His life had indeed been suburban. Watching his spiritual (or dispirited) brethren on television, he thought about it, bit by bit, slowly, almost carefully, like a tide inching up a beach, withdrawing, inching up a bit farther upon the old, old sand.

He had grown up in the suburbs of Long Island, and he had spent his adulthood there, crossing the latitudinal stretch of the land deposited by the glaciers of the last Ice Age to earn the money in New York to earn the upper middle class dream of spacious homes, garages, lawns, the cars, and all the suburban amenities for the family. As if he turned the pages of a photo album (he was of an age in which he drew connections to photographs more than videos), his memory settled on vignettes of himself and his wife and growing children by some poolside, making light talk with company and giving readymade smiles to the lens. The faces of his wife and children at once so clear and yet also the masks of un-beings. Yes, the masks were clear. Barbeques in which a neighbor in a Hawaiian shirt or a T-shirt bearing the logo of some team plopped the sizzling meat on a wide, white paper plate, and the survivor, in that so recently forsaken life, took his portion of the ritual feast back to a sun dappled table. (Thinking of that, an actual hunger caused him to salivate, and he clenched his throat as if controlling a vice.) And the vistas of streets, the towns, the masses of leafed or unleafed trees, speeding by the train on the way into the city, or during his return, a homecoming effected sometimes in darkness, sometimes in light. How many times had he made that redundant journey? How many miles had the crossed? "I could have been to the moon," he laughed softly out loud to himself, the declaration of someone who admits he had surrendered for so long to the absurd. An absurd journey that had reached no destination, he saw now, which had settled nothing in his being. And, yes, the homecoming, the deep, unsettled atmosphere of the family, in which he had played his role as breadwinner well enough, had been attentive well enough to wife and children, but finally had not been able to grasp something essential of their spirits and so they had not grasped or seen into the equal portion of his.

The family. Here, on TV, a man called his wife, but the survivor, The New Man, did not call his. His son and daughter were in appropriately expensive colleges, one in Boston, the other in Virginia, and he wondered at what point in their day the news had reached them (it had reached everywhere almost instantly, hadn't it?). He tried to imagine them paused with worry as they watched the replays of the collapse of the Towers. And his wife, called to the national hearth of the electronic screen, was she on some phone now, distraught in her loveless way, seeking information that might prove him alive?

He had not loved her in a long while as she had not loved him in a long while. Or rather love, first the enticement and the pleasure, had become something more complex, certainly disturbing, then as necessary and onerous as some sort of tax, without whose application life could not have been supported but whose levy could be despised. It was not an unusual story.

One thought of tides again; the tide of a passion retreating, returning slightly, retreating more, a cycle repeating until a great stretch of arid beach was exposed and became, on the coast of their marriage, the normal, unwatered terrain, no longer a beach with tides but a desert, visited or rather inhabited by a man and woman's damaged emotions, regrets and omnipresent, repressed longings that touched this world in distant sight, like thin frail clouds overhead in the blazing, callous sky. Longings that grew into the calm of resignation and habit.

A reporter stuck a microphone into the face of another man calling his wife on a cell phone. The man coughed—from an ingestion of the dust of debris and an excess of emotion—a declaration: "I'm OK. I love you."

It was just what "the news" wanted. The New Man wondered if this survivor spoke a true feeling. Of course catastrophes often made false feelings true.

A week ago, perhaps a little more, in bed with his wife, the man who had preceded him, the old New Man, had looked into her eyes as she had looked into his. Their bodies had fallen alongside each other after what had became the sporadic—even rare—occasion of sex and their faces had exchanged a smile. Now, at the end of this day of warm September, as the TV went from declarations of the displaced on cell phones to, once again, the burning Towers, the hordes in their flight from the city, The New Man imagined himself and his wife in some bed in some room in the Towers that morning, on the floors above the burning, the look being exchanged between them the lie of a satisfaction attempting to deny the catastrophe that burned below and which would soon consume them. This was a terrible image to him, filled with too long a history of truth, and he recoiled from it, trying to re-imagine the sad lovers (almost as if he were not one of them) in a room in the height of a building in Brooklyn or Queens, watching from across the river the Towers burning, rote eroticism stayed by this herald of the collapse of empire. His spirit, damaged, bitter, and not a little selfish, was trying to remove both himself and his wife from the apex of a hell. But, as the Twin Towers had done that morning, this escape imploded, collapsed, its rubble strewn throughout his denial and his heart. He tried to close it all by saying aloud, as if she were in this room in New Jersey with him, "We'll both survive and go on."

3. Dead Presidents; By Any Means Necessary

Something from the flood of the news of the day came back to him. The majority of the ATMs in the metro area were down. He counted the money in his wallet: $144. He counted it a second time. It would not go far. The New Man cursed himself quietly. Or cursed reality. Perhaps for the first time he understood the logistics of what he would have to undergo in order to assume a new identity. No: not a new identity, a new life.

In the spring of 2000 ("God, a year and a half ago," he thought) he had for some weeks gone through a spike in his normally dull angst, a spike sharp enough to make him tangibly entertain just how he might leave it all. He had established some money in an account his wife knew nothing about. He had gotten a bonus he had never mentioned at home. His escape money.

Why not just divorce? He would never admit it to himself—at least he hadn't, for years—but divorce was a confrontation he could not face. And he could not face the fact of this cowardice. Though perhaps had he lived a different life, one of less dullness and pretense, he would have been less the coward. But all this is unknown.

At any rate, that spring the pull of the normal had tugged him away from escape, and he had remained in the routine of his life—and paid his psychic taxes.

Now, finally, he would escape. No: he *had* escaped. Now he would use the money.

But he would have to have *some* sort of identity…. He pondered the as yet unknown to him process of getting an ID within the undercurrents of a trade that had certainly flourished in the last decades of the just departed millennium as more and more illegals had swarmed into the country. Ironic that he too now would be a seeker—a beggar—in that torrent, face the etching out of a new illicit place among American society. Though was it illicit? Was it against the law to become—The New Man?

On TV, they were talking about the backgrounds of the hijackers: all Arab, it seemed. The New Man paused. *Already* the guilty were known? Or were the zealous authorities merely branding everyone with an Arabic name who had been on the manifest of the four hijacked planes? As he considered the possibility of xenophobia and even government skullduggery, he recalled that in the years at his job for the highly successful import/export firm (which now in an instant had become nonexistent), he had not only heard stories but had come across evidence of the dishonesty of governments. Not that he had discovered any bodies, but certainly he had been presented with machinations to which no government would admit.

"It's in the interests of trade," said a colleague. "It gives people jobs."

True, The New Man considered, as the face of Osama bin Laden filled the TV screen. The still portrait, the quiet dark eyes, the long homely bearded face that might have been one of El Greco's images, the face in fact that seemed quite gentle, was replaced with a brief video of the jihad's guerilla leader at some training camp for terrorists (the viewer was informed) in the outback badlands of Afghanistan—the country that had suffered under the Mongols, the

British, the Soviets and which, apparently, if emerging "official" rumors were correct, would soon suffer under the millennial might of the United States of America.

Bin Laden gently brandished some sort of automatic weapon, its dark polished surface having the rich glint of an accessory in a fine home; though this home was a place for deadly things. And yet there was this smile from the man, a smile that bordered on a laugh as he crouched and aimed the weapon at some unseen object. He might have been a humor-seeking Marx Brother, posing with fake beard and Bedouin getup, camping it up as the terrorist who would bring down the high-tech, infidel West.

In the next moment bin Laden was replaced by a newscaster who was plainly a minion of that West, the white, unbearded face talking about the damage at the Pentagon and then thrusting the microphone at a military man who had been inside when the plane hit. Tall, broad, with a blond buzz cut, the officer related that after hearing about the World Trade Center, he had joked with a comrade, "I guess we're next." In the bizarre fulfillments of the day careless predictions of disaster had come to pass.

But the face of bin Laden, the scion of a rich Saudi family turned warrior for Allah, rested persistently before The New Man's inner vision—and was reflected on the next channel to which he turned. Here was a tunnel of electronic fun house mirrors, a portrait repeated. Within that flesh was—the declaration of the day went—the mind that had hurled those planes at those Towers, exploded the life from thousands of bodies; estimates of the death toll were ranging above 5,000. The New Man found himself peering into the eyes on that screen, trying to decipher the mad insistent evil brilliance of this lone man.

.   .   .

Bin Laden was replaced by the smoking skies where the Towers had stood. But as he regarded the ravaged rubble of this aftermath, The New Man's thoughts drifted back to the finances of his position. Credit cards. Identification. He looked again at the bills in his wallet. The six redundant Andrew Jacksons (who had practiced his own religious wars, on the American Redman), one Hamilton (cut down through the chance of personal violence), two Lincolns (a face as calm as bin Laden's, but more sorrowed, wiser; *he* had waged a war of the innumerable dead) and the four bills with Washington (whose white "do" suggested the coiffeur of an elder among The Three Stooges), were a sort of identification, he reflected. The government used the face of dead presidents to announce a promise of payment—

He shook his head. Where was his mind going? Well, it went to the motelkeeper—because The New Man was abruptly linking this low-end hotelier of foreign extraction to someone with connections to black market IDs. A bit of racial profiling to be sure. But The New Man did suddenly consider confiding in this man, imagined himself leaning close over that counter and spelling out his predicament in a low, sincere voice, the voice of man who bravely sought spiritual cleansing, a divestiture of all his earthly past.

In another moment he was reigning himself in. To confide in someone who oversaw the hideaway in which he, The New Man, had sought as the first sanctuary in The New Life? That would be very, very careless. Confidences—if any—would come with those who would be there an instant and then forever departed. Then, more strongly, he told himself, there should be no confidences at all, period.

He bluntly resolved to take care of what needed to be taken care of, in any way necessary, while maintaining his secret.

His attention was caught by the small black leather bag he had carried down from the vast height of the World Trade Center. With a sort of masculine flippancy, Wilson had always referred to it as his attaché case. On the floor, it leaned against the wall just below and to the side of a window in which the smoking signature of Manhattan billowed in these last hours of the day. If the old New Man hadn't gone those ten flights down to fetch it…. It was uncomfortable to face salvation by brute chance. And yet, this was perhaps his first "truth" as The New Man.

He went over to the bag, grasped the handle, raised it with a feeling—and a remembrance—of its weight. It had slapped against him a thousand times as he had fled downward, all those flights to the street, but he had not been aware of still clutching it at the time. Why had he not just flung it aside, as an encumbrance? Had he felt an unconscious responsibility to finish carrying out his favor to Wilson? Would he have flung it aside if the bag had been his? Memory told him there had been other men clutching their attaché cases. One tries to bring as much of one self along in any emergency—any escape.

Suddenly it came to him—at least consciously: *Wilson is dead.* Why hadn't the thought occurred to him before? He shrugged, a gesture more resigned than callous. Yes, Wilson was gone. No one could have survived on that floor.

All the better for me, I guess, he thought. This bitter reality was a perverse gift—from whom? From what? The New Man was not the fool who would thank chance and he lacked the belief to thank God.

As he hefted the bag it seemed heavier than he had remembered it. Well, he was worn from the day; at the beginning of his flight there had been the strength of the adrenaline rush of the need to escape death.

He placed the bag on the bed, unzipped it, though not before brushing a residue of fine dust, ash, whatever, from it; a residue that might have been the object's own "memory" of escape. The New Man found the bag stuffed full of papers. In those first instants these pages had meaning only in that they had been the reason for his survival. If Wilson had not called…there would be, now, no New Man.

If he had gotten to the elevator to go back up to his office a few moments earlier; or had the plane hit a moment later….

Throughout the long day, which now seemed like a year, he had not thought of that instant of impact until right now, near sundown. He recalled rocking, swaying, holding the bag, not knowing what was going on. He had been informed in very short order by the osmosis through which events outside one's physical realm are brought across the connected chaos of disparate groups of human beings. Informed, not precisely, but enough to know he was in peril. And he had turned from the elevator, whose heartbeat light still blinked on the wall, but believing with an instinct he did not question the cry of some voice that yelled, "It's not working!" and had sought the stairways, clutching the bag.

Now, as he removed some mundane business papers from the maw of the dark, worn leather, he thought that if on one hand it was the mark of his salvation, it was also a weight from his other life. He should have dropped it off in the debris and ash of lower Manhattan. Then he had the sort of paranoid—and practical— revelation he'd just had concerning credit cards and ID. If he disposed of it here, in New Jersey, and it were found….

The New Man, angry at himself (for no rational reason), and the unforeseen difficulties of disappearing, slapped the bag off the bed. It thudded on the old, faded carpet and a long rippled tongue of papers and folders fanned out from the dark interior.

The New Man stood looking down at this oddly neat display. He glanced back to the window, at the smoking sky now in dimming light. He sighed. A more immediate concern struck him. He was hungry. He'd had a hurried, skimpy breakfast so many hours ago—ages ago, in his old life. Now his psyche as well as his body wanted food again. He left the room, the pages of Wilson's effects like the train of a décor that had been incongruously placed.

4. Dining Out

The motelkeeper was looking up at the TV behind the counter, so he presented the back of his partially bald head. On the screen was something The New Man had already been presented with several times that day: crowds of celebrants in some Middle eastern country (no American broadcaster seemed sure exactly where), joyous, shouting, waving Palestinian flags. One woman seemed a particularly exuberant flag waver. Her body was hidden in traditional grab, save for half of the face, where very western glasses sat broadly on her nose as she gave forth with the rapid yipping cry that signifies a special fanaticism in that culture. An American reporter's voice was saying, "It's hard to believe, to conceive these people are actually celebrating the tragedy—"

The New Man watched the motelkeeper watching the TV. In a moment the other turned to The New Man. "I am ashamed of those people."

The New Man wondered if this were sincere or not. Who could know? He might have believed his "resurrection" had gained him heightened senses, an intuition sharper than the dull weight of the past, but the reality was otherwise. If he had some new perception, he was not habituated to it enough to wield it.

He said to the man, "Where are you from?"

The other might have taken that as a threat, but answered with no hesitation. "Saudi Arabia. That was my father's country. My mother"—he looked back to the TV—"was from Afghanistan."

It was a perfect Hollywood background for this Middle Eastern man in America on this day of September 11, 2001. His father from the natural country of bin Laden, his mother of the country in which bin Laden had created himself.

The motelkeeper went on: "This is terrible. It will be hard for us, for any of these countries, now. People" (The New Man had had the abrupt worry the man would say "you people") "will hate us. They will certainly be…" (he chose the euphemism) "suspicious."

The New Man made a gesture with his hands to show that he at least was not suspicious. But he must say something. "What is your name?"

"Ahmed."

A common enough name from that part of the world. The New Man tried not to hesitate in reply. "I'm…Theo—Theodore. But I guess you know that." He nodded to the registration book.

Ahmed gave it a glance that seemed to say he would not pry into another man's business even to look at his name—though he had addressed his guest earlier as "Mr. Newman."

"Call me Ted." He was painfully aware how artificial this sounded, how obvious that he was trying to act natural.

Ahmed stuck out his hand. The New Man shook it: the first flesh he had touched in his new life—the hand of a foreigner, ignorant of The New Man's transformation.

"And you got out of there," said Ahmed, looking back to the TV that once more showed the infernally smoldering ruins. The ruins might already be appearing like the logo of an event rather than evidence of the event.

"I'm lucky, very lucky," said The New Man. But he did not feel lucky at all. He felt himself at great risk. "I got out of the city right away. I knew I'd be stuck there if I didn't."

"Were you afraid there would be more attacks?"

Actually he had not thought of that once. Just of getting away from the collapsed past. But he lied: "Of course; you didn't know…."

"Your family must be relieved. Astonished." Ahmed's eyes were wide, ready to receive "Mr. Newman's" agreement.

"Yes. Yes. I said they were on the west coast—" Had he in fact said that before? With relief he saw Ahmed nod. Ahmed did not ask why The New Man's family was on the west coast while he worked on the other side of the continent. If he did ask, The New Man could just say they were on a vacation, that he had been unable to go with them due to work. Meanwhile, he was saying, "But I might have to stay here a few days." He wanted to make up a less vague excuse for not moving on.

He did not need one, as Ahmed said, "Yes, no planes, all over the country. Only military in the sky. It is like war."

Bin Laden's face returned to the screen. The New Man and Ahmed stared. Bin Laden was once more giving his shy, Mona Lisa smile.

"Where can I get something to eat around here?" asked The New Man. It was an easy thing to pronounce, but this question, coming from a need that was not a lie, seemed to make Ahmed regard The New Man cautiously, as if now he sensed something not quite right. Though almost immediately the motelkeeper said, "Go outside, at the end of the block"—he gestured toward the right—"cross the street. On the next block, same side, there is a good place. You'll find something there."

This last sentence had a curious ring to it: as if among the food offered in this establishment only here and there would The New Man find something to his liking.

He thanked Ahmed, went out onto the street, shutting the door on the apocalyptic infomercial the TV had become.

Twilight was settling in. The dim east was smoky with destruction. In the brighter west, still vivid in the aftermath of sunset, the sky had the poignancy of a farewell. After walking a hundred feet or so The New Man realized he was not only crossing the border of day into night, but the border of the familiar. The streets were thronged with people of predominantly Middle Eastern descent, with a fair sampling of what appeared to be the relocated peoples of what had once been called the Indian subcontinent. He had not noticed this at all when arriving at the motel. Perhaps there had been less people out then. Or more likely that he had been so involved in his flight—passage: from the past and present to…?

Arabs, Indians…crowds that moved in front of shops that had the air of a marketplace of some Hollywood movie from decades ago. For many were dressed in the clothes they would have worn had they been in their native countries, halfway round the world. Men in billowing pants and long shirts worn outside the pants that came down to the knees; women with shawl-like costumes and covered heads; men with turbans, fezzes…. But any Hollywood version of exotica was never quite accurate—and perhaps The New Man's interpretation of this "reality" was stunted by his own cultural limits. He was immersed in a foreignness that he sought to identity and catalogue. Many of the shops had letters in both English and Arabic—and other languages. Some shops lacked English all together in their signs. Through the windows of these shops The New Man could see that the shopkeepers inside were of the same racial brew as the crowds outside. He seemed the only "white" on this block. "There goes the neighborhood," he joked, actually saying this out loud; but his displaced spirit did not feel amused. He was invaded with a sense for which he had no personal or historical perspective. An Englishman walking amidst one of the Crown's colonies a century ago would have known this—but not have felt as displaced as The New Man. That Englishman would have had to walk in the tumult of some Congo forty years ago to know a similar sensation.

The New Man reached the small restaurant, its neon name in Arabic across the front window. In the middle of the window, in smaller letters, in softer neon, was the apparent translation: "The Traveller's Rest." (Curious that there was the double "l", like the English would use.) An odd name. And all too ominously appropriate for The New Man, who had the sensation that he was being, well, watched, about to be found out.

At any rate, he was a traveller in need of rest, food—and other things.

He went inside and instantly felt many eyes turn to him. As his race marked him out on the street, it did in here. A young, dark haired lovely woman in smart western clothes (yes, he was starting to translate this environment to himself as if he were in another country) conducted him to a table, smiling curiously at him. She wore a perfume that made him think not of flowers but stones, rocks in a hot light. For a moment he regarded her with a sudden loss of the situation and his place within it; the appearance of beauty has this peculiarity….

He was thankful the table was not in the middle of the crowded place but off to the side, and set in a somewhat dimmer realm. He felt a peculiar safety in being on the periphery. And he was thankful that the menu was in three languages, English being one of them.

Though he looked at it without comprehension at first. He was becoming frightened. He had wanted to lose himself in the vast country of America, in the vast country of the future. How could he lose himself in this neighborhood?

Or in this time. The ubiquitous TV, a totem intent on a plethora of images, blared further scenes of the day's carnage. The New Man's eyes, among these many foreign eyes, could not help but turn to these changing but connected visions. And he resented this pull. The destruction of the World Trade Center was the chaos from which had come his freedom; but to have to witness it over and over again, or at least its aftermath, seemed like a telltale glaring clue, even an accusation, by which he might be found out. The universe might have been saying: *This will be shown until someone notes your escape—*

Apparently another patron or two had a problem with the loud, insistent coverage. A voice in a foreign tongue shouted out and then another, seeming to agree with whatever the first said, and the smiling pretty dark haired woman lowered the volume on the TV so that one could not hear it at all in the soft din of the restaurant. With the lack of sound, The New Man could suffer the images that remained as somehow disconnected from—from what? The now redundant commentary, but something else, too.

He pushed himself away from the allure of visual destruction and sought to tend to his hunger—which now insisted on his attentions more than the day's events. But the menu's English was not so helpful after all. Yes, as Ahmed had said, he would find "something" amidst this offering of foreign dishes. Yet if the selections were in English, most of them he had never heard of. He thought of asking the waitress for help, but did not want to call attention to himself. He scanned the menu again, trying to imagine what this or that dish was; eventually he did find some that were not entirely foreign to his experience.

The waitress returned. Her smile was less curious and so more pleasant as he ordered. And The New Man had melded the aspect of her beauty into the ordinariness of her job. She noted his selections with a manner that intimated his presence was not at all strange.

As he waited for his meal, and his hunger, unfed now over the long flight of the day, began to truly gnaw at him, he began to listen to the talk of the small crowd. There was enough English among other tongues to hear the expected: about New York, the Pentagon, the plane crashing in a field in

Pennsylvania—a voice asserted: "The government shot it down. It was going right to Bush." There was an earnest wave of babble in various tongues. From those who spoke in English or at least occasionally did so, there seemed to be a general consensus this terrorism was to be condemned, but a distinct faction voiced cynical opinions. "America only cares if it loses its business, not its people." "They thought they were safe. It's only the Palestinians who get their houses knocked down." "They think because it's a city of big buildings it can't fall."

Now and then a face glanced at The New Man. He avoided these looks. But forced himself to stare back at one very dark skinned man with a thick moustache who studied The New Man with the caution of an anthropologist. The man soon averted his look. The New Man felt a tired triumph, the sensation of solving an annoying difficulty—though one which he would have to face again.

The waitress came with his food, her pleasing face giving no evidence that any unpleasantness existed in the room. She refilled his water glass with an elegance, a smoothness of motion he found captivating. He had not recalled drinking that much water since sitting down. In truth, he had been scorched and parched from the compressive fury of the day

She left with her smile; he began to eat. The food and his hunger were complementary partners. For a while he gave attention to nothing but his belly.

Two soldiers dressed in camouflage uniforms entered the restaurant. They were young and black. There was a distinct pause, at least a broken sort of lull to the babble in the room. The New Man had the sensation a catastrophe was about to break out. –Or that "they" had come for him. But then one of the soldiers called out to a waiter: "Mahmoud—!" and a tall, gaunt middle-aged man came to the soldiers and gave a quiet, friendly greeting. He led them to a table. The soldier who'd summoned the waiter kept talking, a bit too loudly, and The New Man learned they were from a National Guard base just outside the town. But would two members of the National Guard be dining out in the "Arabic quarter" on this night of September 11? And then The New Man said to himself: Like I am?

The talkative one was directing his companion's attention to the menu. "I had this shit in Desert Storm. I was all over: Kuwait, Egypt. Some of it's weird, but I know what's good—"

Desert Storm? The young soldier should have been a boy then. Well, perhaps he had been eighteen and was now a young looking twenty-eight. As The New Man continued to study the soldiers, he saw the quieter one was indeed younger looking than the other. Food was brought and the talkative soldier dug in with gusto, his companion following more cautiously, but soon with apparent satisfaction. The New Man returned to his own dinner.

But in a moment he looked up and saw the older soldier walking toward him. The New Man's heart constricted. And felt utterly choked when the soldier said to him, "Excuse me, sir, don't I know you—?"

Was it the look of horror on The New Man's face or a genuine sharper perception of memory that made the solider say, just as he reached the table, "Oh, I'm sorry, sir. You looked like an officer I knew, in the Gulf War."

Perhaps this still young black man linked everything to that decade-old moment of American glory. The New Man, attempting not to show his infinite relief, said, "No, I was never in Desert Storm."

"Sorry to bother you."

"That's all right."

But, mistaken identity over with, the soldier suddenly peered at The New Man as if really seeing him. "I guess you've never been here before." He said it in a very friendly manner, but The New Man felt threatened.

He said, "I'm from New York."

"New York?" the soldier repeated, questioning, though with awe.

"I got out—"

"Were you—?"

"I was in the first building that got hit." Why was he telling this truth? Because he had the instinct the truth would best help him hide?

If The New Man had spoken softly enough, several diners nearby had heard (their attention had already been focused on this meeting of two men who did not, racially, belong here) and stared at The New Man with surprise or sympathy stealing over earlier expressions of distrust.

The soldier exploded loudly and called over to his companion, "This guy was in the Towers!"

So the entire restaurant stared at The New Man. There was a hush. He was on stage. He stammered softly, ostensibly speaking to the soldier, but really to the wider audience that listened. "I was low enough below the fire. Though it was still a long way down…." (The first sentence was to assert his luck; the second, to assert that he was worthy enough to struggle for it.) "The city was closing up. I got across the river. I have to wait—" He stopped, the faces of the two soldiers, the faces of the relocated Muslim world upon him. He seized the only escape route available. "I don't want to talk about it now."

Who could argue with that? With genuine sympathy and embarrassment the soldier took a few steps back. "Sorry, man, sure." He returned to his seat in an almost reverential manner. Gradually, very gradually the faces in the room turned from The New Man; they would allow him, after he had nearly been killed, to collect himself. While The New Man had to collect himself for another reason. He looked down at his food.

As conversation returned to the room it was softer, and more indecipherable; certainly his presence—and story—had altered the tenor of the atmosphere. Less English was being spoken. He had the distinct feeling that derogatory remarks directed against America had been checked for the moment. The crowd let The New Man eat in whatever peace was possible, and he did indeed eat, if somewhat uncomfortably, but also with the thought that he had overcome, successfully, a hurdle.

When he finished, paid his bill and left the dark haired waitress her tip, this woman who had soothed him with her manner, he felt he had been subject to the involuntary metamorphosis of being sequestered in the cocoon of tragedy. As he rose to leave, the restaurant became even quieter. It had been as if, after being identified (no pun intended), the diners had given him the courtesy of not informing him he should be a dead man. As indeed, in a very real way, he was.

As the door of the Traveller's Rest closed behind him, he sensed rather than heard the increased din the release of his departure had allowed. A man who had passed through catastrophe had been among them. The New Man began to walk back to the motel. If he ever returned to this restaurant he would have to consume his meals in the glare of an event he was using for transformation.

During the short walk back he thought of the soldiers. *I could have told them I wasn't in Desert Storm, but in Vietnam.* But he had not wanted to foster any camaraderie of arms.

Desert Storm. There seemed a strange cycle of things. Or not so strange. They say history repeats itself. He could recall that evening a little more than ten and a half years ago, in 1991, watching on TV the beginning of the attack on Saddam's forces in Kuwait. From early August, 1990, George Bush—Bush I— had manipulated an international coalition against the dictator of Iraq. Now Bush II would be gathering global acquiescence to seek the elusive but palpable enemies planning redundant destruction from their (alleged) Afghan redoubts. Luckily for the second Bush there was, as for Bush I, a clear face (right out of Central Casting) for the villain behind it all: then Saddam, now bin Laden—

And with a serendipity that abruptly shocked The New Man, just as he reached the motel, a page of a newspaper, twisted like a Möbius strip by a warm wind, blew across his path, unraveling then concealing then unraveling the face of bin Laden, the long, calm, bearded El Greco face that had sent determined maniacs for Mohammed out into the technological hell of the West.

The New Man picked up the newspaper page and straightened it out. It was an Arabic paper. He could read the date, but understand none of the text. It was today's paper—and it was chilling coincidence that bin Laden was pictured. Of course a paper dated today could have none of today's news…. A late edition? He didn't think so…. What would this paper be saying tomorrow, of today's news so spectacularly wrought by this man?

Would America seek him out as vigorously as they had chased Saddam out of Kuwait? Clinton had tried to bomb bin Laden's camp in Afghanistan in 1998, along with that "chemical" factory in Sudan, but Osama had lived to fight again.

The New Man thought that the success of Desert Storm might give America too much confidence going into this operation, never mind that the experts, only a few hours into the upheaval of the day, were already predicting rough going. Afghanistan had repelled the British and the Soviets (with a little help from the USA, ironically: "The enemy of my enemy is my friend," the Arabs say). A hard land where farmers still used oxen, which had known invasions and civil wars, now oppressed by the theocratic Taliban, a land that might not yield so easily to Patriot missiles, laser weapons and smart bombs.

With the light, soiled weight of the page of newsprint in his hand, The New Man wondered if the Desert Storm veteran at the restaurant would soon be tracking across the mountains of Afghanistan and find there a more complicated horror, one so old and entrenched it would suffocate the new invader. That American foot soldier of the millennium might also reflect that for all the "success" of Desert Storm, Saddam remained in power—and a year and a half after the Gulf War, Bush I was defeated for re-election. Then again, as The New Man looked at the Arabic signs on now closed stores, he noted that to serve leaders who must pass from the scene after a brief rule is the grace of democracy.

The streets seemed less crowded on his return to the motel than they had before sundown. Well, this was natural. The New Man was glad for the lessening of human traffic—and yet it made him involuntarily a bit leery of any figures that did appear. On his way to the restaurant he had seen many people, both men and woman, in foreign dress, but now it seemed that every single figure on the street, every dark pedestrian outline wore the costume of another country, another culture—even another time. It was as if with the dark The New Man had thoroughly entered a world daytime had only threatened. Perhaps this was only the result of his now strained imagination, the necessary paranoia of the fugitive.

Yet his imagination would not have the pained luxury of working too long; he was nearing the motel. Though before reaching it he was arrested by the sight of a tall, dark silhouette, dressed in what seemed the garb of the desert, flowing robe and burnoose, standing in front of an appliance store where a bank of televisions, turned to different channels, played, without sound, a collage of the day's events. The face of the president, the planes hitting the Towers, the cautious expression of Colin Powell, the celebrants of the America-hating world, a family in a hovel in Afghanistan. The damaged *Cole* of last year in the waters of a Yemeni harbor, a close up of bin Laden blinking slowly, saint-like, the burning Pentagon, a soot covered man interviewed in New York. And the kaftan-shrouded figure stood there, his back to The New Man, taking all this in, the panoply of images a cacophony to the eyes of The New Man; but this foreign watcher of the West's gathering of terrible news seemed calmed into stillness—or expectancy?—by what he saw.

The New Man walked on.

At the motel, there was a temptation to go in through the front, at the registration desk, to have contact with Ahmed again—assuming that Ahmed still stood watch at this hour, while the TV played the disaster over and over again behind him. But perhaps The New Man did not want to face another TV of indiscriminate images. He went into the courtyard of the motel and climbed the steps to his room. The key did not fit into the lock right away; his hand trembled. He had the abrupt fear he had lost even the past of this afternoon. Then his hand, key and lock coalesced and he was inside the room—and grateful to be so.

5. Wilson's Bag

He had left the lamp on by the bed. It was not bright enough to flood the room; it made a shelter of light on the bed. He did not flick on the overhead light. He went to that vague cone of lamplight and that place of rest.

The New Man sat on the bed, picked up the remote from the night table, hesitated over whether he wanted to see—and hear—that collage the desert-dressed figure had studied outside the appliance store. Then he looked over the side of the bed. He had forgotten: the bag and its spilled papers lay on the floor. The fan of papers was like the display of a delicate arrangement: almost Japanese.

With a profanity that was a sigh he bent over and picked up a few of the sheets.

There were business letters to and from Wilson, lists of products exported and received—shoes, radios, concrete…. An incessant list of things: artifacts. The New Man had the nearly mystic revelation (mystic but common; though, if common, profound) that these artifacts of ours were ultimately useless. Or perhaps what he meant was: temporal. Had he not seen at least the suggestion of every imaginable object strewn over the streets of lower

Manhattan, defiled and covered with ash? A bicycle wheel, a shoe, a woman's jacket, a piece of a table—on and on.

He bent over, grunting, to pick up the rest of the papers—to straighten up, to put this nonsense of the past—yes, the past—out of the way.

Then, when he had it all on the bed he laughed to himself. Had he not been saved by this? He had done the favor of retrieving this effluvia and thus, at the end of the day, was alive.

Chance.

So perhaps his new life was due more to chance than to premeditation.

He began to put the papers in the bag—and was suddenly struck by what he saw on one page, and then in the text that continued on to the following sheet, and the next.

Abruptly he was rapidly scanning one page after the other, astonished to the point of profanity again: this time fierce, loud obscenities that might have carried to any ear outside of his room—and then he fell abruptly silent, the silence of the TVs in the appliance store windows, the silence that bears the flood of many sights. He looked into the dimness in the corner of the room. Finally he spoke once more to himself, muttering, "I don't believe this." He said it weakly; and, despite denial, he was possessed by resignation—knowing that some new truth he had entered had displaced all disbelief.

The first pages that had arrested The New Man described CIA backing of the Mujahideen against the Soviets in Afghanistan in the 1980s.

It was a document that began like an historical text; for the briefest moment The New Man thought this no more than background information Wilson or someone else had dredged up as pertinent to doing business in a certain political climate; but the text evolved into such particulars that The New Man had to believe this was either utter fantasy or utter truth.

A report from a nameless U.S. government writer read: "I have to say I found it disturbing or at least ironic that while we attempt to interrupt international flows of narcotics, in *some* cases in Afghanistan we not only look the other way, but a few of our agents actually bring pounds of good dope to the Mujahideen. It seems many of them like to be a bit stoned before they go into battle. I can't say this is looked upon with favor by the apparently rigidly pious Muslims who lead them, but I guess that here too the higher-ups look the other way to get a job done."

Another report, equally anonymous: "There were suspicions—and incredulity—when this young man bin Laden showed up, just graduated from school in Saudi Arabia. He had studied civil engineering. He offers not just himself but his money—millions. His family runs a construction company in Saudi Arabia—a billion dollar business. The father came from Yemen as a bricklayer, somehow became friends with the king (that alone is fantastic) and wound up with contracts to build roads and holy shrines. Osama bin Laden is one of fifty plus children—Daddy Laden's wealth made him wealthy with wives. The father died in a plane crash near San Antonio, Texas, in 1968. (Did we—or anyone else—have anything to do with this? Just asking….) Bin Laden inherited millions. Did the other sons—I hear there were twenty-four—get as rich?

"Anyway, bin Laden shows up in Afghanistan, with not only his money but the backing of rich Arabs—daddy's connections?

ours?—and the Mujahideen have the backing of millionaires, got roads built, get munitions, etc. The Arab world wants to get the godless Soviets out of this territory as much as we do. You can almost feel sorry for the Russians. It's becoming their Vietnam."

On another page The New Man found: "Last week I spoke to a French agent who'd spent some time with bin Laden. (What are the French doing here? They complain about everyone, are reluctant to support anyone, but they are everywhere. Then again, they seem to have some attachment to the Arab. That Camus thing?) He told me bin Laden said he had believed he had understood the words of The Prophet, the will of Allah when very young, had strayed from piety as a youth (no unusual tale, really) in the flesh pits of Beirut (I can think of better— safer—places to carouse) but that now he was becoming pure again. Well, a few million bucks make the road to Mecca a lot easier.

"So between bin Laden, other wealthy Arabs, stoned Mujahideen, and a mountainous country, the Soviets will be here a while. As I guess we will be."

The New Man slapped the pages down on the bed. How the hell did Wilson come by all this? What did he have to *do* with it? The New Man's imagination put together a scenario in which the company that had employed both himself and Wilson had been used in some way by the CIA for its international connections. But it seemed like the stuff of a cheap movie.

Though the pages that followed brought the matter somewhat beyond the material of a Hollywood potboiler. The New Man was discovering a psyche and a psychology here which popular thrillers never reached—something of a cross between Conrad's *Heart of Darkness* and the interior perambulations of Henry James.

"The following is unconfirmed but it should be passed on. It may be true. If it is not it still displays a mindset that at once denies this 'legend' and yet feeds from it. Allegedly it took place in 1977. It could have been a year earlier or the year after. Bin Laden is on some youthful escapade in Beirut—he's twenty, twenty-one. In the bed of a prostitute—the story usually goes she was sleeping after the act; some version put it just before dawn, the end of her working day—in her bed bin Laden sits bolt upright and hears a divine command. He leaves without paying her. (How did she act? Was she angered or submissive?) Bin Laden returns to all the holy things he learned as a child. The Soviets invade Afghanistan in December, 1979. Bin Laden goes there as part of his divine mission."

So like a lot of people bin Laden was getting it on in the '70s, thought The New Man. He read on: "It should be noted that a popular version of the story has the prostitute of foreign origin, at least with some mix of European. Part French, go some versions."

So the French were indeed "everywhere," thought The New Man. They preceded us in Vietnam, and now a half French whore leads bin Laden into Soviet Afghanistan and then to the jihad beyond.

The writer added: "I just realized—isn't it just before dawn or at dawn they are supposed to pray? His 'divine call' was probably only the local call to prayer. Anyway, it's fitting, right?"

The New Man ran a hand over his eyes, for a moment picturing that long bearded body enwrapt in the limbs of a woman. And (perhaps the strain of flight had made him delusional) he thought he could almost smell the sweat of two sexual bodies. He was repulsed at the force of his own imagination and cast away the images and its olfactory intrusion.

Another report: "We debriefed a wealthy westernized—at least sympathetic to the West—Saudi woman who knew bin Laden when he came back from Afghanistan. There had been talk of him marrying her. It would have been advantageous to both families. But it seems the woman—and her family—were untraditional and would not be forced into the match. She said that one night during the Gulf War there was some gathering at her parents' home and bin Laden was there and he pointed out the window to where the sky was lit by explosives. He told her, 'That is the light of Satan.' (Though don't Muslims have another name for Satan? I can't recall it.) This woman later left Saudi Arabia for a career in finance in Europe and the U.S."

Was she in one of the Towers when they came down, when the Light of the Fallen Angel was obscured in the darkness of dust and rubble of the financial district?

The New Man pressed the tips of his fingers into his brow and massaged the bone of his skull. This was just too…extraordinary.

As if a reflex against reading further, he clicked on the TV. A youngish heavyset black woman, a survivor, was half sobbing, telling her story. "I just can't— I keep seeing those faces on fire." Her eyes seemed agonizingly entranced, fixed on images that could not be erased.

The New Man clicked off the TV and returned to the mysterious pages of Wilson's.

The reports jumped back and forth in time, returning to bin Laden in the Afghan war, then the Sudanese exile of the mid- '90s, well after the Gulf War. These dispatches of incidents—

and speculation—were interwoven with an exploration of human nature, political and psychological machinations The New Man would have thought at odds with the usual classified reports. Though what did he know about such matters? Perhaps many covert official documents delved into the psyche of their subject more than one knew. Perhaps at the base of conflicts, ideology and spying, there had to be…literature.

"Of course, above all, it's irony. We aided the Mujahideen and bin Laden aided them. He had millions. We had blank checks. He becomes the visible hero. We become the scorned—because we go into Saudi Arabia and Kuwait in 1990 and '91. (Not that we weren't in Saudi Arabia before, just not in such massive numbers.) We supported the ground that formed him, that helped him to his fanatic's fame."

Another report: "After bombing the camps last month one of our sources said that bin Laden had been there only an hour before we rained down the apocalypse. He does not stay in one place for long. He moves around, especially since the bombing of the embassies. He's like a sand dune in a windstorm. He very rarely uses cell phones. No faxes or e-mail. It's said he has a double. What a job that must be. If you get killed as bin Laden's double, do you get into Paradise? Do you have to wait to use *his* virgins?"

The New Man stayed on the image of bin Laden with a cell phone. It was too incongruous. The lean dark, bearded face intense against the thin black tool…or sending messages by e-mail, while somewhere an American government analyst searched through the billions of electronic messages of an entire planet for a word that would alarm and give some way to trace the identity of the sender.

Further on, the writer said that bin Laden relies mostly on messengers now—this archaic touch seemed perfect. A word spoken to one who would travel to another place, however far, and deliver the message faithfully.

The New Man read on. "The millennial New Year's Eve has passed and nothing has blown up. The public will quickly forget—those that it registered on—about the terrorist we nabbed crossing the Canadian border who intended to blow up the airport in L.A. But on the verge of a new century (we should stick to centuries; a thousand years is too far to plan ahead) we have to think: what does bin Laden envision for the world should he succeed? Not that I think he thinks in terms of our conception of "success." Success to him is just being faithful. If you kill the infidel it's good, if you die fighting it's good. It's win-win with him. But: if the West is driven out of the Arab world, would Allah be satisfied? Would bin Laden be satisfied? Would he be pure enough to keep to his sphere, or would he be like Hitler, wanting more? That's what his sort usually does. He'll give it all the right religious reasons. His type can't be settled, can't live in peace or in a truce. They have to go on, fight outside their borders, make every country their concern: every border their own. (What is a border, before God?) Bin Laden has his own concept of the Master Race, you might say."

The New Man had to pause from this disparate stream of commentary. He flicked on the TV again. And there he was, bin Laden, the revolutionary risen from a whore's bed, speaking softly while a British accented translator spoke: "It does not matter what the West calls us…Allah willing—"

He pressed the remote violently; the image was killed. He returned to the pages of Wilson's bag. And read of the fantastic plot to tempt bin Laden in a exchange that mirrored the speculation The New Man had just read: how indeed would bin Laden react to the West's withdrawal from the Middle East?

"At the meeting one of us threw out—it was more a joke than anything—'If you said to bin Laden, we would leave Saudi Arabia, leave the Gulf, *if* he gave himself up to us—would he do it?'

"'We're not leaving,' someone said.

"'We'll make him believe it.'

"'We lie?'

"'As if we haven't.'

"'And he's going to believe this?'

"'We'll convince him.'

"'He's a fanatic. That doesn't mean he's naïve.'

"'We swear on—God.'

"'He'll believe our God?'

"'I don't know. You never know.'"

To The New Man this string of dialogue seemed to have the dichotomy of being both true and false. The report continued: "Then we all laughed and went on to practical things. But I found out later this ridiculous plot was put into effect. Various emissaries of ours met with emissaries of bin Laden's. It was turgid going. (And surreal; it had to be.) Then, if what I heard is to be believed, bin Laden actually consented to meet one of ours in some forsaken place in Afghanistan. Our ambassador was— a cleric. Well, that was appropriate—and calculated. Maybe UBL" (The New Man had noted that these documents often spelled bin Laden's first name as Usama) "would believe a man of the cloth, even if he were still an infidel. So our man of God swore to God (and swore to bin Laden) that if he surrendered— the whole bit. Bin Laden didn't speak for a while, then said, 'It is easy to die for that.' And he was told he did not have to die, just turn himself over to American custody. But bin Laden said if he agreed to this he would demand to be put to death by the Americans immediately. He would not tolerate the humiliation of courts, Western law—and punishment. He would give himself up but only with a quick death.

"The way I look at it; there was too much of the whole Christ thing—the killing sacrifice—in this."

Well, the long, bearded figure, the El Greco face, could be the El Greco Muslim Christ—"Anyway," the report went on, "I don't think the cleric was expecting any kind of agreement (if all this is true). He said, 'So you agree—if your terms are met?' Bin Laden said, 'Yes. And you swear to your God?' 'Yes,' said our ambassador. (I wonder if there was any hesitation.) But our man said he actually 'felt bin Laden would agree to this, but then he got to talking theology. I know he was avoiding the proposal; that he would not agree.' ('Proposal.' Our cleric must have searched for that word.)

"And then, maybe bin Laden was wisely playing a game. He knew we would have to go through the proper channels, the everyone-deserves-a-fair-trial routine, put on a good show for the world. We could do it no other way, he could do it in no other way than the opposite of us, so—

"fSo it goes on like this: During some discussion about the powers and graces and names of angels, bin Laden suddenly said, smiling, broadly smiling, 'You are from Iblis. How can I believe the father of the lie?' 'Father of the lie' is right out of the Bible: Jesus' title for Satan, if I'm correct. Bin Laden just ended it, he walked away. Maybe, speaking of Jesus, UBL was making connection to that scene when Jesus is tempted in the wildness by the devil. The devil offers him everything if he would worship him, Satan. But *we* were offering sacrifice; we were offering to make him a Jesus, not to worship us. And we weren't offering him riches. We just offered him his goal. But, of course, we were not truthful. It wasn't an offer, it was a—disguise.

"Our man came back—and went into therapy, telling an uncomprehending Company shrink how he had blasphemed in swearing to God we would keep our word. Of course we would never leave the Gulf, and bin Laden knew that. Perhaps he wanted to believe us, allow us to make him the greatest martyr of all, but he knew it was 'Satan' tempting him, trying to make him turn from the real way to get the politics of God done: war and terror. But I must stress I really do not know *if* the scene between our priestly ambassador and bin Laden actually happened. I only know for sure it was suggested. Let's put it this way: who would have thought we would have actually tried to kill Castro in all the ridiculous ways we did try to do it? So why not try to 'kill' UBL with a fanatic's sainthood? Let's hope bin Laden isn't around as long as Fidel. I don't think he will be. Bin Laden lives too close to the edge. He wants the pan-Islamic world of Mohammed. Castro is content with his little fiefdom."

It was becoming too surreal. It was like a tale out of *1001 Arabian Nights*. The reports were in differing type, on different sorts of documents—or copies of documents. The last report had been stamped "Classified—Eyes Only." This was too much a cliché. Couldn't anyone made a stamp like that and—? And yet. The New Man studied the dates of the documents (though not all were dated), indecipherable signatures here and there, a scattering of acronyms he had never heard of, and large initials often scrawled at the beginning or end—or in the midst of the text, apparently to affirm corrections—of many of the reports.

Could Wilson, the commonplace looking Wilson, a Long Island suburbanite like The New Man (had been)—could Wilson actually be connected to such events?

At the end of the upheaval of this day, The New Man reasoned it was not at all so impossible. Did not the CIA—or other intelligence agencies—use agents who had a plethora of foreign contacts? Wilson, in attending to the company's business, had often traveled abroad. Though as far as The New Man knew, the company had not been shipping watches or ballpoint pens to the Taliban.

The New Man was almost wary of looking at any more pages. But of course he did.

The matter grew more surreal. He was confronted with columns of numbers. A code?

The next page began with "Recall"—like some ominous command. This was followed by more columns of numbers. What had to be "recalled"? Did the second page have something to do with deciphering the first? Or did one have to decipher the first page to decipher the second? He went to the third page. It was utterly blank—as if the abrupt whiteness had been meant for the reader to gather thought. Or as if all that had preceded this, the tales of bin Laden, the numbers of letters, were of a nothingness—

He considered the columns of numbers.

"Recall."

What he recalled was…himself.

6. A Youth of Numbered Days and Foreign Hours

As a young man, he had been something of a mathematical talent. Children are taught numbers as being attached to things: If you have one apple and buy two more apples, how many apples do you have? When you talked about apples or books or candy there was an earthly draw to numbers; but the interest of older students fell away when numbers were stripped of things. Why should we feel compelled to find the answer to 78 minus 59? But some had become more fascinated. Numbers were a universe unto themselves. They didn't need the "lesser" image of things. In high school and college he had explored and mastered the most arcane—or revolutionary—systems of mathematics. It had been a world that had blessed him in a manner apart from human emotions: a pure world, without ideology and delusion.

(Unless, of course, one considered mathematics itself delusion, that its surety was merely a mask—a thought that came to him now and then when on the heights of mathematical clarity. He noted it, went on with what he had....)

His teachers had acknowledged his prowess; one had even predicted the possibility of genius. At the very least, he had considered he would become a professor of mathematics.

Then, upon graduation, had come Vietnam.

It was 1968 and he had weighed escaping the war that seemed so ridiculous in its horror and thus more cruel to the immediate fortunes of the country. It had not only been the fear that his own blood would be shed in Southeast Asia that had caused him to regard arguments for the war as unsatisfactory. He had regarded the Vietnam War as he would have most wars—with eyes that peered from the mathematical: the activity of combat as opposed to the pure manipulations of numbers and symbols. For him to go serve in Vietnam just did not add up.

Well, it was 1968 and King was shot and then Robert Kennedy and in the summer the Chicago police beat protesters in the streets while the Democratic convention nominated Hubert H. Humphrey to run against Richard Nixon. The madness of the time seemed not just in Vietnam, but throughout the homeland. The New Man considered flight to Canada—but ultimately he had not considered it strongly enough. Perhaps, as much as he had been against the dictates of the madness of the time, he had been bound by a visceral and blood allegiance to the awful folly and fate of the war his country had created: a surrender to the fate of his generation and place. He was called; he went. As the presidential election neared, he arrived on foreign soil. He entered the natural, deadly labyrinth of the jungle; and that complicated terrain mirrored more than himself.

When he returned with the end of the summer of 1970 (he still remembered that blue of the sky when he stepped off the plane at JFK, a certain blue that made him say, "It's autumn"), the country in a sort of exhaustion from the sixties (of which the four murdered students at Kent State that spring had been the final symbolic violence), he had been, to use the overused word, so traumatized by his experience in Vietnam it seemed that all his youthful powers, his easy and admirable faculties, especially his link to the world of mathematics, had been ravaged, violated, severed. He had shot his weapons many times into that jungle in that foreign land, and though he had never once known if he had killed a man—or woman or child—for sure, he knew that men had indeed fallen at the chorus of gunfire in which he had sung; he was a guilty choirboy in a fusillade of death that had brought down other human beings. In a sort of instant karma his spirit had been silenced by the silence his side had given others. He lived with a guilt never quite balanced with the fact that he had needed to survive. Kill or be killed. He had been ripped from the better world with which he had occupied his spirit. And he could not get back. He had been presented with the violent fact that the inner sanctuary that had nurtured him was a frail thing in the brutal world. Each day he had been pulled into that brutality. It had become his everyday face. Finally it had drowned him.

He had also been wounded physically. Not disastrously. He had seen his fellow soldiers die. Though he had not made any bosom buddies, though he had not wept as others did over the corpses of their friends slain in an instant (dead in the split second between lighting a match and lighting a cigarette), living eyes and body blown asunder, often flung so disparately over the earth it seemed this human being had never existed at all. The few days in which he had been fitfully sequestered in a hospital in Saigon he had stared up at the fly-specked ceiling, in the hot uncomfortable air the fan blew at him, and had imagined angles and the intersection of angles laid mentally upon this mundane firmament, but ultimately he had felt the Angel of Mathematics had departed from him in a horrible sundering, abandoning him just like those companions in arms who had been obliterated in a moment. The geometry of the insect stained ceiling was a farewell hieroglyphic.

He had sorrowed in his way, for those murdered comrades, though it was not a sorrow for any one for them but for something in which they were all held. And this sadness continued inside of him when he returned to America and did not return to the world of numbers but began to coast, eventually with success, through the world of business. Eventually, in 1980, after a decade of dull transformation, he took a position with the firm that had its offices at the World Trade Center, supplying the importation and exportation of useful items of the late 20th century all over the world. Numbers had become attached to things again; they were not of that other, purer world, their metaphysic subsumed in the everyday.

But here, now, well into the night of September 11, 2001, it had been thirty-one years since he had returned, defeated, from 'Nam. (He wondered: *Has it been thirty-one years to the day?*) Now he was The New Man, and he looked at these columns of numerical permutations: a beckoning. Plato had once said that no matter how much a man is debased there remains forever a spark of purity in him that cannot be extinguished. This is what murderers face in the last hour before execution: more than the fear of death, the recognition of the betrayal of that purity they themselves had possessed. The New Man had lived for decades with that last bit of purity smoldering in himself, his everyday life kept from its flame, seeing it as no more than a vague glow over some far horizon. Now, as the ruins of the Twin Towers itself, flame and the smoke of debris flooded through the island of his spirit. He directed a long unused concentration at the columns of numbers. They were exact, and stark, and steady and austere. It was as if he had turned a corner where the past had finally flooded into the present. And he began to work.

7. The Hours of the Self's Unused God Before the Devil's Face

He worked very slowly at first, and he seemed to travel painfully through the past of what had become of a habitual weariness, his psyche still wounded by an old oppression that had won him by domination and had continued its rule through his resignation. But no resignation knows total surrender. There had been moments, instants, fleeting stabs of spirit, when he had, for instance, looked out from his office at the long high façade of other buildings in the city and, in the gridwork of windows, in the unequal rectangles of many structures, solid visions of mathematical series came to his mind, an apparently random geometry he could coalesce into a pattern—almost resurrecting the geometry that had departed in the hospital in Saigon. And then he had torn himself from those visions, or their strength caused him to fail them, as if he were a man looking upon the blatant loveliness of a woman he should not at all be contemplating: because he was not capable of the bravery of any further action toward the embrace of his passions.

But now: the blood of Vietnam, the human beast that had ravaged his days, had slammed up against another bloodletting, in the unseen bodies of the thousands fallen in the debris of the Towers; and the violation of that past had also met his singular desire to become The New Man—and to have effected that becoming. At least its beginning.

There was a writing tablet by the phone on the night table: like the remnant of some quaint custom of which no one any longer partook but that had to be displayed to honor an old courtesy. Beneath the flourished script of the motel's name at the top of the page The New Man began his calculations, his deciphering, noting—in the way one notes an absolutely inconsequential thing that insistently takes on the aspect of an inexplicable profundity, like an oddly colored pebble on a beach or the butt of a cigarette on a street—noting that someone had scrawled a phone number in a very heavy hand on the page that had been on top of the page that presently faced him. The impress of the number could be read easily enough if he looked at the paper at a certain angle. Irrationally—or with the old instinct of an intuition—he traced the number along the impress; and, with the ease of a man following his lust into a consummating act, slipped these numbers—factored or square rooted or rearranged—into his calculations.

A man on a quest takes all signposts into consideration.

And worked away timelessly. It was a further moment in his metamorphosis. He was an athlete in the race again, pushing hard with long unused muscles; now he was a lover grasping a woman he had for so long ignored. And while she had remained yet lovely for all her isolation, he had aged, and become weak, but not so weak that he could not storm to the task again, or at least enter the fight. And consider that effort might once again make him strong.

He found himself at times shuddering, at times suffering silent tears, at times muttering to himself things that he could not remember a moment after speaking them. He paced the small room, he found himself pressing his palms with all his strength on the surface of the dull walls; he tasted the sweat that beaded his lips. Was the air conditioning still on? Sweat was flowing down his armpits. He caught a glimpse of himself in the mirror: pained face, yet with eyes struggling honestly—yes, honestly at last, with freedom.

Strange or not so strange that this code, in which the ghost of the phone number seemed an outlandish key given him by chance, the gift of a paranoid's or an ascetic's dream, should present him with some sort of liberation. He sought to cleave through the mystery of the columns with disciplines that wove fractal geometry and complex equations for chaotic systems. Numerous times he thought himself about to break through, to make it all collapse into a common coherence, but in another moment he saw it was a case of nothing more than "almost"; like a turn in a maze after which one expects to find an exit but does not and so one is left with the fact of simply going onward. As the hour passed midnight, those moments continued: the cry of breakthrough becoming the soft curse of further toil. His disappointment was greater than he could have imagined, while his persistence, the insistence in him that he must solve this puzzle (for indeed, it was obviously connected with his new life), was also greater than he might have imagined. And more pleasurable. Though "pleasurable" was an inaccurate—at least a poor—word for this.

In college he had taken a course on codes and ciphers. Technically a code is a substitution of one word for another: "ant' could mean, say, "Monday." A cipher has letters or numbers substituted for other letters or numbers. The simplest cipher might have the number 26 indicating the last letter of the alphabet. Though the more common alphabet ciphers had the most frequent occurring number—or letter—in the cipher correspond to the most frequently occurring letter in a particular language.

The New Man remembered—and it was with irony, in this day and time—that it had been the Arabs who had pioneered cryptography a thousand years ago. Some Arab scholar whose name he could not recall had detailed the alphabet substitution cipher, with a method now termed "frequency analysis."

So this was his next tact. He left the complexity of the systems he had applied to slog through simpler but tedious trial and error. But this too led him to only another turn in the maze—or a corridor with a dead end.

He paused, in one of the later a.m. hours, and, without thinking, as if it were part of his mathematical effort, clicked on the TV. There was the smoke, ponderous, thick, rising and drifting across the skyline of lower Manhattan after the collapse of the second tower. The camera's vantage point was at a distance, probably from across the water. As often as he'd seen this scene from so many views since he'd witnessed the event in person, The New Man's eyes and heart were held a long moment once again, poised as if watching the birth of a thing he still could not comprehend. And when he was about to finally change the channel, he was held by a broadcaster's unusual words that broke into this scene—which he suddenly realized, had been eerily silent.

"More than one person has said that the face of Satan could be seen in the smoke at this time. Perhaps this is understandable in the emotions and terror of the moment."

Satan. The New Man, as perfunctorily, as superficially religious as any of his kind, was uneasy at the synchronicity of the devil's name occurring in the reports and now here, on TV, connected with the Towers. He gazed into the replayed, televised smoke cloud of destruction and was struck with the elusive perception that for an instant a face did seem to linger in the roiling dark, the shifting topography spewing upward into the violated air. A face—no, that was ridiculous—but, yes, a face. A trick of the shifting chaos of the smoke, of course, the same chance effect of nature that causes one to see objects upon the eroded surface of a rock. The only difference here was that the supposed demonic face could not be held and examined, but, in another moment, was gone. It was a vision more apt to the drifting changeability of clouds. Then again, it was held on film, replayed. He watched it replayed several times on screen, the broadcaster saying, a little amused, and perhaps a little worried, "Well, do you see it?"—and, satisfied he did not have to hear any affirmations from his audience, he moved on to something else. The New Man clicked off the set with the image or almost-image of the face in the smoke.

A face, yes, but Satan's? He had to think of bin Laden's alleged remark in the report he'd just read....

But what did Satan look like, anyway? God's perennial protagonist, star of Milton's molding and mocked figure of Halloween getups. Was it that latter image in the smoke, the elongated, sneering, horned face? Ridiculous. A face, yes, for an instant, but hardly God's nemesis, the original unholy rebel. The New Man would have more likely said the face in the smoke had been a blank, bland slate of the human visage upon which the seer wrote his own inner demons. There was a mirror in the smoke of destruction: inexorable, ungraspable, shocking—immemorial. More disturbing, though, The New Man considered, was the fact that the TV reporter had even broadcast such an image and commentary. It may have been justified by the extreme horror and tension and surrealness of the day, and it was apparently true that many had claimed to see the devil in the smoke of this destruction, and so it was perhaps utterly suitable commentary—for this hour of the morning, when there were yet some dark hours to go before the dawn that moved incessantly across the Earth. But all the same it struck The New Man with a great unease. Some confession of the demonic was chattering away, if reluctantly, from disparate mouths. He flicked on the TV again, and, my God, there it was, on another channel, but with no commentary: the shifting, almost-there face—until the cloud of destruction twisted and no face could be seen any longer.

This was followed by the umpteenth interview with one of the hordes of rescue workers, a big, gaunt-faced man with a fireman's hat and the soot on his face smudged like some Gothic makeup to accentuate his cheekbones. "From somewhere in the pile we thought we heard— It took us hours to get through it—nothing—" he blinked at his words, at the recent vision, as if his spirit was confronting realities he could never have possibly considered.

Indeed, the voices of the interior as well as exterior world could mock one, and lead to "nothing" at all. The New Man flicked the TV off again. He slapped a hand to his eyes, driving away Satan's ethereal face. And returned to the cipher. Its message was also continually almost there, then gone.

Sometime after in that timeless time of dark, while the dawn did not yet intrude, he perused backwards over his calculations (he had scrawled so many pages now), back to the first page on which he had written the numbers of the impressed phone number and considered it again. He had, almost as an exercise, something to warm him up, get him started, used the phone number in his figuring. He had left it off hours ago. Yet—

Something in those numbers hinted at....

He had tried the fractal route earlier, in which larger systems break down into smaller systems that mirror the larger—in an infinite progression that seems endless. Now, abruptly, using the phone number again, he fashioned a key in which a large picture swam into his view and then a smaller on and so on—and a message emerged.

It was such an abrupt tearing away of a veil that he shouted aloud, in the pre-dark dawn, on the verge of the morning after September 11, 2001. It seemed his pen raced across the paper as fast as his deciphering mind.

Further down towards dawn, but with the world outside still in darkness (he had the strange thought that across the river the face in the smoke had not so much dispersed as grown larger, if more tenuous, so that if he should look out at it he would see it as a constellation of heavenward flowing ash, the dark matter of this immediate upheaved universe), The New Man came to the end of the columns and began to put together the words he had deciphered. He had understood that before he had gotten far along in this step that the words coming upon one another made no sense in the order in which they had been placed: here was a further code. But with instinct and surety he applied the fractal pattern once more. The New Man had the sense that this was overkill, an exaggeration of camouflage for a simple communiqué—but of course the importance of it, at least to the party sending it, must be realized.

The message told the receiver (in this case, but utter chance, The New Man) to meet an unnamed party…*on September 12, 2001—in the very town in which The New Man, again by chance, had come to become The New Man!*

Chance? Coincidence? This stretched all such boundaries. It was the impossible odds used so frequently in Shakespeare and bad movies.

The New Man was struck forcibly. He felt as if he had not escaped at all, that he was in fact being led, even imprisoned. He was faced with admitting to a paranoid's fantasy. The images and sensations of the descending escape through the building, coming out into the bright sky being violated by smoke— Was the Moms Mabley-woman on the bus some bizarre overseer observing The New Man, the rat in the maze? And this motel, that restaurant ("The Traveller's Rest"—My God!)—even the face of Satan—the terrorist attack itself. Was it all—? What? What?

He clicked off the lamp by the bed. He wanted to face this enormity in the dark.

Awful instincts in him knew that if he had fled into *this* with the abruptness of chance allowing him fruition of a long held desire, that focal point had had its madness; how could he disavow its further direction?

As his eyes adjusted to the sudden absence of light he was aware that outside, in the world, the sky was becoming tainted with the approach of dawn. In this less-than-dark he agonized, and then tried to face the situation as dispassionately as possible. Million to one odds are sometimes met; a hundred million to one. Consider Lotto, Mega Millions, those commonplace games of chance—that Wilson, yes, occasionally played, claiming he'd buy an island if successful. The New Man recalled once explaining the odds to Wilson, saying it was literally a waste of time to buy a ticket, that this was irrational, that Wilson was being "mathematically impaired."

But who was having the last laugh now—even if from the grave? This message of a meeting…. With whom? For what purpose? Considering the dawn that came like a threat, The New Man had the wild idea, the wild fear: to be murdered, like the unhappy hero in Kafka's story, for some guilt that no one describes but which all condemn? Of course, The New Man was "guilty"—of shedding or trying to shed a half century plus of identity.

Trembling a little, he went to the mirror. The room had become dim with light. In that dimness he peered at himself. A rose by any other name…. But he was trying to not so much shed himself as to assert himself. He looked back to the bed, the reports, the strewn pages of his calculations. He had the sudden thought that not once in those columns of figures had there appeared the zero, that integral numberless number that had been the invention of the Arabic world. Only in the phone number, with the New Jersey area code, had there been that great, pure roundness of nothingness—

The phone number. His heart seemed to stop, clasped in an unspeakable horror. He looked toward the phone. To convince himself as to why he could not commit the daring act of calling that number, he said it was too ungodly an hour.

He gave an odd, mumbled laugh. Ungodly. It wasn't just the hour that was—demonic? Why was that word so insistent now? Perhaps he was being harassed by Satan's image.

Later, later in the day he would call. He promised himself. Or dared himself. He would find the number wholly attached to this sudden new drama of his life, some number someone who'd had the room before had written down,k called—but then, how *could* it be coincidence it had fit the code?

To distract himself from finding out further impossibilities and also to consider something essential to this entire mystery, he dwelt upon Wilson. Or rather what Wilson had *seemed*. A man indistinguishable from the hordes (The New Man's old self among them), who had also commuted from Long Island into the city. Wilson had lived in Babylon and frequently the old New Man would encounter him on the train in the morning. Coming from farther out on the Island, the old New Man would be immersed in the distractions of the newspaper or the comforts of a half sleep or the strained wakefulness of some anxiety anticipating the day at work. So he and Wilson would share that final rush across the island together, crossing the border of Suffolk into Nassau, entering the drear functional complex of the LIRR at Jamaica and then the brief dark passage under the river into Manhattan. Both men always tried to get an express that would make no stops between Jamaica and Manhattan. The New Man recalled the conversations between himself and Wilson about the annoyance of missing that express. The image of Wilson's unremarkable face, hovering in the slight swaying of the train, floated in The New Man's consciousness.

Of course, even when Wilson and the old new Man were on the same train, it was not likely they would, from two different stations, enter the same car. But now, thinking back on it, it seemed that Wilson had done so an inordinate number of times. After the hours of revelation the night had caused him to suffer through, The New Man was plagued with further evidence—at least suggestions—of some conspiracy against him; or not so much against him as pushing him through a conspiracy whose purpose he had never been told. Of course, his frequently encountering Wilson might have been due to the entirely unextraordinary fact that he, the old New Man, had usually stood in the same position on the platform at his station every day, and so had gotten on the same car, while at Babylon, Wilson went to the same spot on that platform every day and it just so happened that these two positions apart in space and time had had the effect of ultimately joining the two men in the same cars. In other words, it was the work of one coincidence, not many.

Though because The New Man had just plunged through—and relived—heady orders of mathematics, he wondered why, if the above had been the case, he and Wilson had not *always* shared the same car, for indeed they had not. This could be as suspicious as the two men often sharing the same car. Perhaps the train did not stop at exactly the same point each day. There had been times when he had not seen Wilson on the train but had spotted Wilson in the crowds at Penn Station. There, in the thick press of humanity hurriedly proceeding toward the day's work, would be the glimpse of the common face, sharing the expression of mundane urgency with the rest of the crowd. Sometimes Wilson had acknowledged the old New Man's glance. If they were a distance apart, Wilson might give a brief wave, continue on his way—though again, that led to the same subway both took downtown. Other times Wilson would not notice the old New Man and would continue onward, though the old New Man would perhaps see Wilson on the subway; here too they might share the same car—but with the subway more crowded than the railroad, they could be sharing the same car and not notice each other—

The New Man's thoughts paused and stumbled back. Perhaps Wilson *should* always be on the same car on the railroad but *chose* not to be; perhaps Wilson was aware of…*something*, and had his reasons for meeting up with the old New Man or not meeting up with him. Perhaps Wilson often spied the old New Man at Penn Station when the old New Man did not see Wilson, just as the old New Man would see Wilson but Wilson not notice the old New Man—or perhaps Wilson was pretending not to see him—

This was an infinite fractal series, with myriad examples compressed into and mirroring the whole. But was this chance or purpose? Or was it sometimes chance, sometimes purpose?

At any rate, The New Man had rarely encountered Wilson on the way home. The two men usually left work at different times. Or, to be precise, the old New Man usually left at the same time, but Wilson seemed to leave at various times.

He could read nothing into Wilson. A face in the crowd, the usual demeanor and interests of a man of his time, his job, his age. A few years older than The New Man, Wilson was an average looking man of average height. He wore a dull long dark blue coat in the winter. He liked to repeat jokes he'd heard the night before from Leno and Letterman. A Mets fan, he bemoaned their failure to overtake the Braves every year. When the wild card Mets finally made it to the Series last year, Wilson had been cautiously enthusiastic, and not really too downcast by their loss to the Yankees in five games—"Though they should have at least gone to six games," he'd said.

He was in his second marriage with no children; there was a grown son from the first. He had come to the firm later than the old New Man, about a dozen years ago. He had some varied international experience. He had dropped references of consulting work in South America, Europe and Africa. After the collapse of the Soviet Union, the firm had sent him to Eastern Europe. Perfect cover, The New Man now mused—but for what?

Exhausted with it all, The New Man left off all thought. His mind had been furious with circumstances, visions, mysteries. In the creep of dawn he closed his eyes and sat and listened to his own breathing. And, perhaps as a sort of protection, he clicked on the TV. Soon he opened his eyes.

But suddenly the shock of the reports, the cipher, the mystery of Wilson were all reduced before the shock of seeing his wife on the screen, talking pitifully in a hoarse voice and roughly pushing tears away from her cheeks.

"I just have a feeling he's alive, for some reason he can't get in touch with us—"

In his horror his impulse was to slay the image, shut off the TV, but the hand that grasped the remote was paralyzed.

His wife continued to speak. Her eyes were glassy with tears. How vivid, how fleshly was this electronic image.

She had not been able to reach anyone from his office. Her son and daughter were rushing home from college. "You don't expect—you can't believe—" In a stream of vague fragments she conveyed a despair that should have only come out of a deep love. And this perhaps shocked The New Man as much as actually seeing her on TV. Shocked and angered him. He knew (at least believed) she had no love for him; this anguish was more out of the violent disruption of the habit of their living together than the sorrow of the loss of the other's presence. They had lived apart together.

"When he left this morning—"

When he had left that morning she had been in bed. He had exited without farewell. That had become habit for both. He resented she claimed some narrative for something she had not witnessed, in which she never partook.

They had not so much disliked each other as realized, with the incessence of the day to day, the inappropriate horrors of cohabitation, admit that something deep in the psyche of each was disturbed and disrupted and even disgusted by the continual presence of the other. Yes, not so much a dislike, certainly not a hatred, but a wish to flee—a wish for a moment of abrupt liberation, a moment that habit and children and work and society never seemed to allow. Because both the man and the woman were never bold enough for their own desires, excusing themselves from freedom on the almost welcome ground of helplessness. Perhaps, had the husband been horrible to the wife or the wife horrible to him, the victim of the horror would have been forced to freedom, but the old New Man and his suburban mate had been bound and thus doomed by a civility each thought necessary. A mask that must be shown others; or perhaps they needed that mask for their own souls. And the moments when the dissatisfaction was buried deeply, a shared hour together, a chance and happy conversation, a long moment, say, of more than passable sex—these were respites that further cemented the couple within the imprisonment of one another.

But how dare she carry on this way. She could have feigned

sorrow and certainly she might feel a little genuine sadness about his disappearance, his possible death—but not this.

Perhaps The New Man was resenting that his wife might indeed have deeper feelings of sympathy, empathy and love than he possessed. Confronted with the possibility of his own vacuity, he was stricken. That body of flesh, the electronic image in which so much of his past was ensconced—no, the disguise of his past—was a condensed accusation of the duties he had abandoned.

She went on; he did not hear her. Or rather he heard, but the words had no meaning—they were their own sort of code, and he had no wish to unravel it.

The unseen hand that aimed the mic said, "I can't imagine how your children—"

He aimed the remote like a gun and the TV died.

What was he doing to his children? He would, of course, get back in touch with them again— Actually, he had not even thought this once. He would defend himself by saying he had had to be occupied with survival, flight. He had to establish himself anew before— But if they knew he still lived, his wife would know…. Without consciously thinking about it, he had decided they were now old enough to suffer a little until— That is, *if* they would really suffer.

He slumped on the bed and wept. He was caught in the madness of his escape; the paradise it had offered had been violated—even more thoroughly than the code in Wilson's bag.

And then what the code had relayed worked at him again. He had been summoned to meet some unknown party for some unknown reason later this day, whose light now flooded fully into the room.

Wait: why did he think *he* was summoned? Why this conviction—this belief, even this faith—that matters collapsed upon *himself*?

The blow of the terrorists upon the World Trade Center had offered him an utter freedom—it had seemed; now he felt utterly bound, as far from freedom as he could imagine. Without strength he slammed his hand on the bed. "I'm trapped." He wept, weakly, on this first morning he was The New Man. Finally, weakly, he stretched out on the bed and with a thin blanket over him slept with surrender the sleep of the ravaged. He awoke with great fear, his face and shrouded torso within the rectangle of sunlight a window cast across his body. The light seemed a brand of an irrevocable, new flesh. The New Man listened with resignation to the sounds of the world outside which he wanted to both elude and shelter him.

Wednesday, September 12, 2001

8. *Preparations For Crossing the Border*

His first thought was the meeting; his second, immediately following, was: at what time? The deciphered columns had not said. Had there been something he had missed?

Like a man returning to punishment, he retrieved the pages strewn about the floor. Could they really still contain the message he had unraveled last night? Here, in the light of day, the pages seemed airy, almost pure, quite apart from the stark, venal labyrinth of the hours of dark.

But of course the message of last night remained.

He returned to the phone number.

With the greatest fear in his gut he jabbed out the numbers on the face of the dark phone. He did this violently, defensively. Immediately a recorded voice came on telling him all circuits were busy and he should try again later.

With relief overshadowing disappointment, The New Man put down the phone. Of course, with the "collateral damage" caused by the collapse of the World Trade Center, and the hysteria following the disaster inciting a flood of calls, it was not surprising that in the New York area the phone system was swamped, or inoperative.

He showered, put on the same clothes he had worn yesterday—well, what else did he have? They were dirty, rumpled, but they would have to do. Ruefully, he looked at himself in the mirror. It was a less surreal study of his image than the one he had pondered just after dawn. Though hardly less disconcerting. He was bleary-eyed and unshaven. He had had only a few hours of sleep. But the trap of his new freedom made him too restless to sleep; it pressed him onward.

He needed to shave. He rubbed the palm and fingers of his hand across the stubble of his chin. He should have picked up a razor somewhere yesterday—though in those sudden hours, who could have been thinking about tomorrow, this very day that he now faced?

He went downstairs. There was Ahmed. Well, here was something in his new life that was repeated from the day before. He thought Ahmed looked at him a little quizzically, as he turned from the ubiquitous reportage of the attacks on TV. The New Man knew he should say something, but what?

It was Ahmed who spoke. "Did you get any sleep?" Of course it was plain "Mr. Newman" had not slept well at all.

"A little." For some reason he smiled as he said this.

Ahmed gave a sympathetic look at man who had been rent by yesterday. "Will you be leaving today?"

"Yes—I mean…I can't be sure—exactly. I'm trying to…get in touch with someone. The phones—".

"Yes, they're all screwed up."

In another situation The New Man might have been amused at this foreigner's ready use of the colloquialism. He drew out his wallet. Money would stay questions. Ahmed made a staying gesture. "Mr. Newman, I am not worried about money—this is a terrible situation for you. We will take care of it later."

But was this a test? Was Ahmed being only formally polite? Did he expect another day's payment anyway, believing "Mr. Newman" had the obligation to override any politeness?

But The New Man was too exhausted for any games, any rituals of interpersonal—and intercultural—diplomacy. He pocketed his wallet. "OK. I'll settle when I leave."

Ahmed's kindness did seem genuine. He was already saying, "If you're looking for a place for breakfast—"

"Oh. I wanted to tell you: that place you sent me to last night was very good."

"I knew you would like it. But for breakfast—" he suggested a place in the direction opposite that of The Traveller's Rest. "They even have bagels," said Ahmed, presenting this staple, originally of the Jews, as if a daring luxury in this Arabic neighborhood.

Into which The New Man would walk, this bright, warm, late summer's day. Though not before Ahmed had offered him a disposable razor that he rummaged from a drawer. Was he always so solicitous of his guests' needs, or did he feel especially sorry for Mr. Newman? Or was he simply trying to show that all Muslims weren't devils? The New Man took the razor with thanks and commented to himself if he had struck out into a new world to grasp his "freedom," he was in the position of being somewhat dependant on "the kindness of strangers."

He returned to his room and shaved. But gifts can have their drawbacks. He cut himself twice with the cheap razor (he hated these type of razors). For a moment he stared at the streak of blood on his skin. Was this somehow the same blood that had run through his body when he had begun his other life yesterday morning?

Yet bloodletting can be a sort of cleansing. He went out, feeling a little less scruffy, tapping his chin and cheek with a tissue to make sure the blood had stopped.

From a car stopped by a light he heard the radio blaring the fact of "a body miraculously alive" being discovered in the debris of the Twin Towers. The driver, apparently Arab, staring straight ahead with the monotony of habit, showed no emotion as he paused at the light; he drove on when it turned green.

The New Man paused by a newsstand, where a lean, white-haired Indian gentleman looked at him, somewhat warily, as if he knew this rumpled man, with the red streaks of razor cuts, was a survivor of the attacks the newspapers glaringly detailed, in digitally-pixilated-snatched-from-TV portraits of the burning Towers and fleeing people.

"*AMERICA ATTACKED*" headlined *The New York Times*.

The New Man shook his head, as if he could not possibly purchase these mementos of the Inferno, and hurried on.

It was the sort of place where people would stop for breakfast, to get something on the run or to sit on one of the few scattered small tables. It was also a store, like a deli.

The patronage was similar to that of The Traveller's Rest. The New Man gave little concern to the stares that were directed at him. Among the exotic menu (in Arabic and English) tacked behind the counter, he did in fact order a bagel with cream cheese, coffee and, on further thought, scrambled eggs. A very American, well, at least a New York breakfast, even if the eggs were seasoned in a way he had never tasted. Alone at one of the small tables (he had the feeling no one wanted to share it with him), his face profiled from the street, he ate with great hunger.

He considered what he had to face this day. The message had left no time for the meeting. The New Man wondered, tapping an instinct that now prowled in his being, if the time could be drawn from the digits in the phone number. If one multiplied or added, or subtracted…. With a conviction that was a leap from logic (or logic reaching something it simply could not explain to those it had left behind) he found that adding the numbers left him with a three in the ones column; as was the case when he multiplied the numbers; as was the case when he subtracted the added sums from the multiplied sums. So it was: 3 o'clock.

"Why not, why not. Go with it," he mumbled to himself. Two or three customers briefly looked his way, with questioning dark eyes. But The New Man was in the safety of his own secrets.

Three o'clock. It was now eleven in the morning. (He was sure the appointed time was 3 p.m., not a.m.)

An hour later he was back in his room. He tried to sleep a bit, but by one he was sitting up, flicking on the TV, darting through the channels. Returning to the motel, he had tried to see the impress of yesterday's events on the faces in the street; and perhaps some of those faces (as in that deli) tried to see something in him.

Across America, across the world, suspects were being detained right and left. There were interviews with the "loved ones" of the doomed passengers of Flight 93 that had crashed in Pennsylvania. Via cell phone calls, some of the passengers of the hijacked airliner had learned of the planes crashing into the World Trade Center. A number of the passengers were determined to fight. "Let's roll," were the last known words of one of them. And then, on the screen the face of a man in Pennsylvania saying he had watched the plane fly right down into a field. The government was denying rumors it had shot the plane down. By the time Flight 93 had crashed, the Pentagon had also been attacked. Jet fighters were in the air with orders to shoot down any plane that might be threatening Washington. Present reports said there was a long debris field for Flight 93, suggesting to many the plane had exploded in the air before it had crashed.

News other than the attacks on America—but not unrelated—crept into the continuous coverage. In Jerusalem, at 1:30 a.m., an Israeli tank had entered a West Bank town, razed a police station and the offices of the Palestine Authority. Two other towns had also been entered forcibly by the Israelis. At the end of this violence, eight Palestinians had been killed, among them a nine year old girl. An aide to Yasser Arafat accused Israel of executing these attacks under the cover of the international attention given the terrorist incidents in New York and Washington, D.C. The Israelis said the police station had been "a center of terrorist activity." Israeli Prime Minister Sharon declared the military action would have occurred "regardless" of whether or not the attacks on the Twin Towers had occurred. In counterpoint, on the border of the West Bank and Israel, Palestinians shot up a car, killing one Israeli settler. "More than two dozen Israeli settlers have been killed by Palestinians since the beginning of the Palestinian uprising close to a year ago," a reporter intoned.

It seemed likely that America would bomb, even invade

Afghanistan if the ruling Taliban did not turn over bin Laden. The Taliban, the most unsympathetic of regimes, issued a plea for sympathy: that America not inflict destruction on a land whose "people have suffered so much." There were shots of farmers tilling drought-plagued soil with oxen, children at some game among the ruins of buildings riddled with bullet holes. In whatever hell they live, children play.

The New Man flicked to another channel. A Manhattan photographer who had taken countless images of violence all over the world had found himself on chance assignment in his own neighborhood. An assignment quickly subsumed by the history that happened before his eyes. His lens caught ash-covered firemen in the rubble, the billowing descent of papers (white, stylized helpless birds in the dark smoke), and a man in a suit with a briefcase, looking up at the burning Towers. His back to the camera, the man nonetheless conveyed a world of expression with his body. He had arrived at the edge of the apocalypse while a moment ago he had expected nothing more than another day at work.

The New Man thought: That could've been me, standing there with Wilson's bag after I got out.

He flicked off the TV and laid himself back down on the bed. The absence of sound and images made him confront his solitude. The room was flooded with the bright light of the middle of the day. The light that reaches Earth does not care what occurs on the Earth it reaches.

In that light The New Man closed his eyes and the images of yesterday, only barely accessed since his flight, flooded his psyche, perhaps instigated by the photographs that had filled the TV screen. Yes, when he had come out onto the street there had been the flutter of descending papers, though only now, in recollection, he focused on it. At distance from the Towers, he had looked back at the deluge of descending whiteness amongst the consuming dark cloud, and it was as if he were seeing a shower of white flowers flung down upon a grave that was not of unmoving earth but of an inferno. He might very well have been the mirror of that man with the briefcase, poised before a destruction that had upheaved much more than another day at the office.

But those white, soundless, fluttering papers against the dark hot smoke. He imagined, if he had not retrieved the worn bag, the pages of reports and code exploded into the air of lower Manhattan. Some would be lost to the catastrophe, and others might be discovered at random. Would any of those discoverers catch a glimpse of the mystery The New Man faced? Probably not. For the most part it would seem nonsense. Well, the code would be, not the reports….

Speaking of codes and ciphers, The New Man's imagination worked further. What if…that vast, descending flutter of paper from the destroyed Towers were itself, in total, a message, some message from, well, God, for want of a better word…which, if gathered and pieced together and pondered might tell of, might reveal—something?

But what cryptoanalytic sequence could be applied to that? The New Man sighed, rested his head in his hands, the fingertips pressed against his eyes.

In a moment he had flicked on the TV again. The UN had postponed a meeting scheduled for the following week, a conference that would have been attended by eighty world leaders. And the annual meeting of the International Monetary Fund, set for the end of the month, had been cancelled.

Arafat was firmly declaring that Palestinians would not rejoice over the carnage in America. The master of old terrorisms, he had a new authority to hold. But whatever the official admonition, surely there was dancing in the "Arab street."

The New Man looked at the clock. He should be leaving soon. He had gotten a map of the area from Ahmed. The motelkeeper had pulled out the map from under the counter—another quaint courtesy (like the writing pad) that The New Man felt few guests used. He recalled the days when you used to get maps from gas stations.

He wasn't sure if he should take a bus or walk. He had not wanted to inquire about a specific location; that might have made Ahmed suspicious. Temporary sanctuary at the motel was believable, if odd, but to be seeking obvious destinations in the neighborhood…. Ahmed might think "Mr. Newman" could be some white collar dope smuggler—whatever.

"Mr. Newman." The New Man smiled grimly to himself. He looked at the map. According to the scale, the meeting place indicated by the message was about two and a half miles, perhaps two and a quarter, from the motel. A half hour, no forty minutes, should be plenty of time to walk it. Well, better allow fifty minutes, close to an hour, in case he took a wrong turn. But he also did not want to arrive too early. It might not be safe to hang around an as yet unknown place and call attention to himself.

Yes, it was time he was setting out…. He looked at the inexorable presence of the hands of the clock and felt the sharp pain of a man beset by time. In the silence of The New Man's anxiety, the ticking of the timepiece was terribly loud.

And yet, this instrument seemed the antithesis of movement. These hours did not change as we stared; but with the briefest turn away…. Whatever name we carry, the hours face us with stern number.

9. *Meeting the Mirror*

The day was hot. Summer remained. As he walked, The New Man noted the still rising smoke in the east. He thought of TV shows he'd seen as a kid in the '50s: the Indians making smoke signals to carry messages. This, of course, was a messageless plume. –Or no, it did have a message, only a wordless one.

He stopped abruptly, squinting in the light, studying the smoke. Here it was thin and grey, there thicker, darker. One could suppose its message was that no American was safe.

He thought, moving on: "Am I American?" What is an American? Like every American save those Indians just recalled, his forebears had come to this country in a time that could be marked. Whether Pilgrims or 20th century (or 21st century) immigrants, all save those "Native Americans" could name a time *before* the passage from Europe or Africa or Asia.

Or the Middle East. As he walked on, he noted the dark complexioned faces studying him. Perhaps some of them had the hatreds of the terrorists who had brought down the Twin Towers and were uneasy at the presence of this lone representative of "the enemy" in their—settlement. Perhaps many of those eyes were uneasy at his presence because they knew themselves the minority and could expect harsh judgement from the majority, which this stranger represented.

He had to give a silent laugh. In a country of minorities, he was a minority of one. Theodore Newman, without ethnicity, without the passage across an ocean, a border. No, he was sort of a Frankenstein, created out of the artifacts of disaster....

He looked at his reflection in a shop window. Perhaps he could pass for a fairer skinned Arab. Indeed, more than a few of the Arabs were fairer than he. Of course, he knew he was marked by more than skin color. He had the distinct aura of apartness.

But what indeed was it to be an American? At various times in his life, especially in the Vietnam era, and in watching TV this last day, he'd heard protestations of "I am an American," or "We are all Americans." All of his life he had felt himself living *in* America...but he could not have said he felt *of* America. Perhaps this was a passion he could not share, as he had not been able to share a passion for and with a mate. Perhaps these voices, these hearts and minds who so claimed their identity spoke the words to convince themselves; and perhaps they truly felt it. And perhaps no man or woman or child could truly know themselves, in solitude, as American, but only in the aggregate, as an echo, a mirror of the larger group. A tree is of itself, and it is of the forest. An American could only be an American in the midst of America—

But an American was an American in London or Bombay or Patagonia. Even apart from the home soil, an attachment to America and its existence was assured. There was a fact, a thing, an *us-ness*, a psyche from which one had emerged. And even if one lived in exile, such as the expatriates who claimed a greater joy in foreign lands, they were still Americans, as a man or a woman still comes from one mother no matter how distance, time and even death intervene.

.   .   .

A turn in the streets brought him to a neighborhood which itself seemed to have suffered a sort of disaster in the past. The disaster of having no future. There were plainly unoccupied apartment buildings. They were structures whose echo of life was a sound long departed,

Other buildings seemed to support life precariously; one man emerged from a particularly benighted building as if he himself suffered the isolation of a survivor. He blinked sadly at the light and hurried down the street. There was some abrupt metaphor of kinship here—The New Man tried not to dwell on it.

And, not unexpectedly, here and there were lots strewn with rubble. Their debris and stillness and shadow in the bright day was like a landscape of the moon, without atmosphere, facing the sun.

It was in the sky over one of these lots that The New Man got a better view of the still ascending smoke, and the great emptiness of sky itself where the Twin Towers should have been. He stopped again, and stared as if in a sort of involuntary reverence. What if the terrorists (though this already seemed too clichéd a title) were able to bring down all of America? What if there were no America? Impossible, of course. Could a few thousand Islamic fundamentalists, shrieking the fury of their jihad, storm through the country and make the women of Iowa walk about veiled? But then, every empire, no matter its height, had crumbled. As had the great swath of Islam itself, that had once stretched from Spain to the border of China, while Europe had stumbled in its dark ages, in its own medieval oppressiveness after Rome's conquering glory. If there were now a billion human beings who recognized the spiritual call of

Mecca, the power of being the world's primary influence had passed to Europe, and then to America. More comforting for Western minds to look at the proclaiming fundamentalists of Allah as the virulent remnants of a way of life that cannot enforce its faith throughout the globe of the new millennium. No one can enslave half the population—women—anymore; no one can refuse the allure of blue jeans or put more faith in the Koran than the weather report.

All these thoughts while looking at the emptied sky.

And yet, and yet... The New Man studied this great space across the water which ugly buildings partly hid, the space the two tall, clean, modern skyscrapers had left and the smoke that twisted to the vagaries of the wind. He was on the verge of seeing something in absence.

A wind did come up then, stiffly, and things were blown about. Before his very eyes, and as if sucked towards him, the pages of an Arabic newspaper, swirled in little whirlpools of wind. There was a sense of déjà vu. Oh, yes, last night (so long ago, it seemed) as he had returned to the motel: the foreign paper blown to him by the wind. Now he saw the bold headlines of this paper in the alphabet so unlike his own, and the photographs of the burning Towers, the firemen in the smoking rubble. Did the headlines applaud or condemn the act? With whom did the spirits of these writers ally? The face of Bush II, the American nondescript face who had gained the supreme power through the chain of influence he had inherited from his father (and the anachronism of the Electoral College), or the long bearded El Greco face of bin Laden (was it last night he had connected bin Laden and El Greco?), one of fifty-two children, who had inherited an even great wealth from his father, friend of the king of Saudi Arabia?

Of the two scions who had inherited so much, it could be said that bin Laden had chosen the new path, the path his own, one different than the father's. But how "successful" would the offspring have been without that original "venture capital"? The New Man thought of the reports from Wilson's bag. In the '80s, the young Saudi had been one of the saviors (along with the CIA) of the Mujahideen. With his wealth, bin Laden had brought in equipment and had built roads in harsh Afghanistan. Now, as the godfather of Al-Qaeda, he bankrolled the terrorizing of America. Could he have risen to war hero and godfather if he had been some penniless Palestinian, some abused Lebanese, one of the helpless hordes of the Arab street in the second half of the 20th century? It is said that no one now can achieve the American presidency without a campaign chest of hundreds of millions of dollars; so, too, no effective terrorism without the funds....

In concert with his thoughts (or, perhaps, their source), the swirling pages showed him the face of Bush and bin Laden more than once. The New Man wondered at the strangeness of a universe that linked the arrival of his new identity with these two human beings whom he would never meet.

Then the wind took half of the pages away and left the others still or slightly twitching on the ground as these gusts from nowhere died. The New Man shook his head, thankful for the silence of images and unreadable words, the fluttering of papers like the soft sighing movements of a dying thing; but The New Man was occupied with the tasks of the living. He went on, looking for an address.

He soon found it. Or found it no longer existed. More precisely, the building that had had that number wasn't there, only its rubble. He concluded this rubble was the place because the buildings on either side of the debris-strewn lot bore, respectively, a number lower and higher than the one he sought.

He had escaped a building that had fallen into rubble; now he had arrived at ruin of greater age.

Whom or what was he supposed to meet here? He had crossed the empty street to the lot, feeling like a gunfighter going to a showdown in which he had a good chance of being killed. Another Baby Boomer TV image of the '50s.

But perhaps it was better to be in the open than to enter a building, where, unseen by anyone, some horror could be enacted upon him. Standing on the sidewalk in front of the lot he looked about. Not only was the entire street empty, it *felt* empty. He realized he had seen only a handful of pedestrians the last ten minutes. Though there were parked cars here and there along the street, a child's bicycle by the entrance of one building and some apparently well tended flowerpots by the stoop of another building. Again the gunfighter image: everyone had shut themselves away from the impending violence.

The lot spread out before him, like a jagged opening in the terrain of an old habitation.

The New Man looked at his watch. If this was indeed the place, he was ten minutes early. (Assuming he had been right about the time.) It would be an eternity to wait those minutes. But he had no choice save to face that eternity.

He found himself staring at the numbered face of the dial, in the sort of musing that is common when we see common objects—and their purpose—for the first time, or see them in another light. His first thought had been: Would "they" be punctual? His fancy had him meeting some Arab terrorist and he had read somewhere that nonwestern cultures are insulted if expected to conform to the imprisonment of the clock the West so strenuously heeds. But then, the terrorists who had executed the hijackings yesterday, the total annihilation of the World Trade Center and the severe damage to the Pentagon—they had certainly been punctual enough to catch those flights…. They had had the will to grasp the sheath of time for their purposes.

He continued to stare at the watch. Perhaps he did not want to confront the vista it seemed he had to enter. The golden minute hand moved ever so slightly as the dark racing second hand swept a complete revolution. The old New Man had certainly been punctual for decades: there had been all those commuter trains. And standing there, he was palpably, sadly struck by that: how the clock had ordered him. Yes, it had always been Wilson who would occasionally miss a train, not the old New Man. (Wilson would arrive late at the office, flippantly blaming the railroad.) But the inferno of yesterday morning seemed to have obliterated time. Until The New Man had deciphered that message. And here he was, early for a meeting—with the unknown.

He felt conspicuous standing on the sidewalk. He started to walk into the lot, amidst the rubble. He thought that this was all too much a mirror image of the aftermath of the destruction of the Towers. Of course, this destruction had happened some time ago. The rubble was weathered. Weeds grew.

As he entered the lot far enough so that the buildings on either side began to block sight of the street, he saw that the area of debris was larger than he would have expected. It stretched across the width of the block to the parallel street on the other side. It was a field of rubble lined by buildings.

And the lot, as one studied it, had its topography. There were mounds, little hills. There were rough paths. There were boulders of debris, great fragments of buildings that were marked by graffiti: English obscenities, foreign words (obscenities, too?) and symbols that were the idiosyncratic cuneiform of unknown artists. The words and symbols gave the impression of street signs—well, not quite. Crude milestones, markers, along some sort of ancient journey: the remnants of a people who had passed here in bitterness and suffering.

Had it been a passage going toward something, or fleeing something? Or was every passage both?

The New Man had carefully walked about a third of the way into this field of ruin when he sensed rather than heard movement from the street. He turned quickly. On the sidewalk he saw, just coming into sight from the corner of a building, a dark figure robed in what seemed a stereotype of Arab dress. A cloth stretched about the head; the end of the cloth came down across one shoulder. The torso and legs were covered in a loose dark billowing material that reached to the knees. Whatever could be seen of the legs were covered in baggy pants and a sort of boot that reached up to just past the ankles. But most striking—foreboding—about the figure was that half of its face was covered. The eyes, nose and the lower part of the forehead alone could be seen.

This figure, out of another time and place, stopped before the lot, gazed into its interior, in which The New Man stood. Across that distance, two pairs of eyes met each other. The New Man felt more conspicuous than ever, now—a target. He felt about to meet an assassin.

The figure entered the lot and began to walk toward The New Man, who summoned up the courage of a man who thought himself lost, so he had nothing left to lose in standing firm. He was thinking the man's appearance was just too—too weird: surreal. As ludicrous as the message that had brought The New Man to this place.

The figure moved carefully but quickly through the debris, until the dark robed body, the half hidden face stood before The New Man, who might have been thinking that to hide half the face was to hide the totality of it. The visible half might be extrapolated into any number of faces.

The figure was tall, very tall, perhaps half a foot taller than The New Man. This height added to the intimidating aspect of the concealed man—who said, in an accented voice:

"Wilson." It was not a question. The voice fell flat and ominous in the air between them The dark eyes seemed beyond all expression.

The New Man gave the briefest, inaudible sigh. It was a prelude to deception. "He's dead."

There seemed a sort of surprise in the dark eyes of the dark figure—and the flicker of an inscrutable threat. The New Man added, "He was in the Towers."

That was all that was needed to be said. Of course, it immediately passed the exchange to a dangerous level. "Who are you?" said the figure.

It was a question that had more levels of meaning than the questioner could know. (Or could he know?) The New Man said, "I'm Newman." (How false the name sounded to him.) The eyes of the half masked other received that without expression.

"Wilson asked me to get something for him. I went down—I wasn't so high up." (Why did he need to explain?)

The other considered this; some unnamable expression entered the eyes. "You know—Wilson?"

"Yes." The New Man kept his face stern, his voice placid.

It was obvious he, "Newman," had come upon information he should not have had. But then again—with fear and paranoia beating equally within him, The New Man mustered a seeming bravery, at least a savior faire; trying not to sound like an echo, he asked, "Who are you?"

The figure paused on this question a long moment. Then: "My name means nothing—"

The New Man could well agree there was not much in a name. He said, "I can't see your face. You can see mine."

Indeed. The tall figure looked fully on The New Man's face; the gazed upon identity-shifter felt this concealed man looked into his very soul. It was a sensation engendered by the situation, but still….

The man gave a sort of laugh. With an abrupt gesture the robed figure indicated a passage further into the lot, paused a moment, then walked on without looking back. The New Man followed that gesture with resignation in his heart. He knew he was destined—or rather he could only choose—to move forward. He stayed about ten feet behind the robed man; he might have been following an apparition across a wasteland, a figure that moved with the casual, slow certainty of habit across light drenched ruins.

They passed a boulder on which a faded American flag had long ago been spray painted; now it suffered under the slash of a great, rude black "X"—a mark of disapproval almost as faded.

These were the physic signs of the landscape.

The figure headed for a little valley between two hills of debris—and The New Man was thinking: "Out of sight so he can kill me?" And had more reason to think that when the valley almost magically twisted into a sort of half cavern in which the figure stopped—and so The New Man did, too. Here they could be seen only from a limited vantage point. Perhaps from one or two windows of these seemingly desolate apartment buildings—perhaps…. But no eyes could save The New Man from the fate to which he submitted (not that he submitted to fate, exactly, but the situation; he *would* defend himself), as the tall man stripped some of the dark material from his face and looked back at The New Man with an expression that joined scorn and mockery.

If The New Man's mouth did not fall open it should have. Apparently, here before him, was the most reviled and celebrated individual in the world at the moment: Osama bin Laden.

The mind forks down abrupt and manifold paths. Even as The New Man refused to believe that the incredible events of the last day could become this surreal, that Osama bin Laden could be walking the streets of New Jersey in order to meet someone named Wilson in a vacant lot, he accepted (or at least took the attitude of: *Let's see what happens now*) this new amazement as he accepted the fact that he had pierced a cipher with a phone number and thus placed him where he already was and had led him to this meeting.

The long, bearded face began to laugh—and laugh and laugh. There was the mouth with its darkness and its slightly discolored teeth. The laugh seemed to fly up and fill the atmosphere of this rubbled arena. The New Man felt he was being humiliated. It was a personal humiliation and one he had to share with the America of which he was not sure he was a part. Osama bin Laden, whose minions had attacked America, who had brought down the Towers, the totems of the West's Sodom and Gomorrah, the idols of Mammon, stood in this blasphemous wilderness alone and unafraid, laughing before The New Man amidst this ravaged outpost of the New World, in the smoking shadow of the land he had transformed.

The New Man's mind would have run on farther into the chaos of this absurdity, but the figure so suddenly revealed stopped laughing and spoke—and changed the "facts" The New Man had suddenly grasped.

"I am not him."

"No?" Though it was not quite a question. Or the question might have been: *Are you my madness?*

"I am his double."

Just like that it became the substance of a bad, dark comedy. Yes, there had been something on the news, about bin Laden moving about every few days, about how he had a double (hadn't Wilson's reports said so, too?)—maybe more than one. Apparently Saddam Hussein had a double, why not bin Laden?

Abruptly The New Man felt less paralyzed; the real UBL would have been unbelievable; a double fit more aptly into the nature of the past day and a half. But still, this was nothing less than the macabre humor of existence.

"His double." He laid the word out flat, like a target.

"Yes," the other nodded, with apparent satisfaction. A

peculiar smile formed among the dark beard. It was as if this mimicry were a sort of coup.

The New Man looked and looked at the face. It was so like the El Greco image…. "So you keep your face covered—not to look conspicuous?" He would use the weapon of the sardonic; but on the precipice he walked, it seemed a pitiful weapon.

The man seemed to pause over "conspicuous"; then he grunted. "Do you have what Wilson was supposed to bring?"

The New Man had nothing but his own questions. Carefully he said, "What's that?"

There was no direct answer. "You read the message?"

"I decoded it, yes." The New Man had to declare he was not a mere reader.

The Double did not seem surprised at this feat. "But you do not know what is known *before* the message?"

Codes and ciphers were one thing; The New Man did not care for cryptic talk. "How could I?" He laid down his ignorance like a virtue.

But now the Double was curt. "You have his things? Wilson's?"

"I have—the bag."

The Double frowned, then widened his eyes with the thrust of a word: "Where?"

The New Man realized this was a sort of strength. He would not be killed as long as— "Someplace," he said. He felt himself studied from the height of that face. Beyond that face, the rich, end-of-summer sky was like a halo without borders.

"So you do not know anything?"

Actually, The New Man felt he'd come to know a good deal. "Except what was in—"

"Why did you come?"

"Because I deciphered—" But it was a repetition that was not a reason; translation of the columns had been more a result than the source of his acts.

The Double made an exasperated noise. He looked past The New Man, looked about at the cul de sac of rubble—and suddenly upward, at a noise in the sky. The dark silhouette of a plane moved quickly across the sun drenched blueness. "Fighter jets," said the Double, mockingly.

"Yes," said The New Man, "You were very successful."

"We?" As if the noun were a mysterious entity. A pause, then: "Yes."

The New Man might have asked if somewhere in this human spirit there was not remorse for the killing of thousands of people—but if this was a double, he was only the reflection of the one who had done the deed, not the doer himself. Though by giving himself to be that reflection didn't he approve of the deeds of that image? The New Man said, "So successful they are ready for anything now."

The dark eyes were stern. "No one is ready for anything. Allah is ready, that is all. *You* cannot *know*—" He pointed fiercely at The New Man.

"So you are no more ready than we are." Even as he waited the instant for the Double's response, or evasion, it was The New Man's turn to consider the use of "we." Was he only pretending to share in the psychic damage done to America?

The Double said, "We are ready to accept the future."

The future seemed a strange world to use in that apocalyptic landscape, with the surreal meeting between a man who was escaping a lifelong identity and a man who posed as another man. For the future is always a question of identity. The question of what will befall us is actually one that asks: What will we make of ourselves; what—whom—will we be in the circumstances that come?

The New Man said, "Why was Wilson supposed to meet you?" This was a euphemistic question. What he wanted to say was, *What the hell was Wilson doing with—for—you?*

The Double scowled at him. "You are not the one to tell."

The New Man would not accept he would be given no answers. "If you were supposed to meet him, why was he— *there*…when—"

"He wasn't supposed to be." The Double was stern and disapproving—and, perhaps, disconcerted. But he said this loudly, as if threatening The New Man with an accusation.

Though somehow The New Man did not feel threatened. In the pause after the other's outburst he had the calm of the sane before the mad; and perhaps the Double may have worried he had misplaced anger over the preferable control of calculation.

Standing his ground in this little alcove of ruin, The New Man had to be fraught with the mystery of Wilson. If Wilson, possibly a traitor to his country (or a double agent?— Again, a matter of identities), the commonplace man of Babylon, the Long Island commuter with U.S. intelligence briefs in his bag and pages of code, if Wilson had known and yet had been there, had been high up in the tower, in the zone certain to be hit by the plane, if Wilson had been there, perhaps…. The thought came to The New Man: if Wilson, suddenly overwhelmed by his betrayal of his country, knowing in those last moments he could not stop the attack, knowing he could not simply call the cops or the feds and say "Two planes are going to hit The World

Trade Center, the jihad is bringing them down," perhaps the least he could do was die with the innocent: one truly guilty life (more guilty than the hijackers) thrown amongst the unsuspecting masses. And so at the last minute he had ascended high up to accept death—and more: left a sort of warning afterward, a trail and the old New Man had been chosen—by chance?—to be the one to carry the message into the apocalypse.

"What did you want from Wilson?" The New Man said to the Double. That simple question gave the air between the two men the sense that The New Man was edging toward the upper hand—despite his vast ignorance of so many things.

The Double would not immediately reply. He was groping back to the strength, the protection of a menacing calculation. "I am not here to inform infidels."

But this seemed an affected declaration. The New Man said, "Haven't you already 'informed' us?"

The Double gave a satisfied smile—or was it something less than satisfaction?—and looked toward the burning sky of the west. He said, "There will be many more messages."

"Like what?"

"The next day and the day after will show it."

Noise came from the sky again and the men looked up again. It was the fighter plane once more—or another. The Double laughed and shouted up to the unseen pilot. "What can you know, looking down from the sky? Allah looks down on you, and sees all that is hidden." He waved his arms and gave an odd giggle after this sudden proclamation.

To The New Man this was wholly histrionics: puerile, ridiculous. Sheer madness. "Where do you go from here?" He was demanding a fool reign himself in.

Perhaps The Double did not quite grasp the idiomatic question. He gave The New Man his mocking expression—which pressed the latter to other questions: "You to walk around New Jersey like that?"

"What do you mean?" The Double actually seemed genuinely puzzled.

"What you're wearing."

He drew himself up. "It is what I wear."

"You look like the angel of death."

"You know nothing of angels."

"And with the face of Osama bin Laden."

The Double burst forth with "So you know Osama's holy. I am proud to—" But it was a passion that was abruptly confused. He cut himself off and in a more measured tone said, "In jihad we are all faces of one mirror."

"A crowd," The New Man drawled with mockery. The Double warned him with a look, but The New Man added, "Of images—idols. I thought—"

It was a telling instinct that had made The New Man choose those words. The Double was angry. "We are not images, we are men. *You* are images: your TVs, your movies." Abruptly The New Man recalled that Arabian figure looking at the televisions—"faces of one mirror"—in the window of the appliance store. Had it been this Double? Who was going on: "In the center of your city there are advertising images as tall as buildings. Women uncovered. You send it to the sky—that you are sinners."

Now, less from instinct than the desire to confront this righteous outburst, The New Man said, "Are *you* not an image?"

The Double fumbled with his words. "I was born with a face, he was born with a face—" he was babbling the obvious, seeking a handle to overthrow facts.

"And he keeps his face and name; *you*...only have the face left."

With a cry from the Double, a billowy long arm whipped out and struck at The New Man. But instinct was still working; he dodged the blow enough so that he was hit only glancingly. He staggered and grasped at the robed form. Yet at first he clutched only loose clothing. He had to grope for the wiry, crazed body within.

The two struggled, pressing against each other, hitting each other with ill-timed punches as they broke apart. The New Man saw an erratically moving face, felt the bony body he hit, and saw the sky, slanted and depthless behind his adversary. Finally, stumbling with their efforts, they both fell upon the rubble.

It was a mutual collapse so simultaneous it seemed orchestrated. The New Man was rolling away from the Double the instant he felt the rough ground. He also cried out with the pain of hitting jagged debris—more pain than the other had inflicted on him. The New Man began to stagger upward, but remained in a half crouch some feet away, when he saw the Double was not getting up at all, but was half sitting up, a hand pressed against an area of blood smeared across his face: the blood of the mirror-man himself, not bin Laden.

The two men regarded each other with predatory—and yet hopeless—eyes. The New Man was aware of the other's breathing, of the glaring dark pupils that studied him with dislike and wariness. Did The Double have a weapon? If he did, would he not have used it instead of striking out with a fist? Perhaps anger had pushed the man to the urge of a more physical satisfaction that a knife or gun could render.

Then The New Man noticed the packets of white powder strewn about, like sudden, small flowers in the rubble. It was obvious they had fallen free from the Double during the struggle. They were a stark, minute purity among the debris. The nearest packet was halfway between The New Man and the Double. The New Man moved to reach for it and at the same time picked up half of a brick so that when the other appeared about to lunge (not with much strength) The New Man brandished the brick and The Double abruptly checked himself. He panted and trembled slightly; his hand returned to the blood on his face (as if pretending the hand had never left the wound). The New Man sensed this was not a very fierce fighter for the jihad. Mirroring the mighty bin Laden had sapped something from the Double's core.

The New Man held the small plastic bag. Its lightness was deceiving in regards to the gravity of its use. "Dope?" The Double blinked his eyes. The New Man said, "Cocaine? Opium? Heroin?"

"I am not here to tell you—" But there was no energy in this; the face seemed utterly exhausted.

"Wilson was to come here for this?"

The New Man's mind sped through the collage of news that had spilled into his consciousness from the TV during the past day. It was known—assumed?—that bin Laden's group, puritanical Muslims, had made no little pocket change on the smuggling of heroin. Afghanistan had traditionally been a major grower of poppy, though in a fiat of zealousness, the Taliban had recently and abruptly banned its cultivation.

But now The New Man's possession of the small plastic bag

seemed to give the Double renewed strength. He lunged again; The New Man (he had put down the brick) could not avoid him; the struggle was renewed.

In this second round of ineffectual punches and pushing, stumbling and tumbling, The New Man felt less anger and urgency. This was not a threat to his life; it was an annoyance. He could not help feel himself engaged in a farce. With a burst of strength he thrust The Double from him. The man landed with an audible thud and the gasp of a groan on the uncomfortable bed of debris, his robed body now streaked and soiled.

The New Man shook with his efforts. He looked at his hands and saw they were smeared with blood. The other's blood? His? Both? He felt the disgust of contamination.

The Double croaked out something that was surely a profanity—or a particularly vicious prayer—and got to his feet. As he rose, The New Man saw that this second phase of the struggle had further divested the dark figure. There was a syringe on the ground.

With the instinct of unveiling a crucial weakness of an opponent, The New Man bent down and was about to pick up the syringe when a more immediate instinct stopped him. He looked back at the panting Double, and who eyed the syringe with an expression that genuinely frightened The New Man. He stepped back as the Double lunged again, this time not to continue the struggle but to retrieve the syringe.

As if allowing another man his doom, The New Man relinquished the syringe. With the small pointed instrument in his hand, the Double stepped back. The syringe's metal tip was blurred by a plastic cap, and yet the end-of-summer light appeared to penetrate the plastic and cause the hair-thin metal to glint. The Double might have been holding a weapon; he was like a frightened Middle European Christian warding off a vampire with a crucifix.

The New Man felt the ugly wetness of the blood on his hands. The warm breeze blew against the wetness.

This surge of sensation, along with the garishness of the spectacle of the Double and the syringe, pushed a wave of repulsion through The New Man. He thrust his hands painfully into the debris, and, with this rough cleanser, scrapped most of the redness from his flesh. He resisted the temptation to wipe his hands on his clothes.

When he had rudely purged his skin from the blood of the struggle, he saw a small black plastic case almost at his feet. As he picked it up the Double shrieked, and The New Man braced for another charge. But both men were past that now. They were locked in a surrender and exhaustion to the bizarre, and a certain, sad fate.

The New Man opened the case. There were three small vials of liquid in it. There was a syringe and the space for another syringe—the one The Double held in his hand.

The New Man gazed back at The Double. "A junkie," he said, flatly.

Perhaps the Double did not know this colloquialism—which, after all, was a bit outdated. But he understood the essence of the pronouncement. His face slightly trembled. A flood of sternness washed over the bearded features. But that resolve was almost immediately defeated, and a sort of lostness followed, and gripped the man, and shook his addicted flesh.

The New Man felt himself clogged by the sickness of circumstance. His new life was all madness.

•   •   •

"Listen," he said quietly, carefully. "Listen." He moved slowly, so as to not alarm this big, sad figure of man. The New Man found a rough, sizable chunk of debris that had once been a portion of a building and sat. "I'll tell you a story."

The Double said fiercely, gasping, "A story?"

"Yes."

"What? Why?"

"Just to tell it." The New Man looked at this mirror-man as if he were himself. Because I—you—"

But he did not have the rest of the words even though he was prepared to say many words. The other, tall, dark robed, and sullied with the excess of a futile struggle, was also a victim of a farce: a sort of strange ally. His co-actor. A man who had taken up another identity. Perhaps that suicide alone had caused him to subsume himself with narcotics.

But if The New Man could not give the reason why he was afflicted with the sudden desire to tell his story he did in fact tell it, beginning with yesterday morning (God, long ago yesterday) at The World Trade Center, the revelation (or was it simply a desire) that struck him after his escape, jumped back farther in time with a line or two of biography: his commutes from Long Island (wondering if the Double knew what Long Island was, if he knew it as anything more than geography); his estrangement from his family (well, bin Laden had become estranged from his); then returned to his arrival in New Jersey, the motel, the reports and the columns of numbers. The Double seemed to shift uneasily with that, as if something unpleasant of himself were about to be exposed.

In every essential terse description of himself, his past and recent acts, The New Man sought to convey his need for a transformation that had become a mockery and a sort of a trap. Yet just why he was baring his soul, so to speak (or at least a painful facet of it), to the Double, he would not have been able to say. Only that it seemed a natural (if one used the word loosely) outcome to all preceding events. Perhaps The New Man wanted to fight the madness with his own odd tale.

The New Man did think, as he listened to himself, that his story sounded trite and superficial, no matter the hints of personal depths with which he tried to lace it. He wondered if he were not exposing his banal life and "transformation" to make the pitiful Double seem less uncomfortable about the spectacle he presented. Though it seemed hard to believe that any sort of consideration for another would invade him now.

Apart from that brief flicker of apparent unease—or of something else—at the mention of the code, the Double stolidly listened to The New Man's story. His face gave no expression of interest, scorn—or solidarity.

With the end his brief tale, The New Man found a more comfortable seat among the ruins—as if he had been given permission to relax, or at least reduce his guard. Thus, with the story done, the two men sat, looking at each other, with expressions that were not so unalike. The circumstance of the ambiguity of identity had worked them into a sort of forced, uneasy brotherhood.

There was the drone of a plane, far off, unseen. And, within sight, the darting silhouette of a bird, its body dark in the light of these last days of summer.

"A strange thing to do," mumbled the Double.

"Was it?" said The New Man, without irony reflecting back

upon the other.

"So now you are you," said the Double.

The New Man considered. "Yes—or another." The Double laughed.

As if beginning his own story, the Double's long, thin arm emerged from the black, billowy garments. It was a cautious emergence. The New Man might take this as a threat. But it was hardly that. The skin of the arm was lighter than that of the face and actually almost shocking to look at against the black cloth. It seemed an arm with little strength; and it seemed something of him exposed that was not part of the mirror of UBL.

The Double made preparations for injecting the syringe: taking a vial from the small plastic box, tying the bicep with a black strip. His face took on an expression of purposefulness and calm. With repulsive fascination The New Man saw the veins on the thin arm begin to protrude from the Double's flesh. Though as he injected the syringe into a vein, The New Man blinked, closed his eyes a long second (this consummation was too much) and half turned his head away. He did not want to witness something so personal. He did not want to see this evidence of a man's continual failure.

A sort of timeless, peaceful, paradisiacal air had settled over the ruins in which the two were half ensconced, half exposed. The harsh brightness of the sky seemed to have softened with the passage of a curious twist in time. And the returning, distant drone of a military plane, safeguarding the skies and the city below, was almost spiritually reassuring. After the anxieties and struggles of the day, The New Man felt utterly serene. He had plunged across a border in which he had been ravaged; but he had felt an end to it; he could be buffeted no more.

He studied the Double carefully. In this light and against the background of debris, within the hum of the far-off aircraft, the Double's face floated, the epitome of a foreign face in a foreign land. It was every foreign face and it was one alone. The mirror of bin Laden looked back at The New Man with an ease, a lack of self-consciousness. The vaguest smile seemed to drift across these features, as if an integral happiness, deep within the man, were being stirred. Then his eyes closed slowly and remained shut a moment, as if sealing in the sensation, which may then have passed from happiness to pleasure—or vice versa. The New Man recalled once reading that the Beat writer and longtime junkie, William Burroughs, had called heroin "the white powder of God" (strange the permanence of such flotsam of memory).

The New Man watched the Double quietly breathe.

The Double's eyes opened. The smile had become a peacefulness that passeth all understanding. He held up one of the other vials to the light of the late afternoon. He regarded it like a jeweler a gemstone. The jewel, in fact, would prove to be memory.

"My father grew this," he said. The words drifted out with soft, perfect timbre. "We lived in—" He pronounced a name (with a definite longing and affection) The New Man could not quite catch. But the name was not important; as the Double went on, it was easy enough to affix an approximate geography. This mirror of bin Laden was one of the scions of a Pashtun family on the border of Afghanistan and Pakistan, a borderland of the spirit as well as of nations.

The Double spoke with the acceptance of things as they are:

of the poverty that was perhaps more oppressive to his listener than to himself. The Double spoke of the fields of poppies (almost Whitmanesque was this brief vivid image), the child's memory of flowers bent lovingly by the wind; in the hard life he had been granted the bounty of Nature's aesthetic. There was a mumbled image of a little boy leaning over to press his nose among the blossoms. The New Man gave an involuntary shudder at the image: that innocence of childhood lost in the fits and starts of the years.

The Double spoke of the long work of the harvest, of hands raw with toil. "I touched my father's hands when I was a child. I was…" He drifted into a silence that sought a description. He could not find the word, then used an incorrect one: "Always…attracted—to how rough they were, like stones." With an interior and stoned look he studied his own hands, which were doubtless not as rough. The toil of being bin Laden's double would only leave an inner callous.

"I was almost a man," the Double said. He sighed and rolled his eyes skyward, as if seeing the transformations of the past above him. "The Soviets came." He paused. His eyes were sad—even pitiful. They held shards of an old chaos. "The ones who have no God." The Double intoned this as if repeating an old chant.

That was 1979, The New Man thought. In November the hostages in Iran, then in December the Russians swept into Afghanistan. It had been one of those small, intense periods of history in which the world seemed about to unravel, but did not. The New Man wondered if this September (and the fury that would surely come after) will prove another small intense moment of chaos that only *appeared* the doorway to the apocalypse.

The Double continued his memoir of drugs and invasion. Like his father, he fought, if sporadically, with the Mujahideen. "We killed a man together," he said. Father and son had been transporting, with the aid of weary horses, a crop of opium. "He was a young Russian, as young as I was, I think...." The Double's eyes, steeped in the drug, looked down at his own dark booted feet and the rubble. He was seeking the face of the slain in some memory at once integral and distorted with the righteousness of the invaded. The New Man could not tell if the precise essence of memory the Double sought had been found. Perhaps he was simply stymied, stuck on the hard image of that unburied body. An image he needed to cast off—as if it were the reoccurrence of an old illness. The Double shook his head; he muttered, murmured, babbled incoherently. Then, more clearly: "I met bin Laden. He was building roads. He had brought in machines, big machines."

The New Man waited. Here was the moment of transformation. Or servitude. Or perhaps it was not the moment. The Double fell silent.

"When? What year?" asked The New Man.

The Double looked at him in surprise—and almost as if insulted. In the happy languor of opiates and memory how was he supposed to recall years? And The New Man thought: If he tells me the Muslim year, how would I know what that meant? As if telepathic to such thoughts, the Double thrust back: "Your year or ours?" (As if not merely different numbers of years belonged to different peoples, but the nature of the years themselves different entirely.)

The New Man made a deprecating gesture. What did it really matter, the year? On the eve of the millennium celebrations, he had read about the calendars of other cultures. How 2000 was this year on the Chinese calendar and such and such year on the Muslim calendar. There had indeed been the fear that those who followed the latter reckoning would explode something in Times Square, upsetting the telegenic Methuselah Dick Clark's narrative of the arrival of the new epoch. The New Man recalled watching *The Tonight Show* and Jay Leno making some joke about a New Year's parade for one of the Bowl games in California: "Watch out for the Islamic Jihad float." California had in fact escaped terrorism. The New Man recalled one of the reports in Wilson's bag: about a terrorist crossing the border from Canada into Washington intending havoc at LAX in L.A., foiled only because one of the personnel at the border had thought the Arab man suspicious. He had been detained, his car searched. Perhaps it had been a case of racial profiling—which no one complained about. The new millennium, at least its first, immediate years, might be a time for venal instincts, racial or otherwise.

The Double was saying, "I saw him once then, then not again until he came back to Afghanistan from Sudan."

That would be the middle of the '90s, if The New Man correctly recalled the bits of biography of bin Laden that had swept across TV in the last day.

By the time of this second meeting, the Double had lived many years as a man whose principal support had been the trade learned from the father—who seemed to disappear from the Double's story. Killed in the '80s by the Soviets? Or in the '90s by the Taliban? The Northern Alliance? The government of Pakistan, more officious than holy, had pushed the drug business out of their country to some degree. The sowers and harvesters and traders who had lived back and forth across the border, giving lie to the demarcation of maps, operated mainly in Afghanistan now, and the opium business flourished. As the '90s blossomed into an era in which Americans wallowed in their SUVs and dotcoms and tossed aside fellatio in the White House with the remark, So what, we're making money, the Double and his ilk were producing more than half the world's opium. By the turning of the West's millennium, the hard land, the too often invaded country, was producing seventy percent of the planet's "white powder of God."

But before that marketing height, the Double's hand in the trade had been reduced by a new calling. The moment of transformation—or self obliteration—had come. The Double—a father now himself—and one of his sons were transporting a harvest through a desolate stretch of mountains (thus the grind of the poor continues, that mocking, absurd cycle) when they were confronted by armed men emerging from a cave. Bin Laden was one of the men. The man who would become the Double confronted this original image.

"He didn't say it," said the Double; "one of the men did."

He meant remarking on the similarity between the poor harvester of poppies and the rich terrorist. It would have to be someone else, not bin Laden, who sealed with eyes the resemblance. If we look in mirrors (and one supposed bin Laden did only infrequently) it is for others who see us daily to assess more accurately connections between one face and another.

"I was…proud. Osama bin Laden. I knew who he was then."

As did America. Bin Laden had returned from the war in Afghanistan to his native Saudi Arabia a Muslim hero. But right upon the end of that war (1989), in the latter months of 1990,

America was sending hundreds of thousands of troops to Saudi Arabia for Operation Desert Shield—which would become Desert Storm— to rout the villain of the moment, Saddam Hussein, from Kuwait. Bin Laden excoriated the Saudis for allowing the soldiers of the infidel to occupy the lands of the Prophet, of Mecca and Medina. He put up quite a row, in fact, and wound up having his citizenship revoked as he repaired to Sudan with a plethora of plans for jihad. The Iraqis were driven from Kuwait, though Saddam remained in power, assuaging his loss by murdering innumerable insurgents who expected U.S. help for their revolt, but got none. (Some sort of uneasy, grisly echo of the Bay of Pigs). In late February of 1993, a bomb was set off in a parking garage below the World Trade Center. Bin Laden, or at least his cohorts, would be linked to that, and a few other things down the line.

The Double had stayed the night with bin Laden and his men. "He was a holy man," said the Double. The New Man wondered if the "was," this attribution of holiness in the past tense, was a Freudian slip or a conscious perception. Or simply the roughness of one to whom English was a second language.

But the night in that cave: there was the image of sprawled, rumpled bodies. The New Man imagined, in the mountainous womb, the beginnings of an alteration, a mark being laid upon the young opium farmer that he could hardly be aware of at the time, some deep, damned, psychology being struck. Though the Double said nothing further about that night.

The next day the Double and his son went on with their business. But there was a new future looming. The Double, not yet the Double, would be working with bin Laden's drug operation. He would not necessarily have a more profitable life, but a more, well, yes, "holy" one.

The Double pointed a finger at The New Man. The finger itself was a little unsteady—more precisely, it was languid (it seemed about to be moved by the slightest breeze); yet this lack of forcefulness seemed all the more a threat. "All of you: America, the Jews, Israel—you controlled us too much. Osama…" He trailed off with this announcement of the much spoken name as if this last repetition would be the sound that sundered all that conspiratorial bondage. "We *will* get our land back," he said, with dreamy insistence.

The New Man took this without insult. The man was a wretched drug addict, crazed with a past of poverty; and he was a man who could not carry his own name. The New Man felt pity for him.

The change in the Double's opium trade was simple: he was to bring his harvest to bin Laden's men.

Here the story got very interesting—though who knew how much of it was the transliteration of imagination further embroidered by the present flow of the drug in the Double's blood. He described operations in caves, or modern, industrial facilities miraculously placed in the desolation of mountains and badlands in which the misfits evolved from Islamic fundamentalism, the New World Order and the breakup of the USSR worked at making a strain of heroin more potent, vicious—and so more lovely to the addict. Within the initial rush of sweet satisfaction and subsequent intimations of grace was a danger that could only increase the drug's allure. God's white powder became the weapon of the warriors of the deity precisely named: Allah. (Though of course all this was so ungodly.) Burroughs' old description now bore the purpose of enormous and diabolic scope. As The New Man received the visions of the Double in accented English, he thought here was the work of a cabal of demons intent on recreating a narcotic that would undermine the West by entering like a prostitute into the sights of the soul who sought the most immediate, illicit pleasure.

Perhaps The New Man was thinking of prostitutes because of that story about bin Laden he had read from Wilson's bag: young bin Laden getting the call after rising up from sinful flesh. He said to the Double, "Is that when you started?" He looked at the small black case from which the Double had drawn his needle and vial. "Or before?" The West was not the only geography lured by the prostitute.

The Double considered him a long time. There was again the distant drone of a plane. Neither man looked to its source. This was indication of an activity that could not affect them now. The Double slowly opened and shut his eyes, opened them again, as if trying to clear them for another sort of both inner and outer vision.

Surely in the bliss of the drug's course, no addict thinks the drug a burden, scourge or damnation, but a communion of some outside grace taken into the very warmth of the blood. In sentences and phrases broken by pauses—for the Double was deep in the drug now, and it was not so easy to emerge from the strict majesty of that estate—he answered with an echo: "Before?… After?" By this repetition saying that he did not know, or at least thought the westerner's need for time's demarcation not essential to the issue. His conscription into the service of bin Laden's network could hardly fit into the borders of a "before" and "after" the westerner sought. The Double's birth in that time and place fated him for both the drug and jihad. It wasn't even a fantastical concept. "Before" and "after" both fell on the curve of a circle, each point losing beginning and ending.

What the Double did tell The New Man, with pauses that said as much as words or allowed The New Man the spaces into which imagination could fill more narrative, was that it had been a while before he had taken up the habit of the drug whose raw source he had caravanned from fields to badlands and borders. The meeting with bin Laden seemed to have no midpoint in that crossing. It was a personal border, a border of the psyche for that man of the borderland—and when it came, it had not been a difficult passage. The Double had not weighed himself with the imprecations of piety, the hypocrisies that said the drug was for furthering the downfall of the infidels. He had made his living through the poppies, that was all. There was no great evil grandness to it, no sense of international machination, personal violation or the immemorial plant as a tool between Allah and the unbelievers. He accepted the drug within his body as he had accepted the rough distances he had had to travel with his crop; as he would accept his role in the jihad's work; as he accepted his resemblance to the one whose face was now simultaneously the West's Satan and the savior of Islam.

In knowing how to work all these things as they are, he gave himself to the drug at the end of those journeys, not in the midst of them, rewarding himself with this grace and defilement when his senses could allow themselves the cessation of a day of oblivion. At unknown points across the land, the horizon darkening with a peace without calendar, beneath the stars with

Arabic names, he reposed in the stupor in which The New Man now saw the Double recede. This mirror of another man mirrored his own inebriation, a repetition of self that seemed much like watching the spirit if not the body recede into the vanishing perspective of a metaphorical Renaissance painting, a diminishing into a sorrowed point of infinity.

At the same time, the addict's life as mirror to bin Laden was becoming another sort of drug. As American intelligence sought to covertly disrupt the Saudi's operation, as Israeli and Egyptian intelligence did likewise, more and more the Double was pressed into the service of bearing *the* image. His poppy trafficking was reduced—and his forays into the drug increased. –As if a balance that had allowed him to function fruitfully while imbibing in periodic self-desecration had been tipped. "Once," the Double related, "I sat on a mountain for days—like Jesus waiting for the devil. They told me one of the *secret* infidels was supposed to see me. So they would be confused, think bin Laden was deep in the country, instead of…somewhere."

This vignette spoke volumes to The New Man. Like most westerners he had to remind himself that Islam regarded Jesus as one of its prophets, as it did Abraham (who was, indeed, the first Muslim) and Moses. And that "waiting for the devil": the very sight, the very act of being *seen* by the West. And "the secret infidels": all of us in the West are infidels and we don't know it? A blasphemy secret to ourselves. Ultimately, just the image of the heroin-suffused Double, raised and exposed in light and height, a target, a decoy, suggested a mocking of Western perception, suggested how easy it was to deceive reality, suggested we were in bondage to image—suggested reality was something else, after all.

And The New Man had to think of that story in the reports: of the cleric meeting bin Laden, of the theological/political exchange. What if that covert divine had met this Double and not bin Laden? After all, there was the Double, "waiting for the devil," waiting to be seen by one of "the secret infidels".... Ominous, ominous absurdity. And possibility.

Were there other doubles of bin Laden? Indeed, was bin Laden himself one man or a reflection of some "ideal"? A sort of supra-being given life in the moments of Western "seeing" so we could have the excuse of a single target, the excuse of the belief that if that target were annihilated we would be safe?

And the Double spoke of targets and annihilation. Without using those words. Deep in the summer of '98, coming upon Clinton's announcement of his "inappropriate" relationship with cherubic-faced Monica, the virulent air strikes on bin Laden's old haunts in Sudan and his renowned redoubt of Afghanistan found the Double pressed into service as decoy, to confound intelligence reports. But the way in which the Double, relocating himself in memory in the roughness of Afghanistan told it, it seemed to The New Man that bin Laden's coterie placed the Double in one spot and then another with the irrational perception that the "smart bombs" or whatever the infidels were using to try to destroy the warriors of Allah—that the missiles could note the Double and believe they had the very mastermind in their sights. As if the machines, the weapons of the West, had the West's prejudices. The Double spoke calmly of the great destruction that had fallen about him, the flowering explosions, the sharp showers of earth and stone, the thundering, concussive sound (he brought hands to his ears). The New Man guessed the Double had been high at the time, as he was now, stoned into a Zen-like stolidity—and The New Man, wrought now in his own irrationalities, experienced the recall of the rush of words from "The Star-Spangled Banner": "...rocket's red glare...bombs bursting in air...gave proof—" Proof that bin Laden was alive and the Double was alive. And The New Man's next thought, a not so irrational connection, was that somewhere was the stained, blue dress.

He asked the Double: "Were there others who looked like him?" The Double frowned back at him as if not understanding the simple words. Or as if pained *by* understanding them. The New Man pressed: "Were you the only one?"

The Double's eyes blinked; he did not respond. The New Man wondered if he had insulted the Double—but he did not think so. Perhaps the drug had just driven too deeply into the blood. Perhaps—then the Double suddenly said, "You are too concerned with *looking*—"

Well, The New Man was insulted—at least, amused. Didn't everyone—wasn't life—wasn't "looking" the essence of what everyone did? He threw aside his very recent thought about the bondage of image. His mind played back the dozen times (or more) he had seen, on TV, the Twin Towers collapse. He had come down out of that danger, emerged himself from the fall of the Ozymandias-like structures of the West: he had been there. And from his being-there he suddenly knew it was more the *seeing* of the collapse than the fleeing from the collapse, than being in the center of the danger that had made him understand—something. The millions—billions—of people watching those redundant images on TV: some of them had to understand, by that seeing, the hatred others had. The seeing of the act. And perhaps all this, the flight, the seeing, were things The New Man was trying to escape as much as his old life.

At last The Double, as if in a farewell message before his attention wholly departed, said, "Yes." For a moment The New Man had forgotten his question, then remembered as the Double added: "Someone had told me there were others; someone told me there were not." He shrugged—and might have left it there, at that ambiguity, but added, forlornly, "I did meet two others. They did not look like him as much as I did. They were not as tall. I was…the best." After his self-applied accolade the Double sighed. What did number matter? He was "the best."

"The best." It seemed—at best—a phrase too Western. Though it conveyed the situation well enough. At any rate, The New Man saw a maze of Arabian images. Something out of *One Thousand and One Nights*. Bin Laden at the ever shifting center, and these satellites of doubles, the Double here resembling bin Laden closely, the others less so, a scattering of mirrors duplicating an essential image in varying degrees of clarity or imperfection. Like a fuzzy substrate of atomic particles, their presence known but their precise course elusive, the doubles were an orchestration of the laws of Nature that could never be wholly calculated—only in the aggregate were they crudely defined, or located.

Though the Double before The New Man exhibited no quantum fuzziness but had the sorry solidity of life.

The Double's speech grew more disjointed as the drug further claimed him. And yet his story, at least to The New Man, had grown more vivid, more directed to one point. Since the bombing of Afghanistan in August 1998, concurrently the Double's addiction increased and his use as a double increased.

He had been reduced to—or refined to—a man who appeared, whose *raison d'être* to the world of others was indeed image, never mind his own religion's proscriptions against such. He was a tool of the *outside*, of seeing, while he sunk further within the interior of the drug, whose supplies coursed the East and the West—while he lived in the center of that supply. It was somewhat of a mystic's existence—and yet, it seemed, without revelation.

But the apotheosis of all mystics' lives is death. In fact, mysticism is the training for death. While the Double's "death" was an abrupt removal from the center of image and stupor in Afghanistan to this mission across the world, in New Jersey, across the river from the smoking ruins of the World Trade Center, a havoc apparently created by the being whose image the Double, through accident of birth, carried.

Beyond the twisted poetry of it, that sort of worked if one looked at it in a mad way, it did not make sense. To conscript the addicted mirror of bin Laden to pass on to a Western traitor (Wilson?) a supply of heroin—or receive a supply. Or was there some other, "truer" purpose, one the Double could not speak of—or had never known? And yet, perhaps it did carry all the poetic sense of the *One Thousand and One Nights*, or at least the modern, fantastical, forking logic of a tale by Borges.

Wilson: Wilson again. The Western traitor. The New Man, as he watched the Double shut his eyes and remain silent, considered the man he had considered far too little, actually—since it was Wilson who had thrust The New Man into the situation that had begotten such weirdness amidst The New Man's own attempt at transformation. In all of his casual reading, newspapers, magazines, on Islamic terrorism (articles half read during his commute), The New Man had never come across mention that these fundamentalists for Allah had ever employed infidel traitors. Unlike the West's previous enemy, the Soviets, who had courted the unsure or fevered hearts of souls as diverse as the Rosenbergs and Aldrich Ames, these Muslims had apparently never wanted help from those damned by not believing in the God Mohammed had declared as the one true God. History often provides the one glaring exception to a pattern, an instance, an act whose uniqueness is apart from what is prior and what is after; but The New Man was trying to make sense out of the real truth behind the suburban image of Wilson—and could not. For the moment the man himself, middle aged, in plain clothes, the commuter from Babylon (this name the only apparent Middle East connection), the Mets fan, just seemed so apart from the millennial intrigues of the nations of the Gods of the world's three premier religions—and the sudden terror that had, now, in an instant, swept across the West.

Yet Wilson, or at least Wilson's image was elusive, and slipped away from The New Man before this stuporous reflection of a terrorist. Though The New Man knew Wilson had not so much departed as been put aside by immediate circumstances. He was in the very air of all this, and could never be far off.

Indeed, The New Man heard the Double mumble something abruptly, and repeat it—something that sounded like "Wilson." As if the drug were unearthing the original partner the Double should have been joined with in the rubbled lot. The New Man strained, leaned forward a bit, hoping the Double would say more (and more clearly), but this image of bin Laden was again silent.

10. *Other Invaders*

The Double had remained wordless and unstirring for some time, eyes closed. One could almost hear the slight breeze curbed about the immobile obstruction of his body. Then he slightly rocked, swayed by an inner wind. The New Man sensed there would be nothing further from him. In fact, it looked as if the Double were about to keel over—and nearly did; he pitched forward, The New Man thrust out an arm, and stayed the long bony torso of the Double with one straining hand. The New Man pushed the Double back into an upright position. There was the unpleasant feeling of his bony body. The Double's eyes flickered a moment, then remained shut. The New Man slowly withdrew his arm.

He had the sensation of reaching the ending of a very odd, bizarre film, with the lights at the edge of the theatre coming up slightly, giving enough illumination for those who want to leave while the credits roll. In fact, why didn't he leave just now? What was he waiting for? Did he expect anything else from the Double?

As he faced these questions, he was also becoming more aware of his surroundings—in a more, well, practical manner. The black robed, stoned Double, the bags of drugs, the debris, and the end of day sky—

Then, as if he were also becoming aware of the voices of the scattered audience of the theatre, his attention was suddenly drawn to the approach of four men entering the lot.

He was astonished by this invasion of others into what had

become an intensely private arena; and he was afraid. The questions of only a moment ago mocked him. If only he had left—

The men were apparently Middle Eastern—marked by their features and the babble of their language, not their clothes, which were Western. Also, unlike the Double, they did not have beards; two had moustaches. But whereas the Double had seemed ominous in approach, tall, dark robed and bearded, his continued presence had grown harmless, even gentle, while the hubbub of conversation these men directed between themselves and the words abruptly called out to the Double and The New Man were hardly gentle.

The movie wasn't over after all.

The New Man stood up as they neared. Their eyes were piercing, with an aggression that needed exercising. They appeared to be in their thirties.

The Double remained precariously sitting, in a half lotus position of narcotic nirvana. One of the men gestured angrily at the Double and barked out something to the others. It seemed a remark of scorn.

Another said to The New Man: "Wilson?"

Perhaps he should pretend to be Wilson, was The New Man's first thought. But he had, right in front of him, the sad spectacle of a double. He said, flatly, "No."

The one syllable sent a shock through the four men. They jabbered threateningly. One of them demanded, "Who are you?" in an accent heavy with threat and revulsion.

A little less flatly, with the irony of man about to be executed and so is free to say anything, The New Man said, "Newman."

Two of the men repeated, in overlapping, accented chorus:

"Newman?" This was at once stupid and menacing. Each of the four looked at each other: they were angry, surprised, fearful.

The fearful believe they must act—to hide their fear from others and disguise it to themselves. One of the men suddenly strode forward and struck out at the Double, whose tenuous grasp on an upright position was broken. He sprawled, with the faintest cry, across the debris. The New Man felt his own anger overriding fear. The Double had become, in this past brief hour, an unexpected but complementary compatriot. He and the Double were two men with recreated identities, identities created more by events than by will. The New Man felt as if he himself had been struck. He made a motion to go to the Double, but one of the four spoke a rough word—clearly a threat. Two others stepped toward The New Man. He poised himself for the uneven fight. He glanced down at the Double, who muttered some soft sound and twisted his body on the debris, seeking a greater angle of comfort. His eyes flickered. And that was all. He remained in his stupor, breathing peacefully.

The New Man and the four men looked at each other. Perhaps two of the men were younger than thirty, with a hardness of face that had come with a hardness of purpose, not age.

One of them abruptly noted the plastic bags strewn about. With a cry he went to one; quickly the men retrieved the drugs, and they held them as rescued religious objects and glared with great accusation at The New Man.

"Did Wilson send you?" demanded one.

"Where is he?" said another.

Wilson in a way (unintentionally or perhaps with mysterious intent) had sent him, but The New Man didn't answer that question. He chose the second. "He's dead."

"Dead!" screeched one of them. Another screeched in his native tongue. The death of the man who wasn't there threatened them.

"He was in the Towers." He might have been speaking a terrible fact to the naiveté of a child. He said it calmly, as if this gave him a power.

One of the men, clearly surprised, shot something at the others. The New Man had the intuition the words meant: "He wasn't supposed to be."

The upset and confusion among the four made The New Man feel brazen. "He sent me down ten floors to…get something for him."

"What?" A man with a sharp, brown face, thick hair, clipped moustache and wearing a soiled short sleeve shirt with a black and white checkered pattern stepped threateningly up to The New Man, who paused before he answered.

"A bag. His bag."

"Bag?" shot one.

"With his…papers. Some papers."

"Where is it?" demanded the checkerboard man.

"It's not here," said The New Man, with the confidence of the doomed. And then, as he had so recently thought with the Double, perhaps these men needed the bag and would not kill him because only he knew where it was.

"What do you know?" was the next demand.

The New Man was almost honest. "Only"—he gestured— "what I see." He was amused at his own irony.

The checkerboard man looked at the sprawled, scrawny Double as if trying to see this mirror of bin Laden through the eyes of a foreigner. "What does that mean?"

The New Man breathed calmly. He would try to be in control—if not of the situation, at least himself. "There was a message to come here. I came."

The checkerboard man's eyes were narrow. "It wasn't for you."

"Wilson couldn't come—I came." The New Man gave the others a little smile—as if he possessed the impetus of a joke the others could not help being played on them.

But none of the four wanted any humor. "And by coming you know?" This was not the checkerboard man but another, in drab pants and shirt of different shades of olive.

The New Man looked at the face of the man who had said this. It was a wisdom the speaker himself could not fully appreciate. One "knew" by entering a situation with some prior knowledge.

Another asked, "You're Wilson's friend?"

"I worked with him."

"How—worked?"

"Same job."

"Same job—but what did he tell you?"

The New Man thought about Wilson's passionate meanderings concerning the Mets. Should he tell them that? About Ventura's "grand slam single" in the '99 playoffs the Mets finally lost to the Braves by walking in the winning run? He said. "I only read —what was in the bag."

The four jabbered furiously among themselves; then the man in the checkered shirt addressed The New Man again in English, with the manner of a grave and stern judge explaining to a recalcitrant criminal why he must be dealt with in the most severe way. "We did not trust Wilson. He was necessary. *I* thought he could be working against us. When I saw him with you—" He gestured at the Double. He stopped; then, very calmly: "You are like the people in the buildings. Wilson might be dead, you might be alive—"

"I was in the buildings."

The other didn't care. "Those who think they escaped will die later. Today, tomorrow." He made a motion with his head. It seemed the most natural, unconscious movement, as if he were tossing aside an unnecessary thought. But it was a sort of tribal communication.

Two of the others attacked The New Man.

The New Man was still winded from the struggle with the Double. And now he was outnumbered, and by younger men. Though at first the fury and fear of survival made him acquit himself well. A fortunately aimed punch knocked one assailant back, but in a moment all of the four were on top of him. In this thoughtless struggle was the thought he was going to be killed. So he would be murdered by terrorists after all, only a day later. For an instant he had the vision of the Double, steeped in oblivion—or perhaps visions of the terrorists' paradise, with scores of dark eyed, complaisant virgins.

There was a blow to his head, something like a soundless explosion, and almost all sensation rushed suddenly away.

But the small shard, the small remnant he could grasp of life he held fiercely, and when he saw the dark knife raised quickly in the air over him he defended himself with an even deeper thoughtlessness and fury than a moment ago. In the debris his hand clutched a rock, half a brick, whatever, and flung it at the descending knife. The short trajectory was blessed by chance; the knife and the hand that held it were struck. There was a cry, a vague vision of blood (like some vague splattering on a windshield), and The New Man felt the knife drop horizontally upon him, harmless but with the weight of a disgusting potential.

In another instant, within this narrow vision of sight and receding sensation, he heard a shout, a scream, a demand. It seemed to come from above, not directly above, but somewhere off to the side, within the height of the parabola of the sky. The shout alternated between English and, it seemed, Arabic; definitely another language. Of the English he caught: "Police!"

The foreign tongue repeated itself, and then the English again. The New Man felt a sharp kick at his side, cries and obvious curses from the four men, who were abruptly gathering the drugs that were once more on the ground, and then hauling the Double to his feet and dragging him off over the rough terrain. He gave a muffled cry, the response to a pain almost felt. And astonishment. The receding, bobbing head of the Double appeared like a phony face, not real at all. This odd quintet disappeared with amazing swiftness.

In the instant of relief following this miracle, The New Man looked dumbly up at the light of the late afternoon, to the sky that bore no clouds and no comfort. His relief turned to fear: "Oh, God, not the police—" He heard the sound of a car. Was it his assailants' departure or the authorities' arrival? He was deep in some maze, and yet, near its confused center, old forces could draw him back to the old life. His new life had been brief, very brief, it had been troubling, confusing and dangerous—but he wanted it. Or wanted something that wasn't of the old. "Not the po—" he mumbled, gasped and tried to sit up. A sharp pain shot through his side and he collapsed back down upon the rough debris. "God," he gasped. It was a cry that sought something more infinite than any imagined deity. Then, in raw despair, in pain, exhaustion and a deep spiritual bereftness, he lost consciousness.

11. *Rescue, Again*

He opened his eyes to the touch of a hand on his cheeks and brow. He sought to make clear the face above his. It was not the police, but a woman, in Middle Eastern clothes, her hair easing from its head covering, her dark eyes studying The New Man with an expression he could not name.

He could not understand what she said. It might have been a foreign tongue or The New Man's faculties might be yet fuzzy. But he had his own words. They tumbled out: "I don't want the police— I'm all right—"

"I'm not calling the police," the face of the woman said. "They're gone."

And there was the memory, of an instant ago, but across the distance of the vast track of being one sinks into when losing consciousness; the sound of a car door, a vehicle speeding off. "Gone?" he mumbled.

"Yes." She gave the most subtle smile—or not so much a smile as a look of concern and encouragement. She was a comfort that came through his pain.

"Do you need a hospital?"

"No, no—" Again, the aspect of something official terrified him.

"Can you get up?"

These questions seemed more than he could bear. "Yes—"

Desperate to prove he didn't need help from the law or medicine, he clenched his teeth and strained to sit up. The sky above seemed an impossible thing in which to rise, but he did, clenching his teeth to keep from crying out. But the woman could see his pain.

"I'm fine. Fine."

She didn't believe that; but she accepted, at least, he was capable of moving in spite of pain. She said, "You should not stay here—"

"Yes, yes." He had finally caught his breath. "You—that was you—shouting?"

She gave the briefest nod. She gestured to a building on the periphery of the lot. "I saw them beating you." She gave an expression that conveyed this was a very terrible thing to see; and then an expression that placed some of the guilt for the beating on him, the victim. "Why did you come here?" When The New Man gave back a look that must have been pitiful, a look saying *That is too much to explain*, her expression changed back to one of concern. "You should not be seen here." Here again, admonitions against "seeing."

With her aid and The New Man's resolution not to appear so helpless, he leaned on her a bit as she guided him through the rubble toward her building. It was a brief journey that, in his pain, seemed long.

The building looked more than half abandoned. Here and there were shattered windows; some were shuttered.

She appeared to note him noting the desolation She returned to him an expression: *Never mind; it's your safest place now.*

"I am on the third floor," she said, as if this indicated that this little height, that thirty feet of elevation was a space not claimed by abandonment and in more normal array.

There was a rear entrance that bordered the lot. The other side of the building bordered the street. Indeed, for the moment—for the foreseeable future—The New Man did not want to be seen from the street.

The border of the entrance was embroidered with faded graffiti. The door was dented and dark. It seemed thick and heavy, too, but the woman opened it easily enough. "Can you walk up the stairs? There is no elevator."

"Yes. Yes." But he did not want to ascend, he did not want to be in this building. What would he be entering here? Already the one night he had spent at Ahmed's motel had seemed the sanctuary where he now belonged; but expediency left him no choice. He had descended—only yesterday—so many flights; he could now ascend a few. With much pain he climbed the stairs with her. By the last flight he was leaning on her heavily. Her body had a strength that moved naturally within it—within the softness of a woman. Some part of his psyche considered he had not felt this for a long time.

And the brief, but painful ascent made him think of that long descent of yesterday. Steps. Little by little, one went up or down them…..to something *else*.

They were on the third floor. They walked down a dim hallway. Speaking of steps: The New Man felt their steps resonated too loudly. The woman stopped at a door, and called out "Rasil," as she reached to open it; but the door was opened slowly from inside, by a child, a boy—five? six?—with the eyes of his mother and hair as dark and skin as dark. The boy had a beauty and an expression both innocent and wounded, daring and cautious. The New Man didn't quite sort all that out in that moment, but later, when memory rushed over him, he said, yes, that's exactly what his first impression was.

The boy looked up, taking in this man. He stepped back to let his mother and The New Man enter with the stranger. The New Man was barely aware of crossing the threshold. Pain still rode his senses. The woman was saying to the boy, "He is hurt, Rasil, he needs to rest—"

The New Man, within his own innocence (everyone who enters a labyrinth is innocent), was cautious himself. "Your husband—" He was standing free of the woman. The look she gave back at those words—it seemed she received this as if he had intruded on something so private she had been struck—offended.

"He is—not here: gone." She said this looking at The New Man, then at the boy, to whom she added something in their language. Rasil withdrew slowly, a little fearfully. He did not want to leave his mother with a stranger. What would he find when he came back? From a kitchen The New Man heard the rush of water from a facet.

The woman said to him, "He is—dead. I am sure."

This last sentence had a curious intonation, making certainty of something of which she was not at all certain. He said, like an echo, but with a question. "You don't know?"

"I know it as much as I can know it without being told."

And The New Man's wife had told the TV he was still alive. Was she sure of this without being told?

The woman answered The New Man with silence. It was obvious she was uneasy over being drawn to the edge of discussing with a stranger something so intimate.

Rasil returned. Following his mother's gesture, he offered a glass of water to The New Man. The glass was big and the boy had filled it almost to overflowing; water swayed and tottered at its brim.

The New Man took the glass carefully. It seemed that even as he must take everything offered him now, he must take it carefully. "Thank you." He drank slowly, then with the depth of a thirst he had just realized. When he finished he clutched the empty glass at his chest. "I was—thank you—" He was breathing a little quickly from the pain of the climb. His side ached so much it was almost numb.

The woman gave a little smile and took the glass from him. For a few moments The New Man could find no words to speak and the woman and the boy were silent and the three regarded each other, the child clinging to his mother's side.

It was the apartment of a poor family: drab, ill furnished. The New Man stood by a window from which he could see the lot and its topography of debris—and studied in dull recollection the very spot at which he had been pummeled, first by the Double, then by the four men. He had the sudden thought: *Am I looking for blood?* It was strange to him that all the violence he had suffered left no apparent sign in the place in which it had occurred. The debris and rubble there seemed no different than anywhere else.

He had the thought the woman had shouted at his attackers from this window. He said to her, sincerely—and was embarrassed at his sincerity: "I guess you saved my life."

She blinked, and did not appear to regard either his deep thanks or the possibility of his murder. Instead, her question: "Why did they do that?"

"I was there," The New Man lied. Or perhaps it was not a lie.

"I saw you talking to the tall man. A long time."

"I suppose we did." She had made no mention of seeing him struggle with the mirror of Osama bin Laden. He said, "Did he...look like anyone to you?"

She frowned. "Who?"

For the briefest instant he considered he was imagining all this, The Double— But no: amidst this new, surreal life, he had to be certain of something. –Of "seeing." Perhaps at this height she was too distant to discern the bin Laden-mirror—and perhaps she had seen his struggle with the Double, but had judged it a fair match, not requiring intervention.

She said, "This is not your..."—she searched for the word: "neighborhood."

He said, slowly, "No. I've been—I am—displaced." What other word could he use?

She frowned again, then suddenly did not allow consideration for enigmas. "You are bleeding." She pointed at him, with equal concern and accusation.

He was conscious of a great wetness that had abruptly burst at his side. The barriers of a wound that had congealed had cracked. He looked down at the streak of fresh redness seeping along a stain that had already dulled to brick. Dumbly he touched it, then held out his reddened fingers as if displaying to himself the evidence of a peculiar suffering.

"Go in the shower," she said. "I have clothes—"

So he let himself be directed—much as events had directed him since yesterday morning. In a moment he was in a small bathroom. She curled the collar of a shirt over a towel rack, then placed folded pants on the floor beneath. She held out folded

Jerry Cimisi

underwear to him. This must be from the "departed" husband. So, out of resentment for his departure, she would give his clothes to a stranger? He'd take the clothes, though this would feel uncomfortably brazen, unclean, but not the underwear— that was too intimate, too close to the flesh of an unknown other, never mind that they were clean.

He studied himself. His pants were stained, streaked with dirt, torn below the left knee. Undressed, he saw in the mirror the scattering of bruises, the blood. "I look like an old corpse," he said aloud, then hoped she had not heard that through the door. He winced as he got into the shower and the water struck him. He moved his head slowly back and forth under the jet of the shower, closing his eyes. After a while the water assuaged the pain. He kept his eyes closed. When he opened them he saw the tint of redness swirl down the drain with the water. He recalled that scene in *Psycho*. He had a sensation of dizziness. He had been The New Man for such a short time; and he had been so flailed.

He dried himself carefully; but there was blood on the towel. He formed apologies to the woman; and he forgot them. (It was not a matter of indifference; he knew she would forgive the situation.) He dressed himself in the clothes he had been given: tan slacks with a pale yellow shirt. They fit him well. If they had belonged to the woman's husband, they were a contrast to the Middle Eastern clothing she wore.

He had intended to put his own underwear back on but it was just too dirty and it stank. He sniffed at it with a grimace. So he left it on the pile of dirty clothes. It seemed all of his old life had shrunk into a lump of ragged, stained, sweat-smelling clothing. He dressed without underwear. And now he had the clothing—

however clean—of a stranger on him, up against his flesh.

I've got nothing left, he thought. His clothing of yesterday had been stripped from him; and his flesh had been pummeled.

As he emerged she called to him from the small kitchen. "Coffee? Are you hungry?"

He stood in the closeness of the kitchen, feeling dizzy, as if he had not left the warm pressure of the shower. "I don't know...."

"Sit down." It was said softly, with sympathy. She would not press him for the need to make decisions.

He sat at the small table. Directly across from him the boy looked up. He was eating something The New Man couldn't identify.

She said, "It was terrible, those men. Why would they do that?'

He shrugged. "I think they thought I was someone else." This was a portion of the truth; but she studied him with an expression by which he knew she knew he was not telling her something essential.

He looked out of a window. From this room he could see a section of the street. He saw a few passing figures. He noted their long shadows and was for some reason surprised it was the end of the day. Time had been alternately lengthened and compressed since yesterday morning; but whatever its state, it moved.

Some of the figures on the street were dressed like this woman, some dressed as he was, casually: Western. He smiled at that. Clothing that was—had been—"normal" he now placed in a category. And as if he could be *apart* from that, too.

She said, "What is your name?"

When he did not immediately answer, she filled in her own. "I am Haziz." She pointed to her son. "Rasil."

"I am Theo—Ted. Ted." He tried to say it easily, but he blinked his eyes.

She lingered on the first syllable. "Theo—?"

"Ted. From Theodore." He had the vague thought: Didn't "Theo" have something to do with God? Yes: theology, theocratic…. "It's Ted…Newman. But I don't exactly feel like a new man now." He tried to laugh but instead winced at the pun. She did not seem to catch its most superficial level.

She said, "Where are you from?" She meant: "Why are you here?"

"I—I just got out of New York yesterday." He could say this without deception. I was…in the Towers."

Oh…." This sound from her, like a sigh and a realization, was genuine. Sympathy, horror, shock. Abruptly he thought her face arresting. Not so much lovely as something—unfathomable. The dark eyes—they held something….

"My company—" He was back to fumbling at a lie. "We—I got out. The only way I could get out was this way, to New Jersey. I'm at a motel until—until—" So he would not have to lie further he gave a forced laugh. "I guess my life got saved twice in two days." This was certainly the truth, a large truth.

She took him literally. "Did someone save you yesterday, too?" Of course she had heard of people helping others escape the Towers.

"No. I got down myself." Again, truth and lies. Perhaps he had been "saved": by Wilson.

"Where is your family?" It was almost a sharp question.

"I'm no longer married." Had he said that matter-of-factly

enough, tinged with a long ago regret?

She considered that. He thought she was weighing the truth of those words, but the liar often imagines others fixing on the façade of his story. In his tension The New Man heard the breathing of the boy at the table. He had stopped eating and for some time had been considering the stranger.

"I can understand that," she said, quietly. It seemed a curious response; yet it was one that hinted at a sharp facet of her own feelings.

After a pause, she said, repeating something that seemed to have been said a long time ago: "Coffee?"

"Yes, yes." To wake himself up, to give himself false strength, to fight off the weight that pulled at this flesh and being. He had the sensation again of watching, of feeling his blood swirl down the shower drain. A fainter repetition of that scene from Hitchcock.

He looked at her—as the boy looked at him—as she made the coffee. Everyone was silent. Rasil went back to his food. The New Man looked out at the street again. Soon it would be sundown. There was a lovely sky in the west, vivid above a terrible world. When the coffee was in front of him and he cupped his hands around its warmth, he said, "I've got to get back." But as he drank, he seemed to forget his own words—or at least, the intent behind them did not seem important.

"Do you have a car?"

"No." He thought of his car, at the train station out on Long Island.

"Is your…motel far?"

"No." But it seemed far now, in his weariness. "I can take a taxi." He was reassured by the weight of his wallet he had put in the pocket of these new clothes. (Amazing that he had not lost that essential item in all his struggles.)

The heat of the coffee flowing down his throat seemed not to rejuvenate him but explode all barriers by which he had kept the day's weariness at bay. Inwardly, he slumped. He wanted to accept that tiredness, remain within it, until….

She saw the deep weakness of his body. She leaned toward him and touched his shoulder. "Are you all right?"

He tried to nod, then smiled and shook his head. "Just tired. Thank you, again." Her touch, firm and gentle, seemed to drive him farther into a desire for sleep.

"You are welcome." She said this formally, as if mouthing a phrase in a guidebook. Then spoke more feelingly: "Lie down." She pointed from the kitchen to the living room, to the couch. "When you are a little better, get a taxi. Do you have any money?"

Yes." He wondered if the question were less connected with concern for him than her wanting (naturally) to assess what sort of man he was—or, more precisely, the nature of his condition.

A moment ago he would have resisted; now he nodded his acceptance of her offer. She went to the couch, rearranged the cushions. The couch was faded and colorless—in such contrast to her. She moved more quickly than sensuously. He understood, on a wordless level, that she presented a methodical aspect to the world; but perhaps it was a manner that hid what was more vulnerable—and, more essential.

When she finished with the cushions she abruptly looked at him with a bright smile, like a young woman who had prepared a surprise. "Rest."

She was not young, she was not old. He guessed her at

thirty or so.

He took a final sip of his coffee, surrendered, got up, moved to the couch. He felt the boy watching him.

"Rest. Sleep. A little while. You look terrible."

The drab couch was comfortable. It was welcome. He sighed as he stretched out and looked at the ceiling. The light in the apartment had dimmed. He thought he heard a cloud of cries from the street. They seemed an appropriate if odd chorus to the quiet woman and the boy looking at him as if they needed to be sure he grasped the comfort he had been extended.

Breathing slowly, feeling (almost like a recollection) the aches of his bruises, he told himself he would have to leave here soon—what would Ahmed think if he did not show up? And there was the black bag under the bed at the motel. But that was a deception logic tried to comfort his psyche with—here on the border of light and night, if he surrendered his body more fully to "rest," he could not see himself returning through the streets of this foreign New Jersey neighborhood in the dark.

He drifted up out of sleep. The light that dominated now was artificial. He had the sudden disorientation of finding himself in an unfamiliar place—then the immediate past played itself back to him. He heard a TV, once more rehashing the news. "…Twin Towers…bin Laden…firefighters…." He had awakened to this new terrible monotony. He got up and was surprised at the clothes he wore. Yes, another man's clothes….

He paused by the entrance to the living room. The woman and her son were watching the news. Once again the first tower to fall was imploding, sheathed in dark grey smoke. From somewhere on the street by the monoliths, a voice cried, "Oh

God!" and was buttressed by screams. Haziz and Rasil looked at The New Man as if they had expected him to appear at that very moment. Haziz said, "Are you feeling a little better?"

He couldn't quite say that, though he was a little more rested. He merely smiled.

She got up, her body shielding the apocalypse on the screen. At the same time she admitted to the apocalypse. "It's not good you see this—"

He sighed. "I've seen it so many times already. And I lived it, anyway." He gestured to the screen. "That doesn't...compare—" (But he vaguely recalled: hadn't he, this afternoon, considered the importance of "seeing"?)

The boy said something to his mother. She replied. It was an exchange in their language. She spoke earnestly to Rasil. He looked back to the TV in that solemn way in which children will study horror first to comprehend that it is horror, then to understand why it has occurred. On the screen people were running down the street, with billowing clouds of ash and debris following them, like an amorphous force in a horror movie.

Rasil looked back to his mother. She took him up in her arms. He struggled. She released him. She turned off the TV. The sudden absence of yesterday's horror was disconcerting. To The New Man she said, "Should he see this? I try to explain—"

Explain it to me, The New Man thought. He said, hollowly, "Who can explain...?"

He and the woman quietly looked at each other. It was a moment when two people study each other honestly, even rawly, and, if not able to relate in words what they see, there is some connection made—of circumstance, and feelings.

Though their talk continued to skirt this, as if diplomatically.

And then there was the distraction of the boy, who was complaining that the dire vision of the TV had been silenced. But his mother was firm, denying him the news, the horror.

"Are you hungry?" she asked.

He felt so much in a maze he did not know what his body felt. "I have to go," he said.

"Eat something. You can get a taxi any time."

Though he wondered if taxis would come to this neighborhood at any time. And he had to think: Does she want me to stay? Was she...attracted to him? But The New Man believed himself, if confused, to be sadly honest. Haziz was twenty-five years younger, attractive—yes, attractive. He was a beaten 55 year old man. This woman was just being kind.

"I've inconvenienced you enough."

"No. There's food—"

So in a moment The New Man sat, as he had the night before, and ate a foreign dinner. Haziz sat across from him, sipping tea. He looked into the living room, at the dead TV. He imagined the images it possessed.

He thought of the irony: he had fled from his family; now, he sat with a family, whose husband—

"You said your husband—?"

She smiled sadly, as if she could have only expected that question, sooner rather than later. She said, flatly, "I do not really know." Now she seemed less certain of the "death" of the unseen husband. But The New Man sensed there was more to this.

"I'm sorry. It's not my business."

Again they looked at each other a moment. They continued to eat. But, in way, her succoring him had made something of her his business and something of him hers.

The New Man felt an odd comfort here; at the same time, he wanted to leave.

In the local phone book he chose at random a nearby taxi company. As he listened to the phone ring he studied the cover of the phone book—across whose worn cover was handwritten in a foreign script many phone numbers slanted in different directions, some apparently with names (he assumed they were names) attached to the numbers, others not. Here and there the writing was in a feminine hand; most of it was masculine.

The voice on the other end of the phone was as foreign as the script on the phonebook. The accent was so thick he could not be sure if the voice had spoken in English at first or in another language. When The New Man spoke in English the voice seemed surprised—or was it the caller's imagination? At any rate, the voice responded in English. A cab would be there in twenty minutes.

Haziz gave The New Man a bag for his dirty clothes.

"I'll give you these clothes back," he began, fingering the shirt.

"No, no." She said this as if there could be no further argument. Perhaps she wanted no reminder of her husband returned.

But a fleshly reminder called: the boy by the TV (it was on again), calling for his mother. She got a glass of water and went into the living room. In the few seconds he stood there alone, with his bag of clothes, the dishes he had eaten from on the table, The New Man felt an unnamable, almost overwhelming sadness rise up through him, like a flood. He had tried to escape the life of a home; now he stood about to depart from a home. He'd fled a devastation into a maze, and in that labyrinth accident and further violence had dropped him into the realm of a hominess made all the more universal by the fact that the woman and the boy were of a foreign culture.

Haziz returned, looked at him. Without words, uncomfortably—and neither quite knew why they were uncomfortable—they were saying goodbye. From below on the street was the honk of car. But until Haziz looked out of the window and said, "The taxi," The New Man did not connect this vehicle's presence with him. He was being summoned on further passage.

At the door he said, "This was very kind of you."

She smiled. "Why kind?"

"You saved my life."

"I think Allah saved your life—from the buildings. That was a big thing to do. I did a little thing."

He wanted to say if murder were large scale or specific, it was still murder. And at any rate, what had happened to him was more the mystery of Wilson than of Allah, but he merely looked at her, with his own smile, a sad one.

Of course, a believer would say that Allah was behind all mysteries, human or otherwise.

As he left, he saw Rasil peering from the living room entrance. The child's face was beautiful, calm and perhaps curious. And hardly sad to see the stranger leave. The New Man had the thought: when had the son last seen the father?

He was already in the dark hallway when she rushed out after him. "I forgot. No lights in the hallway. Here." She thrust a small flashlight into his hand.

He grasped the cool cylinder. "But don't you need it?"

"Go. They won't wait long—here." She actually pushed her hands against him, urging him along.

This sudden touch seemed almost rude—and yet it was also full of concern. It ripped through a yearning that his present flight kept at bay.

"Thank you." He moved down the hall, the beam guiding him. The labyrinth is full of darkness, one needs one's own light— As he descended the steps in this building that seemed to have no other inhabitants, he felt grateful for the flashlight and also guilty that he had taken the woman's guide through darkness. She probably has more than one, he told himself. If not, she can certainly get another. This led him to think: just how does she survive? On what? In this rundown neighborhood, with a missing husband. Social services?

It took a brief time for him to go down three flights of stairs, but it was a descent that seemed longer. And not once did he think of his long descent of yesterday. In between the recent sanctuary of Haziz' apartment and the taxi outside, The New Man again felt exposed to the ominously transformed world.

But more than sensing the danger of a foreign landscape, he felt a surprising loss at departing from Haziz' apartment.

The taxi driver, dark skinned and mustached, was of an ethnicity common to taxi drivers in the metro area, and he seemed to look at The New Man with no different an expression than many other drivers of his ilk had in the past. But then, in that past, Middle Eastern drivers had been picking up the old New Man around Wall Street, or midtown; now he was in an Arab neighborhood. There had to be the question in the man's mind: *What are you doing here?*

And a question as to The New Man's destination. As they

drove along, The New Man imagined the driver studying his passenger in the rear view mirror. And there was no conversation between passenger and driver. In far more unusual circumstances The New Man had conversed with The Double and Haziz; now, in a situation markedly less surreal, he was at a loss to say anything. Was this why he had fled his old life: it was so common he could no longer have truck with it?

But the lack of conversation could only make the driver more suspicious. Even the Double, who had been confronted with The New Man instead of Wilson, had been less suspicious. The Double's suspicions had been more in regard to a greater whole, some larger picture to which both the Double and The New Man had fragments but not the entire landscape.

The taxi stopped at the motel. The New Man tipped the driver a bit more than he normally would have—but not too generously: that would have made him more suspicious. The driver gave a nod, and a façade of a smile. He drove off. The New Man knew he would be remarking to others about the unlikely fare he had picked up.

He went to the side of the motel, climbed the outside steps to the room, and entered. It seemed odd, returning. Very odd. As if a sense of necessary passage had been broken. Since yesterday morning he had been on the move, always to another place: from the Twin Towers to this town in Jersey, from the motel to the lot, to the woman's apartment— Of course he had left the motel last night to eat, then had returned, and had done the same thing that very morning. But this was different. The meeting with the Double, the attack of the four men, Haziz: he had had an adventure. He had gone beyond the pale. He was returning with the burden of having suffered things. *Should I be coming back here?* he thought.

But the bed was welcome. He sank into it. He was tired again, the aftermath of his physical wounds returning. As a distraction, or rather more as a painkiller, he went to turn on the TV—but then did not. He needed to be free of the world's babble. The terrorist attacks seemed only a disguise for a truth into which he had plunged.

Now where? he thought. *Now where?* He repeated this to himself a few times, as if it might bring him to an answer or sleep. And that became: *Nowhere....* He laughed grimly, quietly. Well, if he thought of nowhere at all, that might settle him into sleep. But sleep did not come right away. His being wanted to savor tiredness and use it as a refuge for thought— and dreams.

The challenge of the code came back into his consciousness. Its intricacy, its, yes, fervor. His struggle with the cipher; his regrasping old skills. He had done that...yesterday. Or, actually, today, in the wee hours of the predawn. But now that seemed such a monumental occurrence. Could he do something like that, even something half as difficult, again? At the moment he did not feel he could. His old sanctuary of mathematics had returned to him in the oddest moment; but now—Though wait: perhaps it had returned because he had cast off the old, dead life?

Will I have numbers tomorrow? he wondered. *Or another day, soon?*

In the middle of the night he awoke and thought about money. The surrealness of the events since Tuesday morning—and this was only Wednesday night—suddenly fell away. The events remained, his situation remained—in a practical light. How was he going to manage being "Newman"—manage financially? As he had pulled the bills out of his wallet to pay the taxi driver, he had seen the immediate future quickly making that small amount of cash into nothing. It was obvious he could not withdraw any money from the joint account he had with his wife. Dead men don't make withdrawals. Of course, someone finding his ATM card might....

No, no, no. That secret account he'd had for over a year—secret, yes, but still in his old name. Would he get away with it? Would some connection, some cyber genius in the banking system pop up and say—wait, this man died at the World Trade Center? There would be the possibility the ATM card had survived the attack, that it had fluttered downward amidst the debris and the ash, had been blown east or west and someone had retrieved it, someone who would steal from the dead—or, rather steal from the living system. But how could that someone know his PIN?

The New Man went on with a fantasy. He imagined an organized group of thieves using some computerized mathematical model to run through innumerable possibilities to arrive at PIN numbers for stolen ATM cards—then stopped himself. Not likely at all. He would simply have to take the chance of using that secret account. After all, he was not a famous missing person.

Even so—when that money ran out? A new job? What would be on Newman's resume? Born on September 11, 2001? If he simply put down his true job experience, his former employee was bound to be contacted. Although, he suddenly wondered, was his old company even in existence any longer? Its only office had been in the Twin Towers.

Of course, he could find some job that didn't care about his work experience. He laughed to himself. He could drive a cab in this neighborhood.

But this was a problem. Even a job at a fast food place required a Social Security number. What would he do about that? He considered once more fake IDs, birth certificates, but he had no idea how to go about this. And he had the instinct this would only draw attention to himself, somehow.

He thought: *I bet the Double would know. Or one of those four men—*

And then, as he stood at the beginning of his new life, there was the fact that he did not want a job anymore. What was such work but a lifetime of dullness? The only work he had ever enjoyed had been the mathematics of his youth, something that was not a job in the usual sense. He wondered if he would have been fulfilled as a mathematics professor at a college. Would he have had the knack, the desire to teach? He had no conviction on that account. Mathematics had been for himself, an enjoyment so private and complete, a purity that might be lessened by extending it to those who did not have his perspective and gift.

He looked down at the black bag beside the bed. It had waited for his return like something indomitable. After all the decades of disuse, his mathematical skill had penetrated the code. But what had he gotten for it? Strange and useless information—and then, beaten up.

But—useless information: The authorities should know about the Double, the heroin, the four men. If he told then, now, perhaps they would be caught—though he doubted that taking them into custody would help bring down bin Laden.

And then, The New Man had to admit, he had developed an affinity—a pity—for the Double. A man whose poverty more than the need to follow had forced him into the life of the image of another man.

The New Man felt his old life had been the image of another man.

He confronted the question: Why did he not simply leave his wife and continue with his original identity?

Identity. Because that hadn't been him at all in the first place? He would still be saddled with—

But wasn't he making excuses for a blatant lack of courage?

At last he fell back into sleep, filled with the food of Haziz, the bruises of other men, and the shards of the dreams of his escape. For he dreamt of the flight from the Towers, dreamt that he was descending even as the building was collapsing, his dreaming mind using the scene he'd witnessed so often now on TV, and which gave him the topography of the roiling implosion. He plummeted down, like some pitiful angel, once of heaven, shot down to earth for something less brave than a sin. He awoke with a start before he reached the hard ground of dream-death. There in the night, in some hour he could not know, he felt an anguish he certainly had not anticipated that long ago yesterday morning when he had escaped the annihilation thousands of others had suffered, and which this pitiless dream had tried to show him.

As he began to drift back into sleep, the thought—the realization—suddenly shot through him: He had seen no one else at this motel. There had been no cars in the parking lot, there had been no one in the lobby. There had been no closing of other doors, no distant muffled talk, drifting down hallways or through walls.

Oh, my God— As if Ahmed's motel had come into existence solely for him, The New Man pushed a surge of paranoia away—yet faced the strange fact of this solitude in the middle of an Arab town.

His eyes scanned the dark room.

12. *A Taste of Honey*

Morning. The bright light of the end of summer woke him like the reminder of something dull he could not escape. He flicked on the TV. Perhaps in the night or early morning there had been other terrorist attacks, a world even more shattered, and it would be easier for The New Man to pass unnoticed—

But no. No new devastations. Not that the world was suffering business as usual. There were still no flights—the air space above the United States was utterly devoid of anything save military traffic. The stock exchange was closed. There were no sporting events. Hundreds had been arrested in connection with the attacks. Then an account of the recovery, yesterday, of a few survivors in the rubble.

He stared a while at the TV, as if it had disappointed him in a promise.

OK, he said to himself, I have to arrange things.

First: clothes. There was the bag of dirty clothes he had carried from Haziz' apartment. For an instant he thought of her as a man thinks of a woman, who for some reason beyond that of her body had drawn his attention.

But the inner pleasure of any such reverie quickly died. The immediate always pressed upon him.

He would just throw the clothes out. He would buy new clothes. He would use the secret account, go to the ATM. He had to. No one would find him. No one.

He needed to pay Ahmed. He rose slowly, nervously, with the controlled breathing of a man about to be tested.

In the nondescript lobby, he found Ahmed watching TV. There was a shot of the Statue of Liberty, and behind the lady with the torch was the absence of the Towers, and the smoke rising from the debris of destroyed architecture and lives.

Ahmed shook his head. "Terrible things." As much as any American, he seemed to be mourning the destruction of the monoliths and the murder of thousands.

The New Man paid Ahmed for his stay so far. Ahmed protested that the circumstances made this unnecessary, but The New Man had the sense that if such declarations were sincere the day before, today they were politeness. Ahmed accepted the money with profuse protest, but he accepted it.

The New Man thought the motelkeeper looked with an inquiring eye at the bright shirt and the tan pants from Haziz. *He's wondering where I got these, where I went yesterday.* He distracted Ahmed with: "There doesn't seem to be many people here."

Ahmed gave an expression that said his guest had broached an uncomfortable topic. "It is slow now."

The New Man was thinking: How much business could a motel do in this neighborhood? It wasn't exactly a draw for tourists. It just seemed incongruous.

Ahmed said, "When I took this place over—many people here. But the roads changed—"

Changed. As if some great interstate had been built a mile off. It didn't make sense. It was...suspicious. It was as if the motel were some kind of stage set...a necessary facade in The New Man's labyrinth.

Ahmed was looking at The New Man with a cautious, and almost begging expression. The New Man's thoughts were going on: *Or, to be more realistic, a terrorist front.* But he said, "I was expecting a call. Have there been any calls for me?"

Relieved, Ahmed looked at The New Man with formal unhappiness. "No. I would have forwarded them to your room."

The New Man feigned his own expression, one of helplessness. "Yes, I know. I was just...." He let his words fade in mumbling; he meant to give the impression of a beaten man grasping at straws. In a sense there was truth to this.

He abruptly said: "I'll be out a little while. "In case—"

There was a muffled roar of voices from the TV as the station switched its coverage from a talking head to the collage of a crowd. Innumerable bodies were behind police barricades at what had come to be known as Ground Zero. Many were holding photographs of "loved ones" (that phrase made The New Man wince, for obvious reasons). Many were there simply out of morbid curiosity; others, by their expressions, seemed lost, even stunned, and were not really sure at all why they had been drawn to the aftermath of disaster. A number of the policemen, alternately sympathetic and annoyed at the up and down energy of the crowd, were on the other side of the barricade, as a guarantee that the authorities had more behind them than a plank of horizontal wood.

The screen broke to a shot of a reporter thrusting a mike into the face of a heavyset woman. "My son is in there—" She gestured wildly, in utter helplessness, toward the terrain of irregular dark, still smoking debris. The reporter, acting more as a sympathizer than a journalist, said gently, "I'm sure they're doing everything—"

"He could be at the bottom of that whole building!" the woman shrieked. For an instant the TV was filled with a human face wholly subjugated by despair.

Ahmed made the vague noise of a man exposed too closely to the distressed privacy of another. He flicked to another channel. Colin Powell talked calmly about the coalition President Bush was building against Al-Qaeda.

"This will all lead to crazy things," said Ahmed.

The New Man was still considering the shrieking mother. He himself could have been buried "at the bottom" and thus never have been "Newman" at all.

"I'll see you later," he said to Ahmed, and walked out into the sun of the third day of his new life.

He tried his ATM card at a bank. A message came on that the system was "Currently Inactive." He remembered hearing on TV that many ATMs were not going to be operative for a while.

But that would not last forever.

The New Man's secret account was at a bank in Manhattan, near the Trade Center. He doubted that bank would be open for business. He would have to find a branch here in this neighborhood.

He went into a delicatessen that served a multicultural mix of food. He stood behind a Middle Eastern man who ordered, in his language, a ham sandwich. Well, perhaps he was not Muslim, or was at least a lapsed one. The New Man pointed to things that caught the hunger of his eye behind the glass. He came out with an unfamiliar breakfast, but whose aroma certainly captivated his hunger.

A turn in the street brought him to a little park—it was as if he had intuited that the very next corner would bring him to a place to stop and eat in a sort of public privacy.

It was warm and he sat in the shade of large trees. "An oasis," he muttered to himself.

On a stretch of grass before him about a hundred feet away, little boys were playing soccer. During a respite in the game, one of the boys held up his left hand, fingers straight, pointing to the sky; with the other hand he made an angled dive at the left palm, at the same time producing exaggerated airplane-like noises. When the airplane hand hit the vertical hand, the boy burst out in laughter. The other boys laughed too.

The New Man watched this with a sudden, grave silence, pausing at his breakfast. In a moment the boys resumed their play and The New Man his meal. But the "oasis" had been tainted by the boys' casual appreciation of cruelty.

He stood up and walked deeper into the park. The sounds of the children were lost in leafy trees and dappled light. He thought of how autumn would come and strip these trees bare; but for now the world seemed utterly captive to a season held poised and luxurious before its decline.

What now? Where now? All he could resolve was: a bank, money. That he absolutely needed. Yes, money is vitally important. Imagine if he had sought his new life without it.

For the past few days he had heard the leaders and pundits of aggrieved, offended, affronted America talk about the financial loss the terror attacks had inflicted. The obvious loss of business and jobs. Indeed. The New Man's company was lost in that rubble across the river. And there was the proposal—that would surely come to pass—to seize the funds of organizations that apparently funneled money to terrorists.

Meanwhile the supporters of bin Laden & Co., the proclamations of bin Laden & Co. had never spoken of money but of God, infidels, the Holy Land desecrated.

The New Man brooded on this vast difference of perspective. On money, on the value of one life. The Western ideals. The West bemoaned the thousands dead. The fundamentalist East brayed with eagerness about dying in battle. So in the West money was important and life was important (perhaps in that order). In that land that bred America's assailants, neither money nor life were important, only something at the end of life. The only good life was the next one, the paradise with its houris.

He left the shady and winding walkways of the park. Further perambulation brought him to a branch of his bank. This is very much like a maze, he thought; every now and then one happens upon an avenue that relieves the long confusion.

The staff in the bank was mainly Middle Eastern. A network for Al-Qaeda? Here and there a non-eastern face looked at The New Man, not so much recognizing kin but in surprise, as if *he* could have no reason for being there.

He chided himself for lumping the darker, eastern world together. He judged the teller he stood before as Indian. She had that dot on her forehead. He wondered if he had ever known what that signified. The New Man, like many Americans these past days, was wondering about things foreign, seeking, as part of a desire for explanation (an immediate explanation), a knowledge of the *other* that could translate into not only a reason for horror, but a backstory.

The woman with the dot on her head gave The New Man a perfunctory look as he made his transaction. She pushed the money toward him with a smile that was too subtle to be genuine.

As The New Man stepped out onto the street fortified with a thousand dollars in cash (ah, the fleshly vigor money gives!), he was thinking that he did not feel horrified or terrorized, but in a suddenly surreal life.

My curse, my passage, he said to himself, and continued on through the neighborhood, with no plan.

Already he had been used to being the odd man out in this neighborhood and he moved along the streets with a lack of apprehension (maybe because he had survived yesterday—and the day before—he thought he could survive anything). He may have been deluded by some vague racial memory, that of a race (or at least vague links to a race) that had established a colonial empire generations ago, an empire now reduced to a vestige, but that vestige was enough to afford him a peculiar safety, no matter that people here felt little hold on them by that remnant, though it tugged at the nonwestern psyche like a colorful, habitual sore. To them, that past was an unpleasant sliver of history upon a greater, more fulfilling age. If both bands of that past, colonial and native, were subject to visceral distortion and legend, they were now the necessary counterparts of this present, and the near future.

He came upon a small shop. A honey shop. It announced itself thus: HONEY SHOP, in English, and, below, repeated the plain, obvious truth in Arabic.

The New Man paused. Displayed in the window were jars of

different shades of honey, from pale to dark, scattered like desirable jewels. They seemed to possess all of the light of the day—and transform it. He had never been in—or seen, for that matter—a store exclusively devoted to honey. He entered.

It was indeed a small shop, somewhat like an alleyway, even a tunnel, with a narrow width and high wide shelves in either side leading to a counter where a man in a billowy white shirt and black embroidered vest sat, reading an Arabic paper with bold curved type above a picture of Bush II. The reader of this paper that headlined the unrest of the day wore black, thick-framed glasses; the flesh around his eyes was distorted by the thickness of the lens.

The area by the counter seemed narrower than at the entrance, enhancing the tunnel-like effect. There was the sensation that by simply stepping into the shop one was being irrevocably drawn to that counter.

There was a small table, like a small island, that cleaved the narrowing path to the counter, set up right at the beginning of the shop, so a customer could pause by it immediately after entering and perhaps have the grace of deciding whether to continue onward, to the finality of the counter, and payment. The New Man took instinctual advantage of the table and stopped there, looking down upon jars of various shades of honey. Some of these sweet wares looked as dark as molasses; some seemed as light as water tinted with a bit of yellow. On most of the jars were inscriptions in both English and Arabic. Some labels were only in Arabic. On these jars the lone familiarity The New Man found were the numbers, Arabic in origin, but which the West feels so much its own.

The New Man lingered by the table-island, somehow wary of

proceeding further, but the man behind the counter lowered his paper a little (the photo of Bush became slanted, elongated, and almost dropped into abstraction) and said, in an accented voice, "How can I help you, sir?" To The New Man the intonation of those words suggested the truer meaning of: *You don't belong here. What are you doing here?*

The New Man could only give the benign response: "I'm just looking—" But on the last word, as if in reprieve, the shop's door opened and a woman and boy came in: Haziz and Rasil. The New Man was dumbfounded. But why should it be surprising that Haziz would come into a honey shop in her neighborhood? At any rate, the momentary reprieve turned into something frightening.

Perhaps Haziz experienced a similar surprise and fear. She stopped, and for the briefest, most subtle instant, her mouth gave the expression of a word it could not utter, but a self-control quickly asserted itself, and she simply smiled at The New Man, as if it were entirely normal to meet him in the course of the day.

Yet she alluded to their singular encounter. "I hope you are feeling better." There was something darkly spoken softly glinting in her eyes.

"I'm fine. I'm fine—" He felt incapable of babbling anything but the inconsequential. Yesterday, in the moments of his being rescued and in his nighttime meal with Haziz and her son (who edged a little closer to his mother and looked up at The New Man, disguising in no way that he, if only a child, had the perception to regard this encounter as anything but normal)— yesterday The New Man had received the presence, the aid, the kindness of Haziz in a battered daze. In those hours Haziz had seemed more a fable of rescue than a mere woman. Though "mere" was an inaccurate word. Suddenly, in that moment in the shop, The New Man, after the years of his loveless marriage, after the abrupt circumstance (like a divine command) of his flight and new identity, in that moment The New Man was terribly, powerfully drawn to this dark haired, dark eyed woman, who spoke to him with a voice that might be intimate and was also a tone indicative of a distinct privacy of feeling.

And the face, the face, lovely enough, and which would be, he thought with a rush, much lovelier if the simple scarf of muted colors and subtle pattern were untied to allow her hair its freedom. The face that was the beginning of the body…the body hidden and yet suggested by a loose garment of apparently light weight, of a deft mixture of colors that was of some traditional design—but, at least on Haziz, it seemed individual, as if this could be only her garment, hers alone. Its looseness did not prevent moments, sometimes long instants, of it clinging to her arms and torso as she moved, gestured and turned—perhaps not so much clinging as resting, giving abrupt definition to her breast, then slipping away, softening that definition so memory had to supply it, until the next moment of movement.

These perceptions of course were all happening in their own instants—that clung, then moved, then rested again on the consciousness of The New Man, so that he was held in the focus of his own sensations even as he was held by the presence of her body. He was indeed within a labyrinth of sensation, issued from the simplest, most straightforward cause: he wanted this woman. It was a wanting whose physical and emotional threads wrapped themselves about his psyche so tightly the singularity of each melded into one another and could not be separated, or even distinguished.

"Are you all right?" Her voice, borne with the disguise of a smile, broke into him.

"Yes—I'm—just—surprised—"

"So—are you here for the honey?"

The now friendly voice (though one with its own motives) of the shopkeeper called out to Haziz. "Your honey has been here since Monday. Did you get my message?"

Again his words seemed to be disguise for something else: *How do you know this man?*

"Yes, I did. I was going to come Tuesday—" Her voice halted on the word of that decisive day. "But—" She gestured and the shopkeeper made his own complementary gesture, one of resignation. The newspaper with the Arabic type was flat on the counter, and one of the shopkeeper's forearms hid the face of the president. "So much trouble," the man said, and the eyes blinked behind the thick glasses. "I am afraid it is going to get worse."

The New Man was wondering why they were talking in English. Was it for his benefit—a sort of polite charade? Not that he saw Haziz as being false, only cautious, wary—perhaps of making The New Man, whose life she had saved, feel lost, even over something trivial.

But as if his thoughts cued a change in speech, some words The New Man could not understand passed between Haziz and the shopkeeper, who pulled out a small wooden box without a lid from behind the counter. There were a half dozen medium-sized jars of honey in the box. The thick, curved jars had been cushioned for shipping with a wispy chaos of straw. Haziz made a delighted noise and expressed obvious thanks to the man. His name, first or last, it seemed, was "Rahman." To Rasil, Haziz exclaimed something that must have been "Look!" The boy smiled as his mother took up one jar of honey and held it against the light coming in from the window. It was truly a golden honey and the bottle seemed to throb with the richness of its color as the hands of Haziz held the englassed shape within the sunlight that streamed into the shop. Rasil seemed to be so happy to be presented with this honey.

Haziz said to The New Man, "He loves honey."

With a burst of salesman-like friendliness, the shopkeeper said, "Everyone loves honey—where we come from." It seemed so obvious he added this qualifying phrase to isolate The New Man as a foreigner.

Haziz gave a laugh, as if compensating for this large statement—and its xenophobia. The New Man said, "A land of milk and honey." He immediately felt a little embarrassed and surprised at himself. For the shopkeeper and Haziz were looking at him a bit quizzically. "Isn't that what they say?" added The New Man, awkwardly. Perhaps the Biblical reference had confronted a religious prejudice.

"Some places have a lot of honey, some do not," said the shopkeeper. "But whether you live where it is or not, you want it." This seemed to be another statement that disguised one of truer intent.

Haziz said, "Mr. Rahman orders special honey for me. It is our one luxury."

The mention of "luxury" seemed to prompt Mr. Rahman's next words: "How are things for you. Since—?"

But Haziz and perhaps Mr. Rahman, for that matter, did not want to go past that "since." Haziz gestured. "Fine, fine."

But then Mr. Rahman, with the most casual boldness, especially considering the presence of The New Man, said, "You haven't heard from your husband?" It was a twofold remark: meant to collapse Haziz' outward demeanor, and put The New Man in his place—a place apart from a Muslim woman.

But Haziz was affronted—and, now, coldly polite. "No." The word dropped into the air like a barrier and a shield. The displeasure on her face loomed, and Mr. Rahman seemed to shrink from it a little, and was perhaps glad of the owlish protection of his thick glasses.

Then abruptly, to deflect her stoniness, he said, booming, "For Rasil!" and grasped some nut and sugar coated confection from the counter. Wrapped in clear plastic, the delicacy appeared to emerge from the very edge of the now unread newspaper.

The boy gave a happy shout and quickly took the treat. The mother's displeasure was still there, but this tactic caused her to carefully submerge it within her features. From somewhere in her garment she extracted a small purse and began to withdraw several bills.

"Just for the honey," said Mr. Rahman.

"No—" Haziz did not want her disapproval to be countered by a gift.

"I like to see children happy." He seemed to want to add, *Children without a father, children of a mother who talks to strangers*—

Haziz muttered an obvious thank you in her tongue and started to pull Rasil away from the counter. The boy had already taken his first bite of the confection.

"Good," he proclaimed.

"Eat it outside, Rasil."

With calculated innocence, Mr. Rahman said, "Does that boy know his own language?"

Here was another affront, another overstepping of boundaries. Haziz said, "He has to know both. He's here now." She was plainly annoyed that Mr. Rahman had tried to assuage both her and Rasil with the treat, only to come out with this.

Mr. Rahman shrugged and made a gesture. "Yes, we are all here." He gave a meaningful look at The New Man.

With one arm Haziz pulled Rasil toward the door. The other arm was wrapped around the box of honey. The New Man felt the fear of her parting from him for a second time. She seemed to understand this, at least sense it. She said to him, "Pick out something. Mr. Rahman has the best honey anywhere. Rasil, finish it outside." With this last word she gave The New Man a look.

So she would talk to him outside.

The New Man and Mr. Rahman watched the door close behind the woman and her son. They moved just out of sight of the shop's narrow window. But dimly, faintly, The New Man could hear Haziz' voice. In another moment he had selected (trying not to make it seem at random) a jar of honey, honey of a dark amber, perhaps subconsciously trying to make his selection the opposite of the light golden bottle Haziz had held up to the light. In answer to Mr. Rahman's query, "You like this honey?"—said with an irony made more potent by the fact that the bottle had no English at all on the label—The New Man answered, "It looks like the kind I put in my tea."

"Oh. I have teas too. Not a *large* selection, but—" Mr.

Rahman waved to the shelves behind the counter where there were small boxes and tins of tea. Even more so than with the honey, foreign labels predominated.

"I have enough tea right now," said The New Man, as he paid what he thought was an exorbitant price for the honey. But then, it was obviously imported. He had the impulse to ask if Mr. Rahman had any Israeli honey.

"Next time you might try some," said the shopkeeper, perhaps hoping to see The New Man again in order to figure out the reason he was in this neighborhood. "Enjoy yourself," Mr. Rahman said with affectation, gesturing at the honey The New Man held firmly and against his body as he exited (as if it might give this encounter some meaning pertinent to his "passage"). But Mr. Rahman could have been referring to the woman outside.

Outside was where The New Man was in a moment, standing before the bench where Haziz and Rasil sat. The boy had obviously just finished his treat and was restless, wanting to go home, a word which he repeated in his own language and in English, as if the counterpoint of two sounds with the same meaning would work his will. His mother hushed him with her own alternation of English and her own tongue.

The New Man said, "Is English as hard to learn as Arabic?"

"We speak Farsi. I am from Iran." At the slight look of surprise from The New Man she added, as if scolding him, "We are not Arabs."

The New Man was abashed. "My ignorance. I guess Americans—"

"See all Muslims as Arab."

"I suppose so. Iran—used to be Persia, right?"

Yes: your word. The Shah, the father of the Shah you know about, named it Iran after the Aryan people of central Asia."

Iran, the motherland of the Aryan race. That was an interesting—and ironic—fact, The New Man thought. Cautiously he sat down on the bench, with Rasil between himself and Haziz.

"I have been trying to teach Mr. Rahman a little Farsi. He's Iraqi." She added, as if in reflection, "He was rude."

"Yes. Not...tactful."

Haziz looked at him with a look that said he did not know the half of it. Then: "You said your name was—Theodore—"

"Ted Newman." How odd the name sounded. How false: it must be apparent to anyone hearing him speak it. Though he was a little hurt she had had to pause to recall the name. "Theodore."

"A nice name." Was it only his imagination that made him feel she looked at him suspiciously?

"I have to thank you again for your...kindness," he said.

"You are welcome." She said this haltingly, as if this were indeed a foreign phrase—as if the sentiment, not just the words were of another culture. "I was fortunate I could help."

"*I* was fortunate. Look: Can I take you to dinner?" There: he had crossed that border.

She stared at him as if this were the oddest thing in the world to say—or do. "Oh, no, I do not think so."

Refusal—more avoidance than refusal—actually made him more bold. "Your husband left you." He purposely made it not a question.

She crinkled her brow. "That's not the right way to say it."

"I'm sorry if I am being as rude as Mr. Rahman—"

She smiled at him. "No, I don't think you're rude. For some reason I think you are confused."

How awful that she saw the truth. He was defensive—and tried not to show it. "Confused? What would I be confused about?"

She shrugged. "I am not sure." She looked back at him, her expression saying, *Will you tell me?* When he was silent, she said: "In a few days…so much has happened to you." She said something—in Farsi—to Rasil to stay his restlessness. To The New Man: "He didn't leave—the way you think." The New Man gazed at her with an uneasy expectancy. Looking to the eastern sky, where the remains of the Towers were still smoking, she seemed to collect herself (before this mirror that could give no visible reflection), then returned her eyes to his face, as if about to be brave. "He had…work to do, he said. I didn't realize—"

Abruptly, her face fought back tears. Her son looked at her with fear. The New Man involuntarily leaned back, then toward her. She gestured him away; she composed herself, turning in profile. He waited as she drew in a deep breath.

"I'm sorry," he said, though he was uneasy in his sympathy.

"You don't know what to feel sorrow about."

This was true. "You can tell me." But he feared what she might say next. He felt the street they were on an awkward stage.

With her face glimmering slightly with half dried tears, Haziz gestured to the sky beyond the immediate buildings of the block. "You see the smoke?"

Of course he did. In such a short time the aftermath of the

terrorist attack had become an ubiquitous feature of the sky. It was not as prominent as two days ago, but it was still very definitely there, more permanent than clouds. He had a sudden clutch of fear—as if she were about to divine his secret.

But instead she gave him hers. "My husband—he was on one of the planes."

"My God!" The New Man said this as soft as a whisper. He had been in the Towers, her husband on the plane— And then he had to be absolutely certain what Haziz meant. She had said: "He had work to do…."

As intuition and revelation coalesced, he cautiously stated, "He wasn't a…passenger."

"No." Her eyes surrendered to a terrifying vulnerability—but did not turn from his.

The New Man was shocked. She might as well have stripped naked in front of him on the street. And to tell him this, here, right after avoiding his invitation to dinner. Right outside the honey shop. He sensed the spectacle-hooded Mr. Rahman peering from just behind the narrow door and had to force himself not to turn and look.

But then, if irrationally, they both smiled wistfully at each other; she was looking at him again, her eyes vulnerable, yes, but almost proud. Or, at least, accepting. The boy studied both of them, as if he watched something very curious that was suddenly happening right before him: a curiousness that overwhelmed even his fear. What he beheld was the not so rare phenomena of two people recognizing each held an experience whose world would be severely misinterpreted by others.

The New Man and Haziz looked at each other a long instant. The boy was stilled, curiously stilled. He was certainly old enough to interpret comments about his missing father, but he either held himself out of instinct or had been instructed by his mother to bear nothing but silence on this subject. His very young face, concerned and awed—and fearful—looked ancient.

Haziz spoke quietly. "You can come to my apartment for dinner." The New Man, still stunned, gave no acquiescence. Her face had the implacable resignation of an idol. "Do you remember how to find it?" It seemed he had no say in the slight nod of his head. He understood she had not so much refused him before but preferred her own interiors for another meeting.

Haziz gave her own nod as she rose and Rasil got up, Mother and son walked slowly away. Haziz gave no look back.

The New Man sat on the bench for a few moments after Haziz and Rasil were out of sight. When he got up he was absolutely certain Mr. Rahman peered out of the honey shop at him, but he kept himself from looking back at that window bejeweled with the elixir of insects.

13. The Prophet

He stood there, breathing in the warm air, looking up to the trail of smoke in the sky. So the husband of Haziz was—had been—one of the righteous martyrs: conspirator in the murders he, The New Man had escaped; and a moment ago he had been desiring this woman. Did Haziz believe her husband was in the martyr's paradise, with its promised houris? He put a hand up to his brow. He felt he had escaped nothing; in fact, he had been more ensnared—in something. How could he continue to move through this existence that assailed him with brutal coincidence?

Though he had to walk somewhere. He was about to return to

the motel when he noticed that immediately adjacent to the honey shop was a bookstore. This advertised itself wholly in foreign letters—Arabic or Farsi?—but the books in its window made its business plain to The New Man.

It was a store that seemed as narrow as the honey shop, and, as The New Man entered (on a whim—or again under the operation of choice, destiny, etc.) he saw he was once more in a tunnel-like store, at the end of which sat—Mr. Rahman again? The New Man was startled. Well, it appeared to be the honey seller, only without his glasses. Mr. Rahman reading, this time, a book. The New Man had the thought that the shops had been formed out of one store and that Mr. Rahman moved back and forth between the two through a simple connecting door.

Mr. Rahman looked up at The New Man's entrance. He began a phrase in his own tongue, then, at The New Man's blank—and anxious—look, quickly switched to English. "May I help you?" It was an expressionless question, unlike the innuendo he had spoken in the other shop.

But *was* this Mr. Rahman? No: the clothes were different.

"Is something wrong?"

"You look so much like— You're not—?"

There was a smile more calculated than spontaneous. "You were just in my brother's shop. We are—twins." He said this uncomfortably; he did not seem to like the word.

"Yes; it's obvious."

"But not so good throughout life. I must be grateful he wears the glasses. Though he tells me I should wear the glasses: my eyes certainly aren't perfect and I am with books all the time. Are you looking for something?"

The New Man didn't know what he was looking for. But said:

"A Koran." Once more his mouth surprised his heart. Or perhaps it was his heart that surprised his mouth.

"So—the terrible terrorists destroy America and you want to know about them?"

"About Islam, perhaps?" He said to himself: *What am I saying?*

"I don't know if I have any English Korans—you don't read Arabic, I'm sure."

"No."

"You can find translations anywhere. Certainly even the United States of America is not going to forbid the Koran."

From the honey shop to what Haziz had told him to this puerile interrogation: the surreality of the life The New Man had stepped into was ruthless. "No, I don't think so."

This Mr. Rahman paused, then said, "So—you came here. For a Koran."

"I happened to be in the neighborhood."

"You have friends here?"

"I—no—I…escaped."

"Escaped?"

"I was in the Towers." Once more, the disguise of the truth.

That made Mr. Rahman pause again. "The Towers?" He gestured warily to the east, as if involuntarily acknowledging a power beyond all personal assessment.

"Yes." Why did The New Man feel as if he were admitting to a guilty act?

"I see…" Mr. Rahman seemed to be trying to imagine flight from the burning monoliths. "But—why—here?" That last word gave this place a geography a map could not.

The New Man retold his fiction again, while he told the truth about his escape.

"And by the grace of Allah you are in a neighborhood of Muslims."

"Life is curious."

"To us curious; to Allah, plain. So: you think Muslims did this?"

"It appears *some* Muslims—"

"That is nonsense. You want to hear the truth?"

The New Man wanted nothing so much as the truth of things, though he was sure he was not about to hear it. "Of course."

"It was the Jews."

"The Jews." The New Man was disappointed. This was not even going to be imaginative.

Mr. Rahman squinted at him. "You're not Jewish?"

"No," The New Man sighed.

The bookseller accepted this denial. He rushed on. "The Jews do not want America to feel sorry for the Arabs, the Palestinians. The Mossad brought down those buildings so America could attack Islam, so what Israel does in our Holy Land will be put in the back of the newspapers. Did you know that morning four thousand Jewish people did not go to work in your Towers?"

"No, I didn't know that," said The New Man blankly.

"Four thousand. Maybe more. They knew."

The New Man said, "Well, I heard there were fifty thousand people in those two buildings. There were probably more Jews than four thousand—"

"The Jews will let some Jews die. It was the Jews who mattered who knew."

The New Man sighed. The madness of the labyrinth. "Four

thousand Jews—people—knew, and none of them said anything to anyone?"

"The Jews protect themselves with silence when it is necessary—though usually they complain." He scowled at The New Man's look. "This is the truth, believe it or not." Mr. Rahman had no idea he had just used a popular phrase.

"You think I'm crazy," he demanded.

The New Man was not thinking Mr. Rahman crazy, only that he was trying to sell a bill of goods. He said, "I do not know you enough to have an opinion."

"But you think it's crazy—the Jews doing this."

"Look. I survived it and maybe right now I'm less interested in who did this than—" But he couldn't finish it. Mr. Rahman gave him a look that said he was going to insist The New Man did so; but then the latter took a sharp turn: "So you have no Koran in English."

Mr. Rahman sighed. "It is possible. It is possible. I will have to look in the back." Then, suspiciously: "What do you know about the Koran?"

"Only that it is the Muslim holy book."

"It is the final word of Allah." For a moment Mr. Rahman disappeared behind a door in back of the counter. The New Man felt the long silence of the empty shop as he waited. Though the wait was short. Mr. Rahman re-emerged, and extended a dark covered volume. Even as The New Man took it, the bookseller, as freely as he had told The New Man about the Mossad and the four thousand Jews in the know, gave a concise summary of the inception of the Koran and Islam.

"The Prophet Mohammed was born after his father died. His

mother died when he was six. He was raised by a grandfather, then his uncle. He married a widow, a wealthy trader. Mohammed served on the caravans of a wealthy widow, Khadijah; he married her." Mr. Rahman said this almost curtly, as if getting necessary but mundane facts out of the way. Then the tone of his voice changed: now he would proceed to the spiritual meat of his story. "He was forty when the angel came to him. He had gone to a cave on Mount Hira. It was the month of Ramadan and Mohammed would go there to think about the terrible thing that men had made of life. And one night the angel Gabriel appeared to him and commanded, 'Read!'" Mr. Rahman spoke this word with abrupt power, and The New Man almost flinched.

"The Prophet said, 'I cannot read,' but the angel commanded him again and there were words before Mohammed and so Mohammed read. A little at a time the Koran would be given to him. When Mohammed came out of the cave, he saw Gabriel with his feet standing on the edge of the sky and the earth, telling Mohammed, 'You are the messenger of Allah!' So Mohammed spoke what he was given."

The New Man was imagining some great, winged, white-robed creature, astride the earth—towering…. As the Towers.

Mr. Rahman said: "There were a few at the time who knew there was one God. These were the Hanifs. The other Arabs worshipped many gods. But even the Hanifs doubted Mohammed. And when Mohammed spoke against giving goods as worship for idols, the traders, the Quraish drove him away. They cared for their profits, not the true God." Mr. Rahman gave an ironic gesture. "There is something wrong that in your language that "profit," meaning money, and "prophet," a man of God, sound the same."

The New Man had to admit to himself he had never made that connection. But he said nothing. Mr. Rahman continued: "Mohammed had to leave Mecca, taking him to where his camel would stop. He said that; 'The choice lies with the camel.'" (Well, The New Man thought, why not a beast showing the divine path?) "Where the camel stopped, there was Yathrib; it is Medina now. It was in Medina he showed us the way to pray. He brought Allah into the ways of what people do every day. He fought in battles—against the Jews, who had turned from the true God, against Arabs who should have known how God had chosen their people."

Surely bin Laden saw himself in this template, as a warrior for Allah.

If Mr. Rahman suspected any of The New Man's thoughts, he gave no indication. "In all this, Mohammed was a strong man. His voice was like music. He spoke gently. He could not bear harsh, loud words. He told us to be modest in all things. He lived as a simple man. He ate dates and bread made from barley. His luxuries were milk and honey. He did not wear fine clothes, and would mend himself those he had. He slept on the floor. After his beloved Khadijah died and he took other wives, he slept with each of then in turn, fairly." (These extra wives, The New Man thought: were they boon—indulgence—or burden? At any rate, Mr. Rahman's "fairly" was too affected, brushing aside a visceral issue.) "He would not waver from what he had been told by God and the angel to follow; and he was merciful."

The quality of mercy, thought The New Man—*different to all of us.*

"Finally he returned to Mecca, where he had been outcast. He and the faithful circled the Black Stone of the Kaaba—which had been used for idolatry—and said with each turn, 'There is no God but Allah!' He was accepted in the place he began. He had brought so many believers with him that others saw he could take Mecca by strength if he needed. Many of the Quraish generals came to the true faith. The Prophet destroyed all idols and left the Black Stone. He kissed it, as now we must do."

The New Man imagined Mr. Rahman's lips kissing this dark mineral surface. It was a repulsive and hardly spiritual image. There was something blatantly perverse about it.

"Before he died, in the middle of the coming of death, he got up and went into the mosque, where he used to lead the prayers, and sat beside Abu Bakar, one of his most faithful. He was humble in the ceremony he had begun.

"It was not until after he died that the Koran was collected into one book, by Zaid ibn Thabit, who took from everywhere the words the angel had given the Prophet: from the memories of men to tablets of stone to leaves of dates. And we have this truth: 'Allah! There is no God save him, the living, the eternal! To him belongs all of the Earth….'"

Mr. Rahman's abrupt lesson was intense, vigorous and compact; its information suggested layers within, and The New Man, not quite prepared to be preached to, had been held, despite his natural cynicism that the passions of others were steeped in a self-deception in even the most meaningful of activism. And he did think, he had to, that this God of Mohammed's had been the God of Haziz' husband, who had crashed into one of the Towers. From the angel Gabriel to that maniacal act…. It was too much to consider in any rational way.

He absently flipped through the pages of his Koran as Mr. Rahman was ending his tale, as if impelled to seek the full word of Allah in complement to the bookseller's condensed account, but his eyes, scanning across the numbers on the pages made him sense—and recall—that here was the only purity *he* had known: the numbers that marked a progression of pages, markers of the text but which could easily be lifted from the text, lifted from Allah, without loss of identity. Here were things more immutable—and, yes, perhaps more spiritual—than messages from Gabriel and the intent of fanatics.

When Mr. Rahman finished he was a little out of breath, his face friendly and a little condescending. He may have taken this infidel's attention to the inkling of a belief. At any rate, The New Man, as audience, was obligated to say something: "You put it very…powerfully."

"There can be power only in the truth." The New Man did not quite believe that; the world had seen enormous power in enormous lies. But he said nothing. Abruptly Mr. Rahman squeezed The New Man's hand that held the Koran. "Read it. Come back and we will talk."

If The New Man was sure he would read at least some of the Koran, he was not sure he would return to this Mr. Rahman, who now appeared to rein in his enthusiasm and sincerity and revert to original suspicions: "If you are still…in the neighborhood."

The New Man would make no commitment as to that. "Thank you," he said quickly, and quickly left the shop. He felt the bookseller's eyes on the back of his neck. His experience with the same *image* of the proprietor of the honey shop and then the bookshop had been like making two abrupt turns in a maze and finding himself in the same spot.

Returning to the motel, The New Man tried to imagine the huge sight of an angel towering above buildings and streets. And then there was the vision of a plane with Haziz' husband, exploding into the robes of the divine.

14. *Angels These, Hurled From a Height?*

That afternoon, back in the motel, The New Man had the choice of three diversions as he waited through the hours before he would meet Haziz—a meeting he both desired and feared. There were the papers in the black bag he might reread to see if they were indeed not of his imagination; he had his new, used copy of the Koran; and he had the TV. He chose the electronic succubus, as it seemed at the moment the less intimate diversion. In hardly more than 48 hours his life had been eviscerated, twisted and turned into something else—by the chance of being in a certain place and time, by a profound decision on his part, and then by further chance, surreal and constant. It is Thursday, he told himself. On Monday I sat in the office, in one of the tallest buildings in one of the world's most important cities; I was occupied with the boring business of objects being traded back and forth between countries; now I sit in an obscure motel in a small city certainly of no fame, with the book of a foreign faith, waiting to see a woman equally foreign, who saved my life. And my entire old life has been cast away. What a difference a day makes, or two or three.

So, not wanting to dwell so much on his life, he turned on the TV, where the event that had been catalyst to his transformation was made so thoroughly public, less private and more like a shared chaotic ritual that had been pushed across a border into entertainment.

Yet he found himself witnessing something a little different. After scanning CBS, NBC, ABC, CNN, MSNBC, etc., that steady stream of acronyms, he was held by a local cable station. Without the high-tech accoutrements and smart videos of the big stations, a youngish reporter said, "Here's some news that doesn't seem to be getting much attention in the mainstream media—" He was thin and pale with thin unpleasant hair and though he wore a suit and tie he suggested unkemptness. In the era of The New Man's youth, those long ago halcyon days of the '60s, this reporter probably would have had long hair and muttonchop sideburns. He went on: "Hours after Flight 93 went down in a field in Pennsylvania, the FBI said it was not ruling out the possibility that the government had shot the plane down—before it might head for Washington or elsewhere. Suspicions this might be the case are based on the fact that the plane left a debris field six miles long, which would not seem to have happened if the plane had simply exploded on impact with the ground. There are definite indications—from cell phone calls—that a number of passengers on board, after they had learned of the attacks on New York and Washington, were determined to fight the hijackers, and the government is saying it appears those brave passengers foiled the hijackers' attempt to use the plane as a weapon of terrorism. But perhaps, a few speculative minds say, whether the passengers foiled the hijackers or not, the government, by then painfully aware of the unfolding terrorist plot, brought down the plane. It has been admitted by the military that at that point the plane would have been shot down had it approached Washington."

He paused, as if understanding what he had to say next would be unpleasant. "This leads to the possibility that the passengers may have foiled the terrorists, regained control of the plane—but the government, not knowing this, shot down Flight 93. Though the more likely case is that the government brought the plane down as the passengers struggled with their captors. That is, if the government did shoot it down—"

The young man paused again and stared into the camera. There was no slick segue into another segment of "America Under Attack." The reporter's stare seemed to ask: "What do you think of that?" Then he said, "We return you now to Ground Zero." Again, the Arabic zero, the rubble and the rising smoke and the grouped and scattered toiling men.

The New Man surfed through other channels, where no mention was made of the government shooting down Flight 93, and he considered the broadcaster's provocative words. It suited the government to leave the combative passengers of Flight 93 pure heroes. Of course, whether the government had brought down the plane or not, those passengers had indeed been heroic: it was heroism to simply recognize that one were about to die no matter what, to fully accept that, to try and not hold on to the next second and the next in vain hope for some miracle. To accept death, and in that very instant try to save the lives of others the plane might be used against.

Could I be that brave? he wondered. He did not want to answer his own question.

While the TV went on, The New Man suddenly remembered: the phone number. He virtually clawed through the briefcase, found one of the copies he had made of the number, and, just as full of fear as the first time he had attempted it, jabbed the numbers on the phone.

He heard a surging sea of static, swelling then subsiding, swelling again. It was like some cosmic noise from the belly, the gut of the universe. And then, faintly, within that primal discordance, he thought he heard a ringing, like some assertion of mind taking hold amidst chaos. But he could not be sure. He let the static and the possible ringing go on a while—he had the feeling now that he would have to confront no one at the other end and so he could stay like that, telling himself he had tried. Any "intelligence" out there would be nothing more than this: inarticulate, helpless—his own mirror. For he looked at himself in the mirror across the room, as he held the phone against his head.

Finally he put down the phone. He sighed. He was relieved. He was disappointed. He was drained.

The New Man flicked off the TV and picked up another appendage of the media, a copy of *The New York Times* he had bought yesterday. In his new life he had sought old habits. Though he had more scanned than read the paper, now he studied it with attention. That issue of September 12 bore the bold, high headline "AMERICA ATTACKED." It had the aura, the sense of a WWII headline. On the front page the Twin Towers were burning. How many photographs were now in existence of the final hours of those buildings?

But inside was a photograph that truly arrested him. A man plummeted down the side of one of the Towers. Against the repetitive vertical surface of the building there was no indication this doomed man had just passed the 70th floor or the 20th, but the photograph rawly conveyed the reality that this unfortunate soul had been hurled down from a great height. The man was in shirtsleeves and seemed to have a smattering of blood on his body.

The New Man was instantly transfixed. He would not have been able to say why. The photograph revealed enough of the man to show he was dark haired, apparently middle aged, but did not reveal so much to keep him from becoming Everyman. Wholly vulnerable and thrust to his death by chance. Quite possibly The New Man saw himself hurled downward, bearing his old name, but for the chance of the call from Wilson.

In the psyche of humankind, certainly in the psyche of the West, beings hurled from heights are angels who displeased God. And then, more recent in the great maw of consciousness and its subliminal seas, the myth of Icarus, whose technology failed—or, more precisely, whose hubris (or naiveté) kept him from seeing the limits of his technology, those lovely wax wings melting with proximity to the sun. The tale was scientifically flawed: the wings would be too heavy, it would be colder with altitude—but it keeps at our gut, as the angels do.

But now, here was this man—as there were others, as The New Man had heard. Those blown out of the buildings by the force of the explosions or who chose to jump to their deaths rather than face the slower, more ravaging and painful death by fire. Here too was a bravery, not unlike the passengers of Flight 93: to accept that death was certain and to choose a "better" death.

And here was the man, replacing the angels and Icarus, and yet inheriting a vital substance of each. Who is without sin and who is without pride—or naiveté? And this had been a man who had had faith in the technology of the day (or who had taken them so much for granted he needed no faith), who had worked within the height of those buildings, who had thought that ascension and the vista the skyscrapers had given was a rightful place, a normal place and circumstance; and then the simplest tearing away, the crudest violence through the will of other human beings, who had lived at a lower height, and yet had come from a greater height to bring that man down.

The New Man pushed the newspaper and that photograph away from him. As he did so, something slipped from the long thickness of this historic edition of the *Times*: a slim, tabloid-sized Arabic paper.

The New Man was actually startled. How had this paper gotten there? By chance, of course, somehow mixed in with the *Times* at the newsstand. He certainly must have perused this paper incompletely yesterday.... –Or had it been a "message" for him to see?

With an intuition of dread, he picked up the Arabic paper. (Only during the past two days had he begun to think of how these foreign mirrors of journalism portrayed the world in which America moved so prominently.) Again, below large thick black headlines the burning Twin Towers—and another shocking photograph of a figure, three figures, in fact, plummeting downward alongside the austere vertical face of one of the buildings. It was a photograph, as horrifying as the one in the *Times*—more so. The middle of the three figures, a body higher up than the others, became the apex of a rough triangle—and that body appeared, *My God, yes, it looked like Wilson!*—with a dark suit, with pants and jacket flapped out at the rush of the descent. A body that looked like Wilson's, a face that could be Wilson's: at the least a suggestion of Wilson that could not be definite because the camera had not zoomed in enough. The

New thought that the photographer (though he could not read the name in Arabic below the photo) had tried to get all three of the figures who had flung themselves or been flung downward, and so had sacrificed more personal detail in order to gather them all in; and, as a result, because of that personal vagueness and the triangular formation, present a spectacle that marked the surface of an allegory.

One of the lower figures, to the right of Wilson, if it was Wilson, was a woman, in business dress and heels, whose sharp dark points seemed like minute horns at the end of her legs. Her body plummeted straight downward, headfirst, with the apparent willful straightening of a diver, the back to the camera, her arms outspread at forty-five degree angles to the head, her hair rushed back—one had the feeling she would, in the instant after the picture was snapped, thrust the arms straight below her head, hands coming together, fingers pointing toward the death guaranteed at the earth below. There was the sense of absolute acceleration about her. The distortion of her shadow that had been cast on the building (the only one of the three who cast a shadow, it seemed) added to this sense of plummeting speed.

While the other man seemed to participate in his death not at all; facing the camera there was the unpleasant visage of helplessness, the arms and legs going this way and that, the torso twisted. The briefest glance might have thought this a body floating without gravity, the helplessness of the body coming from that lack—when, in fact, gravity absolutely commanded the figure. From one splayed arm the dark spread of the fingers might have been ineffectual claws; there was nothing to clutch in this descent. But above all the figure was stark with its obvious surrender to its sad fate of being subjected to this killing descent.

While Wilson—if this *was* Wilson: he plummeted with his legs downward, as if with not so apparent control as the woman, though with more control than the man. One hand touched at his head, as if seeking to keep a hat in place, though there was no hat to grasp or stay. He seemed a figure in a painting by Magritte, a suited bourgeois character at once in control of himself and yet placed in a surreal situation no one could ever control—and yet it might have been a circumstance born of his very consciousness.

The New Man's eyes strained at the photograph. Was it Wilson? One instant he said Yes, another No; another instant he could not be sure. And, finally, that was the truth of it. It could be and it could not be. But it certainly impressed upon The New Man the assumed death of Wilson, who had been at some terrible height that morning, a brutally unforgiving height— And yet, and yet: the most unlikely possibilities insisted themselves upon The New Man. Since the morning of September 11, since that incident of which these three figures were one of the many markers, the aspect of all possibility had changed. Wilson could be alive, he could be dead, he could be one of those figures, he—perhaps, perhaps, thought The New Man, he had not been in the building at all. Yes, Oh God, that thought had struck him before. Wilson had *said* over the phone he was in his office (or someone's office), but he could have been calling from outside, why from his home in Babylon or from somewhere else— "In some town in New Jersey," The New Man said aloud to himself; then laughed with fear and a little mocking at his own imagination—and the possibility of anything being possible. He kept looking at the picture, this triangle of plummeting disparate human beings. Had they known each other? Had they been cast down or jumped at the same random moment? Had one jumped, two been cast down, or vice versa? Before he could overwhelm himself in the mathematical positioning of the possibilities (the two men had jumped, the woman fallen; the Wilson-figure cast down, the other man and the woman fallen, etc.) he made his own plummet from such reasoning. He was in the maw of a chaos for which he could find no mathematical model. He was transfixed with the helplessness of his own descent, suffering some terrible revelations or at least likelihood before the photograph of the plummeting trinity. "Father, Son and the Holy Ghost," he said, again aloud, again pierced by his own words. (A non-religious man, was he making religious connections out of mockery or a yearning to fill some lack? For that matter, what had made him blurt out he was seeking a Koran to one of the Rahmans?) The Wilson-figure clearly was the Father, the Creator, the one who had set all this in motion—or at least had set *something* in motion; the woman had to be the Spirit, the Holy Ghost, irrational but determined (why did he give her those aspects?); the other man, exposed at all angles before his death was the Son, ready to receive what another's will had decreed.

The New Man cursed and pushed the paper away from him as he had pushed the *Times* and the Arabic paper away. At the end of that motion he found himself reaching for the Koran.

Al-Hijr, Surah XV: "And we destroyed no township but there was a known decree for it. No nation can outstrip its term nor can they lag behind….

"And remember when the Lord said unto the angels: 'Lo! I am creating a mortal out of potter's clay of black mud altered.

So when I have made him and have breathed into him of My Spirit, do ye fall down, prostrating yourself unto him.' So the angels fell prostrate all together. Save Iblis. He refused... 'Why should I prostrate myself unto a mortal whom thou has created out of potter's clay—?'"

Allah gave no reply to that but said, "Then go thou forth from Heaven, for hence thou art outcast."

This curse would be upon Iblis—until the Day of Judgement. For at the sentence of his casting out, Iblis had protested: "My Lord! Reprieve me until the day when they are raised." Allah had agreed: "Thou are of those reprieved till an appointed time."

But Iblis would not be thankful for this reprieve. "Because thou hast sent me astray, I shall adorn the path of error for them on earth, and shall mislead them every one."

The New Man put down the Koran. This was too much like the Bible's tale of Lucifer's rebellion for him to feel the Koran was imparting something different. Of course, these were but a few lines in a big book. He would have to take it up again—perhaps go to Mr. Rahman for some pointers, he thought wryly.

And he thought: he could hardly blame the angel Iblis/Lucifer for feeling distraught over having been ordered to bow to mortals. It was like God saying, I spit on this: worship it.

But, above all, his chancing upon the tale, the fundamental narrative of the devil's beginning, the casting out of God's divine but disobedient creature, could only return to The New Man's mind the photograph of the plummeting victims of the attack on The World Trade Center. And within the image, the thought that the angel of the attackers may have come from a repulsion of worshipping what we wanted them to worship—our world, not theirs. And so their anger easily corrupted them into murder. While we—

He caught himself. He was getting twisted with symbol and philosophy. This was indeed the maze. He held the closed book he would open again. But not today.

He brushed away the photograph of the plummeting trinity. Here were aspects of sin and helplessness, not redemption.

15. *New Clothes, Heralds in the Sky, Prayers on the Street*

The New Man looked at the clock. Time was on its march, losing its constant minutes to eternity, but he still had more than a few hours before he would see Haziz. Then the sudden thought, or knowledge returned: her husband had been one of the hijackers. This was bizarre; this was terrifying. Could it possibly be true?

The New Man's spirit, stretched in ways it had never gone, pulled and twisted in a chaos of personal decision and surreal circumstance, could not confront this imponderable possibility for long. In a sort of surrender, or necessary withdrawal, he drew his attention to more practical things—he was still capable of the natural progression from imaginings to reality. The prospect of the deeds of Haziz' husband drew The New Man to the fact that he wore the man's shirt and pants—a dead man's shirt and pants. He looked about wildly for the bag of his old clothing and considered drawing out the stained, wrinkled clothes—

No. He would not wear his old clothes again, and he would not wear the clothing of a terrorist husband. He abruptly left the room and went out, to go shopping.

He had considered asking Ahmed where he might find some

inexpensive slacks and shirts, but The New Man had the feeling that the less Ahmed saw of him, the less suspicious the motelkeeper would be about the presence of his guest, survivor of the Twin Towers.

In the courtyard of the motel, across the empty parking lot, The New Man was startled to see a figure stride up to a door and enter it. In fact, The New Man stopped dead in his tracks. There had been the unease of the recent realization that he alone seemed to inhabit the motel—apart from Ahmed. Now, here was another. But this seemed to make The New Man more uneasy than any fact of solitude.

He frowned to himself with irony. He recalled reading *Robinson Crusoe* (he'd just gotten back from Vietnam; why he'd picked up that book then he could not have said): the shipwrecked man had often bemoaned his aloneness; but, when finally—after years and years (wasn't it decades?) of being marooned—coming upon a human footprint in the sand, he had been filled with fear. Perhaps only then had he understood the safety and purity of isolation.

The New Man made himself walk on. Perhaps the other man studied him from behind a window with equal unease—or with the knowledge of something The Man did not possess.

The New Man had been out enough in the neighborhood now to more than vaguely recall a store, another place of business where foreign and English words were layered above each other in common display; a store whose large frontage was open to the street, where shirts and pants, clothing of all kinds were displayed, practically right in the midst of pedestrians and then extending back into the interior of the shop.

The New Man found it quickly enough, after making two turns with an instinct that seemed to have come out of habit—though in this regard the word habit could barely be applied to The New Man, as he had been in the neighborhood only the day before yesterday. (The ironic thought came to him: "I wasn't born yesterday—only the day before.")

But as he approached the shop he heard a distant cry—not a single cry, but a far, far-off repeated, then altered murmuring, whose words were either too distant for him to understand or too foreign. And he noted that a fair number of people on the street stopped, and positioned themselves facing in the same direction: eastward. Some did this abruptly, others after a searching pause, as if trying to locate a thing far past any distance, any skyline immediately visible. He realized this scattered crowd was obeying an obvious commandment of their faith. The murmuring which he had thought of as far-off was merely disparate, for these scattered voices raised themselves, at first incoherently then distinctly, and now it felt a near thing, though what they spoke—or prayed—was indecipherable to The New Man.

Prayer indeed. The New Man found himself also stopping, here in the midst of the afternoon light of the street that now seemed to have a voice. His attention became focused on a youngish man, probably in his early thirties, who was making calm gestures with his hands and reciting the appropriate formula softly. He wasn't dressed in foreign clothes, but his face was suffused with a foreign ardor. It came to The New Man abruptly: Muslims have to pray a certain number of times a day. He watched the young Muslim bow in further recitation. Then, continuing his duty toward God, he prostrated himself on the dirty sidewalk, a spectacle that made The New Man uncomfortable and which he would later find at odds with the prescribed ritual. There was the impression that with this young man the afternoon's obligation had struck through a claim of preoccupation, that it had found him forgetful, and thus he had felt guilty, and bound to enact his duties even if they were done roughly. To The New Man, this prostrate body, the shirt stretched tight across the back, the pants rumpled, appeared a man mindlessly submissive to a callous summons.

And yet the ceremony had its allure. The man drew himself up, balanced himself on his heels. His incantations were lulling, still indecipherable, and beautiful to The New Man, who continued to study the one praying without hiding that he did so. Once more the praying man prostrated himself, once more he drew himself up on his heels. Continuing the soft words of his ritual, he looked over his right shoulder then his left.

It was at this point that the eyes of the worshipper met the eyes of The New Man. The eyes of the worshipper were inscrutable. The New Man suddenly felt as if intruding, more so for the odd sort of pleasure he had gotten while watching— almost as if a man spying upon a naked woman, who does not immediately know she fills another's vision. The New Man felt a little guilty and walked on. He had the sense, as he left the worshipper, that the man was repeating the stations of his prayer.

The New Man wondered, as he reached the sidewalk display of the clothing store, if its employees would be thus occupied. He did hear, as he reached the sidewalk bazaar of goods, another distant calling: perhaps an end to prayer.

Whether the clerk who approached him inside, dark

complected, with silver frame glasses and a trim moustache, had been released from prayer just before the arrival of The New Man or whether the man had not been at prayer at all—or whether the man was Muslim in the first place—The New Man could not know. Tall and lean, his dark hair receding (there was the sense about him of a man trying to leave the weight of his body for a lightness, at least an austerity), he greeted The New Man with an easy warmth—though The New Man had the feeling it was not so much a greeting but a diplomatic statement that he understood The New Man was out of his realm and so had to be regarded with extra, solicitous attention: an attention just to this side of suspicion.

"Do you need help, sir?"

"Well…some pants, shirts."

The thin man ushered The New Man right outside again, to one particular section of goods on the street, a table of slacks that seemed of fair enough quality: what would be called "western" clothes; while nearby, hanging on racks, were the long shirts that reached down to the knees and were slit up the side to the waist. The New Man was in fact about to ask the man just what these shirts were called. (His attackers had worn them yesterday—but no: they hadn't. Was he already embellishing memory with stereotype?) He found the garments intriguing, suspended by the score before him, so long and still in the light and bustle of the street, each like a chrysalis of some humanoid creature.

But he uttered no questions, for just as quickly as he had directed The New Man to the shirts, the clerk ushered his foreign customer back into the shop, deep into the shop, where slacks, in neat repetition and subtly varying shades—white, grey, light tan, dark tan, brown, black—were draped precisely on hangers; while again, as outside, in juxtaposition, more "native" garments: a tunic type jacket and wide, billowy pants.

The complementarity of East and West was an arresting motif throughout the shop. There were baseball caps, fezzes and turbans, and mantles for women. There was the complete, suffocating chador, the hooded robe with a mesh for the nose and eyes—looking like a Halloween costume; and there were low cut blouses.

The thin man seemed to sense The New Man's amused appreciation of the clash of cultures; at least that was what his smile intimated. The New Man felt the other toyed with the idea of asking his Western customer to try on a fez or one of those baggy, neo-Arabian Nights pants.

And The New Man did have the thought: if I bought one of those long shirts, the pants, grew my beard, then no one would ever, could ever recognize me. I could go right up to my door, and my wife would see a stranger. His next thought was: and I'd probably be arrested as a terrorist suspect with no papers.

In the end, he purchased the known: three shirts (white, blue-grey, the third with thin blue stripes on white) and three slacks (light tan—something like the one's Haziz had given him—dark tan and light grey). He bought underwear. Just as the clerk was trying to interest him in a suit (low priced, but not of cheap quality, the seller stressed), The New Man remembered he needed socks and bought a half dozen. He was about to consider looking at sweaters and light jackets—in another month it would be the middle of October—but by then he had had enough of shopping, and the eclectic mix of Eastern and Western garments now seemed too much of a jumble to sort through, a not quite right miscegenation of apparel that made him uneasy.

As he paid for his purchases, The New Man had the feeling (which had now become familiar to him) that the thin man wanted to pry into the reason The New Man had come to the store in the first place, but could find no good way to lead into this, and said nothing. And so The New Man returned to the streets, to the motel, with his new threads in two near transparent plastic bags that bore the logo of the store. (Yes: an Arabic and English logo.)

In his room he took off the clothes of Haziz' departed husband; he showered, then put on a white shirt and dark tan slacks. It felt good to have new clothes upon his body, clothing no one had worn, including his old self. There was a little of the stiffness of new clothing, prior to the long-folded creases being worked out. They should really be ironed, he thought, but it will do for now.

He folded the clothes of Haziz' husband, and put them in one of the plastic shopping bags. In the simple act of doing so he paused, to think again about this man being one of the hijackers.

It suddenly struck him that he had automatically assumed Haziz' husband to be on one of the planes that had struck the Towers. But he could have been on that plane that rammed the Pentagon or crashed in Pennsylvania. Yet an illogic that had the reality of instinct gave The New Man the conviction Haziz' husband had died within the Towers from which he, The New Man, had fled.

Though it was even more fantastical, he considered, the fact that he would be seeing Haziz again tonight.

To stay this from overwhelming him, he flicked on the TV.

As if in proper, repetitive prologue, there were the workmen at smoking Ground Zero, the reports of "new developments" in the strange new world of "America Under Attack"; President Bush declared that not only would the U.S. topple bin Laden and his terrorist network, but bring down states that harbored terrorism. With this promise—or war cry—America greeted the millennium.

More had come out about the hijackers. A number of them had taken flying lessons in Florida. (Would Bush II declare war on Florida? Hardly, after the Republican triumph there in the election.) And, unlike the cadre of terrorists who had brought a bomb into the World Trade Center in 1993, and who had lived covert lives, these millennial hijackers had lived, apparently, "normal" lives. A flight instructor recalled one student: very friendly and the last person one would imagine as a religious fanatic.

There would be no baseball games, no football games, until after the weekend. This alone was proof that America had been shocked, and shaken to its core.

Russia vowed to aid NATO in any way to help America's vigorous anti-terrorism initiatives.

This was the mark of how history, as time itself, rushed on. The USSR and the U.S. had grappled in the dark pre-apocalyptic Cold War for decades, with the fate of the rest of the world crushed between the determined lumbering interests of these two empires. Now Russia, exhausted after its three generations of the lie of communism, collecting itself after the quagmire of Afghanistan and the economic collapse of the 1990s, had withdrawn from the center of the arena and would watch America struggle with a new foe. To the winner of the Cold War had gone the challenges issued by the new kid on the block: the fanatics of a nearly 1400 year old religion.

The New Man looked at himself in the mirror before stepping out. "My God, I've got a date," he said to the glass, and laughed grimly. One morning he had fled a terrorist attack, now he would be having dinner with a woman who had wed one of the terrorists. He'd been thinking of that too much; he shoved it away. He remained before the mirror studying his face. His reflection looked back at him with the clarity of a mundane truth. Old, but rested, he thought. Not unhandsome. Perhaps.

He leaned more closely to the mirror. Could these past days be seen in his eyes, his features? He studied his eyes as if he could see in them the gathered images of these past two days. But there was only himself, looking at himself.

He gave only a brief, helpless thought to the motel's other inhabitant as he walked out onto the street. If he had only known this neighborhood since the day before yesterday, its mix of Middle Eastern people and its smattering of Asians, its streets seemed already familiar. Though if his "transformation" had not been entirely a metamorphosis, it should be expected that the land he walked upon in this new life would be a different terrain, with different inhabitants.

He came to the lot of debris. The sun had sunk behind buildings in the west. The shadowed rectangle of rubble and the still bright sky seemed to him a herald of the future, the immediate future—the debris suggesting the further possibility of change, of the shedding of old things; while the sky, bright but with intimations of darkening, was the portent of a vast but as yet unknown destination.

A breeze came from that sun-cradling west, cooling the end

of a hot day. He paused by the lot, enjoying the sensation. He wondered where the four men and the heroin-addicted Double were now. Had he thought about them even once today?

A noise drew his attention back to the sky. A plane, catching the light of the sun that was now denied to the earth below, passed slowly through the sky. It glinted in the faint rumble of its passage. It too seemed a herald. Only for a moment did the aircraft appear on a straight path. As The New Man continued to watch, he saw the plane take a gradually curving trajectory. He recalled how the Double had thrown his mockery up at one of these planes yesterday—or perhaps it was the same one. But what could these planes hope to engage? The terrorists did not have their own air force. They had had to use our planes for their attacks. So with none of those in the sky, only this stern military display, the terrorists would be stymied at least from any more aerial atrocities. Though as The New Man noted the smoke still rising from the east (and the scent of it, faint but palpable, a scent that had become habitual), he thought: but the deed was done.

The plane was gone from sight, though The New Man faintly heard if for a few seconds more, like the promise of something relentless.

16. *Prayers at Home*

The New Man looked upon Haziz' building. The light of day had lessened just enough for him to see that one window held the beacon of artificial light—and one floor above it a window also bore the same mark of habitation. The New Man wondered about that other occupant of the mostly deserted building. Then his curiosity gave way to apprehension. It was a feeling akin to his sighting the one other occupant of the motel. Every nearby, unknown being was a potential threat. He considered he might be about to embark on a course that, if fulfilling to his worn if newborn soul, was also dangerous.

In the dimness, he trudged up the three flights of stairs. He had the feeling now that this was an upward path that had become a habit. He guided himself easily along the length of the dim corridor. What had he done with the flashlight Haziz had given him?

He knocked quietly at the door, almost carefully. There was a pause of a heartbeat or two, then Haziz opened the door. Her dark hair seemed to escape in great thick waves from a head covering that was a vivid, light blue, almost the sort of blue one sees in the photographs of tropical waters. She spoke a greeting The New Man lost in his nervousness. She smiled subtly, the corners of her mouth barely ascending; it was a natural, calm expression, her response to his coming to see her, an expression that was something like the release of a worry that he would not come—a relief; and so that subtle smile affected him profoundly and struck him with gladness he would not have felt had she made a show of welcome.

If the subtleties of her face were the focus of his being transfixed, her entire form also filled him with pleasure. She wore a long dark outfit, of a blue at the other end of the blueness of her headscarf. A dark color but of a light material, as suddenly he saw the outline of her legs that a lamp from inside the room cut through her clothes. He gasped to himself and was a little awed. A beautiful woman was receiving him. His apprehensions of a moment before seemed the puerile worries of a childish sexuality. The hair, that smile, the silhouette that climbed up to the unseen hips…. Somehow, inexplicably, this woman, abandoned by a man, living in a near-abandoned building in a country foreign to her, exuded the greatest confidence, not an acceptance of things, but a belief that she could meet whatever came. She *had* met what had come.

The New Man entered. There was Rasil, peering at him from the livingroom. He had been looking at a book. The boy acknowledged The New Man's greeting, the careful pronunciation of "Rasil," with the blinking of his eyes. The stranger had said it well enough.

While The New Man, awed into calm by Haziz, thought, *But I'm not his father. I intrude.* Yet; m it was a thought more an observation than a fear. It was a pity he extended to the boy, and a sorrow.

"Everything is ready," she said, gesturing to the kitchen. "You came at the perfect time."

"It's the time you said I should come." He would grant her foreknowledge of the perfect moment.

"Everyone does not always come at the time they are asked."

It sounded like a line from the Bible—or the Koran? Or the sad wisdom of someone who has been left and cannot call back the departed.

She said, "Rasil and I must pray before we eat."

The New Man was about to ask—what was he to ask? If he should withdraw, avert his eyes, stare at a wall in another room? And so soon after being invited in so warmly by Haziz. But her manner made any such questions useless—unnecessary. In a moment she and Rasil had washed their hands and faces at the sink, positioned themselves on prayer mats in the livingroom, facing a wall that was partly booklined (The New Man would note the books later) and had begun the process of continual worship The New Man had witnessed overcome the man on the street that afternoon. As The New Man had been witness to that stranger's prayers, he had been impressed by the abrupt sincerity of involvement, the palpable devotion (just as he had been made uneasy by the abrupt demand of devotion), right there in the immediacy of the common light and the dirty street. Now, observing Haziz and Rasil speaking quietly, *"Allah Akbar,"* then what The Man would eventually learn was the opening of the Koran: "In the name of Allah, the Beneficent, the Merciful…."—The New Man felt an even greater depth of sincerity from the mother and son, an enhancement or perception of feeling perhaps engendered by his sense of attraction—and gratitude—to Haziz.

A window immediately perpendicular to Haziz was open, and its dimming light—the sun had set—cast a rectangular halo about her head that made her face more vivid, as did the scarf she wore on the thick dark hair. For a moment The New Man thought it curious that Haziz and Rasil did not face the twilight of the window—its seemed logical to pray outward, toward the sky; then he remembered that Muslims pray in the direction of Mecca, as precisely as they can reckon it, and this unwindowed section of the room, with its books and shelves, was apparently the locus of that point of the compass.

He watched them bow, sit on their heels, prostrate themselves—he took in the stretch of Haziz' body within the draping of the fabric. Then back on the heels, prostration again, heels again, the turning of the head right, then left. The voice of mother and son rose and fell.

There were layers of emotion—reaction—going through The New Man as he watched. He had always felt an outsider at religious ceremonies—even when he, much younger, had fulfilled them out of obligation, his family dragging him to church sporadically. He had gone through the ritual of listening, silence, response, and even occasionally song, all with an apartness in his heart—a separateness that was not unlike the purity the faith espoused. He did, now, feel a peacefulness in the observation of this ritual, so smoothly enacted by mother and child, but it was a serenity, a devotion that flowed to him across a border he himself could not cross.

Their prayers finished, Haziz and Rasil rolled up their prayer mats and placed them underneath the worn couch. The New Man smiled at Haziz, a more perfunctory, less genuine smile perhaps than she had given him upon his entrance. He considered that her apparent pleasure at his arrival had to be tainted by the fact that she and her son had to perform something intrinsic and intimate to them in front of a man neither knew well.

"We pray right after sundown. And just before bed."

"Did you do that when I was here yesterday? I didn't see—"

"You were sleeping." She said this as if she were forgiving him.

Somehow this seemed an irony to The New Man—not from any sense of Haziz' forgiveness, but the fact that he had slept through her devotions. He said, "How many times a day do you—?"

"Five. Just before sunrise—"

"That's early."

"Yes. I am afraid a lot of people cheat."

"Do you?"

There was her smile again. "I have overslept sometimes. And children don't like to be woken up. Though sometimes Rasil wakes *me* up—" She tousled the boy's hair. He said something softly to her. He was understandably shy before this stranger. The New Man felt a pang of guilt.

Haziz was saying, "Then we pray just after noon, in the middle of the afternoon or late afternoon. That's three times. After sunset and before bed: five."

"You are…faithful enough to do that every day?" He immediately worried that his use of "faithful" sounded like an accusation.

"Faithful sometimes more than others. At least it's not the forty times a day Mohammed prayed."

"I suppose every religion has to lessen severity of devotion in order to—" He stopped himself; he was sounding too academic.

"In order to what? Get believers?"

"I wasn't inferring—"

"Say what you think."

"That is always a dangerous course."

She regarded him; he could not read her expression. "It is," she said softly, as if she had long ago accepted the burden of this truth. Her regard made the instant too long. Her eyes were so dark they seemed literally black, a blackness so thorough that, like Africans with very dark flesh, her irises seemed to take on the shadings of other colors.

Then she said, "To be devout is not to be blind." And she led him to the table.

The New Man dined well. His appreciation of the food and

Haziz' explanation of just what he was eating took up most of the conversation. She talked about how she had liked this dish or that as a child in Iran. Both The New Man and Haziz were relieved to talk of nothing more serious.

After dinner, Rasil asked if he could watch TV. The New Man understood the boy's request by his gesture toward the set. His mother said, in English, "Only the news is on now—all the channels." Of course, "news" meant one thing alone.

Rasil protested; The New Man caught "Nickelodeon." Haziz acquiesced, but added, "Which show?"

"Arnold. Arnold," said Rasil.

Haziz smiled. "Go ahead." Rasil left for the livingroom. Haziz said to The New Man, "I like that program. Have you seen it?"

"I don't think so." He had the brief reflection of knowing all the kids' shows when his own children were the age of Rasil. This recollection made him sad.

"City children—with very funny lives," Haziz was saying. The New Man didn't realize right away what she was talking about; he was confronting the pain of remembrance. Haziz said, "The boy, Arnold, has no parents, his grandparents raise him."

"That is happening a lot today."

They were nearing an issue neither wanted to talk about though one which each wanted the other to reveal. The New Man said, "When you told me about your husband—"

She looked sharply at him. Would he be brave enough to go on?

He did: "I'm not sure if I'm more shocked *that* you told me, than—than the fact *of* it."

Her face was impassive. He waited. From the livingroom he heard, "Hey, Arnold!" It gave Haziz the excuse to divert her response. "I am glad he is watching something. There is too much news."

"How could there not be—news? After—?"

She didn't respond to this directly either. "He said he wasn't feeling well that morning." (For an instant The New Man thought she was talking about her husband, but then:) "I kept him home from school. I haven't sent him back. It is too soon— I think I will wait until Monday. There are a lot of Muslim children in his class—"

"In this neighborhood I would think there would be."

"The school is on the edge of the neighborhood. This is a— mixture. A lot of Muslims, but also a lot of—others."

"Others."

"Yes. I thought there might be fights between them and the Muslim boys. Rasil—he does not like to fight. He is gentle. His *father*—"

"Was different?"

"Yes. Not that he was…violent. But…." On her face was regret she had gone down this path. "He would—confront." She sighed. She diverted the subject once more. "Do you have children?"

He considered his options, of truth or lies. "Yes. They are grown." This was truth; before she could ask, he balanced that with a lie. "My wife and I are divorced." He uttered the lie smoothly. Then the thought: *Hadn't I told her that before?* He added, while in the power of his falsehood, "For a long time."

"Where are your children?"

"Not in New York. In college." Truth.

"But you remember when they were little."

"Of course." It was as if she had intuited his recent thoughts.

To divert himself from his own abyss, he forced her back to what he saw as pertinent: "You know he was on the plane?"

She paused. "I should not have told you…."

"I am astounded that you did."

She hung her head, not looking at him. "Since Tuesday—I have guilt."

The New Man realized he rarely believed anyone's mea culpa. Hers, perhaps—but yes, he had to accuse her: "You knew that—?"

"No, no." Then she became brave enough—or defiant enough—to look at him. "I did not know what would happen, but I sensed, through the summer—he didn't tell me—that something was planned…." There was neither bravery nor defiance in her face now, only sadness, a depth of personal culpability and helplessness that brought him his own sense of guilt. Through past seasons he had sporadically planned, if halfheartedly, "something"; and now, through a force outside of his own doing, it had come into effect.

She said, "When you told me you had survived, perhaps that made me tell you…." Her eyes insisted: *Don't you see the connection?*

"Didn't you think I might go to the police?" He had the memory of her voice, shot into the air, calling the police.

She seemed surprised. "I did not even think of the police—of you— This, this *thing*—makes me think of something beyond the police, beyond what Mohammed—my husband—"

"Mohammed."

"Yes. Not the Prophet.' She smiled sadly at the coincidence of names. "Though he thought himself like a prophet. He would turn history around. He would say to me, from when we first met, history is many rivers, going into one big river. You change the channel of one river, you dam it up, dry it up, you explode the banks of one (that's what he'd say, 'explode') change any river's course that goes into the big river—and the big river is changed."

"I suppose that is true. So a few days ago the course of the river changed."

"I think what happened was already on course to happen—in some way." At his questioning look she said, "You do not know our world."

He thought of the streets here, where he had eaten and bought clothes, of the Double, the four men, the honey shop and the bookstore. "No, I don't." But he had to add, "All of us are strangers somewhere."

"I am not talking—in the abstract. All this—what Mohammed did, how he talked about history—and whatever you think" (as if she knew his thoughts) "...it's ironic—is that the word?— to me. I studied history. I wanted to teach it. I had some dream, my own dream of changing the way the world saw many things: how the West saw Islam, how Islam saw things within itself. How Arab Muslims saw non-Arab Muslims—like my people, the Persians."

She frowned. "I thought Mohammed wanted that, too. He did. Once—in the beginning. But his mind, his heart—his discipline—he became tempted by...." She almost seemed about to cry.

"What?"

"By the easy thing—I mean the false thing. Even false things are often not easy to get." After a pause in which she appeared to struggle with inner thoughts, and the possibility of tears died, she sought some correct narrative of the past. "He was Saudi. I went to his country for a while to study. I was young, but I already had my...plans—my vision, you could say." She gave a sad expression and she mocked herself gently. "My vision.... And now: this—" Her gesture took in the world of her apartment, herself and The New Man, the unseen son watching the American cartoon (for a moment The New Man caught the TV's voices).

"I had my vision but I was young." It was almost like a lyric in a song.

"As if you're not now."

"I was younger then. I went to—meetings. I wanted to find out what others my age thought. What they were doing. We have been—Muslims—in a strange position for a while. We have bad governments; our faith seems to fight with the rest of the world—or the rest of the world is afraid of it; and we have this wealth from the oil that all the world wants."

"More a need than a want."

She shrugged. "Wants, needs. When you are young you are not sure between them. But at those meetings, the young people there—whatever things they said and did—we *were* the future." As with her husband, she used the past tense.

"For better or worse."

"What do you mean?"

"It's an expression."

She sighed. "I think I know what you mean. We had bad, we had good—more good, I thought." She repeated: "I thought." She went on: "I knew even then most of it was just talk, most of the students would fall back into the useless lives of their parents" (The New Man was thinking: *Has my life been anything more than "useless"?*). A few would become fanatics just as useless. I was looking for the ones who were passionate and practical. I thought I was like that."

"Were you?"

She gave the smile of wisdom gained at a quiet, pained cost. "Not as practical as I should have been." She shook her head, admonishing her past self. "Too passionate."

"But passion—" The New Man began, about to defend something whose quality he himself doubted.

She didn't seem to hear him. "He was like that, I thought: passionate, practical. I met him about a month after Iraq invaded Kuwait, and the West, the father of this Bush, was making their plans. Just like now. History is terrible. It is most terrible when it happens a second time so soon.

"At the meeting there were students…denouncing, is the word, I think, America—and some denouncing Iraq. That is the way I felt. And I said that. Saddam Hussein had made my country suffer in the war in the 1980s. In America you don't even know about that war—"

"We know; maybe we don't know very much."

"Maybe *you* know. People here—they forget right away…if they are not the ones hurt."

"I think that's all over."

"We don't forget. Eight years' war with Iraq. Hundreds of thousands killed. I remember the cemeteries, so many new cemeteries in the 1980s. It was like something new got put into the earth. Something new, but it was death. And now Saddam goes into Kuwait, he doesn't want to stop. I was afraid then Iraq was going to bring the West down on all of us, worse than the Israelis.

"But I was in Saudi Arabia, and I was mocked—among these students—for coming out against Iraq. And what is ironic (I use this word correctly, I think) I am sure most of the loudmouths there (and that is a word I know), most of them, ten years later, more, are in the world of their rich Saudi parents, making business with the West, buying off jihad, looking the other way when they have to."

"And how do you feel about jihad?"

She studied him as if she wanted to ascertain his purpose in this question. "I understand its reasons. I will tell you this: What was done here—" she gestured again, the window, the destruction just beyond the river (history's river, as her husband had said?); "It was not justified. But the anger behind it, not so much in those men—in my husband—but in the Arab world that says to America, 'Now you know what it is to feel threatened—'; that is justified."g

He was quiet a moment. He could think of nothing to ask. On her part, she perhaps worried how to continue, despite her "passions."

"Mohammed was the best speaker at the meetings. He said— he predicted—and he was right—he said the West, America, would come to the world of Islam with hundreds of thousands of soldiers. He said the Saudi government could not refuse its oil partners. He said Saddam would be forced out of Kuwait by America, but your country would be afraid to drive him out of Iraq. He said too many troops would remain in Saudi Arabia, and that, connected to what America always did for Israel, would be America's downfall. The Russians had been driven out of Afghanistan; America could be driven out of Muslim countries. He was right, so right about Iraq, Saudi Arabia and your country. It was as he could look exactly into the future of next year. And he was right about the anger against America for staying in the Holy Land. But Mohammed was wrong when he said the West would be driven out of Muslim countries by the millennium: '*Their* millennium,' he said."

"He might be off by just a few years."

"I don't know." She was silent for a little while, considering things she had not spoken. "Mohammed was at other meetings, and we talked. We met away from the meetings...."

She lost her words then, awkwardly. When found, she stumbled with them, not quite sure how much of herself she wanted to present. The New Man was patient, and a little amused. Perhaps a little jealous. He had the not wholly inaccurate picture of Haziz then, of the young woman of a decade ago (had she been more lovely—or less?—the years from twenty to thirty enhancing one woman, lessening another): dark haired, passionate, with a vision of the Muslim world that even her kindred in Islam could not grasp. While The New Man also had a vision of her, of another sort of life she might have lived in the present tense: unattached to a man, without a child, allowing her a freedom in which he, The New Man, believed, he would have wished to have met her—not thinking in his own passion and reverie that her allure had not a little to do with a maternity and the burden of limitations, the satisfactions and betrayal of love that the twenty year old—or thirty year old— firebrand could not have possessed, merely intimated.

She told The New Man how she and Mohammed, with the fever of youth, had discussed the progress of both Islamic fervor and modernism, a mingling and confrontation that many in the Middle East as well as the West feared might prove the inevitable stepping stones to Armageddon. Hundreds of thousands of American troops massed in Saudi Arabia (as Mohammed had said), the UN giving its condemnation of Iraq; and then, in January 1991, the young Haziz and the young prophet watched on television the missiles strafe Saddam's domain. Mesopotamia was being brutalized by the West's millennial fury. This was a recollection that flowed out of Haziz' past with an earnest sadness. And it was a remembrance that drew The New Man's own memories. A decade ago he too had watched the television war, the safe conflict for the West that was heralded on TV as if the approach of an exciting miniseries. Television had saturated reality with its own inexhaustibility; the war was important not merely for the fact of it, but *because* it was being covered so thoroughly—portrayed—so continuously. It was a coverage that perhaps had heralded what had been happening since Tuesday.

Haziz' look has become rueful. "Our talks before the Americans attacked" (before she had said "your country"; now she pronounced "America" as if he were not its citizen) "…they were desperate, and they were lovely. It gave us the…fever of lovers." She smiled at this cliché, and The New Man was once again jealous, and annoyed. She said, "When America attacked Baghdad we became lovers. 'Allah will forgive us,' he said to me in bed. He was devout. I was more politically Muslim than religious Muslim. Like a lot of the Jews. But I was cautious to go to bed with a man—I had not before. But I believed it could happen before my marriage. I wasn't thinking of marriage. I was thinking of the Muslim world."

She smiled. "He used to call me Khadijah—the name of the Prophet's first wife."

"Yes, I know," he said.

She looked at him, a little surprised. He didn't want to reveal he had only just come to this knowledge from the Mr. Rahman of the bookshop. He said, "Did you like that?"

"It was our…joke."

Was it jealousy that made him say: "I thought you could get killed in Muslim countries, a woman could get killed for sleeping with a man when she wasn't married."

She nodded. "In some places."

"But not in Saudi Arabia."

"We were youth. We were…becoming ourselves."

"And did you?"

She looked at him strangely, sighed. "I don't know. But then, that time…there was great danger from the West. We could all be destroyed—I think Mohammed believed this more than I did. This was our first conversation after…lovemaking." (She did not look at The New Man when she said this word.) "I still remember the flashes of light from the missiles, the explosions on TV…and the way this…destruction flashed on the wall. I saw this—what the TV showed—in his eyes. I always remember that—as if that were his burden to see."

"But you saw it too."

"I did. But I think he saw it so deep inside himself…." She shook her head. "He told me it will seem America—Israel and Europe—they are all winning, then it will unravel for them. They will be brought down."

"That hasn't exactly happened."

"*Then*. But your Towers did fall."

"Two buildings do not make a country." Though he wondered if a great downfall *had* begun. Perhaps its first brutal hour had been in that decade-ago TV war. He imagined the young lovers, their bodies lit from the flash of missiles and bombs on the electronic screen.

She was looking at him seriously. "I believe that a people, a country, a person…can be poisoned and not know it, die and not know they are dying until—"

"The Towers fall?"

She shrugged. "I could see something was happening to America these last years. All the money, SUVs, your dotcoms, up and up your stock market, Clinton happy with that young woman—"

"Who I guess wasn't much older than you at the time."

She smirked. "It was all like a fever when the patient is sick." The New Man had the brief thought it seemed she had used the word "fever" often tonight. "You drew those planes to you," she said.

That might have shocked The New Man in his other life. Now, he said, calmly, "So you approved of what your husband—of the attack?"

"I do not like killing. I did not approve of Saddam in Kuwait. But America used that as an excuse. Why should America own oil? Why should America own biological weapons? Why should America, just America, own nuclear weapons? Who was the country that used nuclear weapons on other people? America."

This may have all been true, but for The New Man it veered too far from the conflicts of the present day. And it seemed all beside the point as he looked at the near presence of Haziz; it was something apart from the desire he felt for her, the sweet wanting that sanctified lust and made it good and almost spiritual or at least a step toward spirit, the unlocking that happens in the psyche when one's flesh wants another's for reasons of more than the tangible body.

"And you're sure he's dead?"

"Yes."

"It seems you weren't sure."

"My lie to myself."

"You want him to be alive."

"He is Rasil's father." A long silence. "No, he is dead. A woman knows."

Here, indeed, was cliché. And perhaps utter truth. She had said it so simply it might have been an observation wholly her own and suitable only to her character rather than that of innumerable women throughout time.

"Which plane was he on?"

"I do not know."

"So he might have been in Washington—or Pennsylvania."

"Yes."

The New Man had to consider this again. If Haziz' Mohammed had been one of the hijackers, he should have slammed into the Towers, and sealed a link to The New Man. This was irrational on his part, of course. "Haven't they already decided who was on which plane?"

"I don't know."

There was another stillness between them. He sighed. "So what happened between Baghdad—Saudi Arabia—and here?"

Her smile was sad and resigned. "Too much to tell—as long as a book. Or maybe I could say it short, I don't know."

"How about in between." But as her expression considered this, he added, "Why are you telling me—so much?" Though even as he said it, he thought himself rude. It was natural.

Natural that he, fleeing his old identity, should be here, that Haziz, wife of a terrorist (would she, or the vanished Mohammed, use that word?) should have him at her table. In the surrealness of the universe, in the coincidences, the synchronicity of life, it was natural.... And he had challenged her rudely. So he said, "No, don't explain yourself. I certainly cannot explain myself."

She did not ask him why he could not; she continued her story, knowing he wanted to hear it as much as she wanted to tell it. And she didn't exactly explain herself, but narrated— smoothly, brokenly, smoothly—a tale with mystery and lack of resolution. The listener made what he would of the story. A decade of some paragraphs, the seminal decade of her life. A girl becoming woman, possessing first an ideal of the Muslim world, an ideal of its betrayal, by others and itself; possessing a man, having him possess her, a pair of beings whose hearts and deeds must inevitably fork—while they became husband and wife. The years as the two diverging paths become subtly wider and wider apart.

As he listened, The New Man felt a guilt that he was receiving the grace of such a heartfelt rendering (almost a confession) of her life. He could not have related his own life in equal manner. If he had more years than Haziz, he lacked the qualities of faith, final judgements, global deceptions and sacrifice.... What *did* he have?—his mathematics, abandoned, only just taken up again—and perhaps already abandoned once more?

17. *The Isolation of His Secret*

The unraveling of the West had not come. But an act of strength, of the hubris of a certain character did come, laid down like a long faulty vein in the body of the superpower—as Mohammed saw it. Like bin Laden, Haziz' young husband was aggrieved and outraged that American troops remained in Saudi Arabia, that pilgrims to Mecca could see, on some horizon, the bases, the complacently armed figures of the soldiers. There would be the reality that Muslims, at some vantage point, would have to pray towards these bases when they faced east to Mecca. Haziz related to The New Man how Mohammed had expressed being struck with anger—"And fear, he said, fear—" at the silhouettes of two U.S. servicemen against a sunset on some plain. "'The minions of Iblis,' he called them," said Haziz. "That means the devil."

The New Man was grounded enough in the common sense of having lived enough years to know that perhaps the sun-limned soldiers had their own fears, whether seasoned "minions" or raw youth who had signed up with the military for courses in computers or any other type of job training. He asked Haziz, "And did you feel the same way? Didn't you think it possible America was protecting Saudi Arabia?"

"Protecting? After Saddam was pushed back? No one from my country has much love for Saddam, Allah knows it. The Saudis wanted to keep supplying the West with their oil. They don't care about the Prophet's land."

The New Man said, "They care about the money America

pays for oil. It's not that they care for *us*." Strange that he put so much emphasis on "us."

"Yes: their interests." She repeated: "They did not care about the Prophet's land."

"You said you…weren't as religious as your husband?"

She briefly seemed shocked by that question, almost offended. Then there was her smile. "At one time I thought I was. But even then I knew his furies, his righteous furies were more about his own wars, inside him." She sighed. "I will say now his ideals were flawed."

"And yours? Then? Now?"

"I was always more practical. I don't think I ever believed that Islam—any religion—needed to be followed down to the most minute things. What to wear, what not to wear, what to eat, not eat. When it says in Koran that women should be modest, does that mean they should wear the chador?"

"What are you wearing?"

She touched her head covering. "This is a rusari. The chador covers a woman completely. The face is all covered—mesh across the eyes." The New Man recalled the odd image of one hanging in the clothing shop, and TV footage of the enshrouded, encumbered women of Afghanistan making their way within the Taliban's world. Their wholly hidden aspect was so surreal to him he could think of no comparison to it, and had to wonder if any human being could ever take up such habit with the indifference of habit.

"Mohammed once asked me to wear it. I refused. I don't think he really wanted me to wear it, only to see if I—"

"Would be dominated by him?"

She shrugged. "He would do things like that sometimes. I

think it was a game for him." The New Man considered Mohammed only played very serious games.

"I thought," she was saying, "Mohammed and I would be good, working together. His religious enthusiasm, my practical…way. We wanted to change things. He said he wanted to change things—or die."

Her eyes looked down, away from him. "After a while, his passions made him foolish. He was not a fool, but I saw he could do foolish things."

"So he wasn't a fool, just foolish?"

"There is a difference—fool and foolish."

"Is there?"

She sighed. "He was like people who want things right, in all places in history, in all times, doing foolish things. Because they're desperate. He was like history. Now I think: isn't that what I wanted, to show everyone history? I was going to write history books."

"Are you still—going to write—?"

She made a gesture. "I can't see…even the future of tomorrow—for myself…." But she gave herself a smile. "I would write a history to show my people to the Jews, to show the world. I would teach history. I would write to show why the Muslim has suffered so much the last century. Why the rest of the world takes one explanation for us and not the whole explanation."

"What is the whole—explanation?"

"It is not simple. And maybe it is—if you can bring all the things together. The Muslims, the Christians, the Jews. Each one came after the other. To explain how they are separate, how they overlap. They are faiths of one God. Whatever name you call God, Yahweh or Allah, God is God. Mohammed—the Prophet—called the Jews and Christians 'People of the Book.' In the beginning of Islam, Muslims left the Jews and Christians alone. Before the Crusades. In my own country, there are Armenian Christians, and the government is fair to them."

The New Man had his doubts about the tolerance of the first Muslims as he had doubts about the degree of fairness being given to Christians in Iran. But he said nothing.

"There are so many things to correct. Most of you in America see no difference between Iranians and Iraqis. To you it's all Arabs. Iranians are Persian and—" She stopped, abruptly thinking of something, something as personal as it was historical.

"The 'fault' of Islam—and perhaps in another 400 or 500 years it will change; Islam is 1400 years old. What was Christianity at 1400 years? Inquisitions. Selling indulgences. The wars of the popes. Islam is still so much an Arabic faith. And if you are Iranian—Persian…if you are a Turk…your life, your spiritual life can be taken over too much by the Arabs. Maybe I felt that more in my life because I married Mohammed. Saudis are Arabs. Muslims are supposed to be of one brotherhood, from whatever country, but there is still the Arab, as if the Arab is the essential Muslim. Though sometimes I think that is a stereotype the West believed in so much it makes us, all Muslims, believe in it too, too much. You know the country with the biggest Muslim population in the world is Indonesia."

"When did the Persians become Muslim?"

"Not long after Mohammed died. In your years, it was 634. Persia was in a chaos of rulers—nine in four years. It was one of those common times in history: a very successful ruler had died, Khosurv Parvez, the most powerful man since Xerxes, and there was calamity, everyone wanted to rule, despots, pretenders—" She laughed. "I sound like a history book?"

"If you do, you're not a boring one. At this point, I am happy to judge a book by its cover."

She seemed puzzled, then laughed again. "A Muslim general in Syria wrote to the Caliph that Persia could be conquered—"

"Through Allah's goodness, of course." He surprised himself that he felt free enough for this dark, clichéd humor.

She gave him a look that said, "Yes, that is the way of the world." What she did say was, "An army of Bedouins, a people who are used to crossing wasteland in the hope of treasures, came along the south shore of the gulf. Their commander, Khalid, set a message to the governor of a province: 'A people is upon thee, loving death as thou lovest life.'

That might have been the message of the planes that had smashed into the Towers. The New Man wondered if Haziz made any such connection.

"The Persian commander Hormizd challenged Khalid to combat. Khalid killed him. And the Arabs began to take Persia. Eventually there was a battle at Kadisiya, a few days that changed history. Thirty thousand Arabs fought 120,000 Persians. But on the fourth day—like an act of God—a great sandstorm swept into the Persian army, blinded them, and the Arabs conquered them."

"Why didn't it blind the Arabs?"

"I don't know."

"Maybe it's a legend—an excuse for killing."

She shrugged. "Battles went on, all over Persia, but the war was won. In one battle, 100,000 Persian were killed."

"The victor keeps the box score." At her frown, he added, "It's an expression. Those who win, write history."

"If I write history, does that mean I win?"

"It seems now everyone can write their version. So we drown in histories, all not quite true."

"I would be true."

"I believe you would try to be. So was it destiny for the Arabs?"

She smiled. "Destiny. Another name for chance."

"Act of God, like you said."

"I did not say that."

"Something about Allah's goodness." But that might have offended her; quickly he added: "But I agree it's chance. It's that destiny sounds better—more dignified. Justified. Yes, whatever you do, is justified. Destiny even makes failure justified. Excuses you."

Destiny: he thought of himself, fleeing the Towers, the handful of hijackers bringing lower Manhattan to ruin: "…a people is upon thee…."

She said, "Somewhere in the spirit of Persians I think there must be some anger—a loss. We were given Allah through the blood of so many."

"And yet you believe."

"Allah is better than the old gods."

The New Man had the unvoiced thought that in some nearing century a newer God would come, and the God of the Jews, the Christians and Muslims would view that newcomer unkindly. And how would that new God conquer?

He asked, "What were the old gods—for Persia?"

"Zoroaster. Ormuzd and Ahriman."

"Zoroaster I know—by name, nothing else, but not—"

"Ormuzd was the god of light who must battle Ahriman, the god of darkness."

"Satan was an angel of light."

"We have all used light and dark for our purposes."

There might have been meaning in that for the two of them, at that dinner table which was brightly (but not harshly) lit, while the edges of the room were dim, as if that lessening (or absence) of light were a danger, at least the warning of a danger. And there was this: The New Man and Haziz, certainly from desperate pasts and brought together by extraordinary, surreal chance, had somehow evolved a sort of light and peace in this friendly togetherness—while, just beyond them, the past The New Man had shed, and the past that had shed Haziz, that past, that realm lurked, and both sensed it and were glad of the light, glad of the talk.

Though a portal of light broke into the edge of the room's dimness. In the open door to the bedroom Rasil stood, tired-looking. Without missing a beat, Haziz went from the Persian gods of Good and Evil to the common needs of her son. "It is time for bed." The boy might have spoken, to acquiesce or object, but the presence of the stranger made him shy.

"It's time for our evening prayers," she said to The New Man. "If you would like to talk a little longer— We say our prayers, I lie down with him a little. You can watch TV—" She pointed to the set in a the corner of the dimness. "Or," she added, as if being fair, "If you want to go—"

"The evening's too young." He almost cringed in saying that. It was something out of an old movie. But The New Man was happy. She wanted him to stay.

His response seemed to please her. "I'll be a little while. He falls asleep fast." She went to Rasil. The door closed behind mother and child. Faintly, The New Man heard the hymn and hum of the prayers he had witnessed only a while ago. He imagined the woman and the boy, humble and sincere: the child balancing a devotion he could not yet understand with the slow arrival of sleepiness, and Haziz, her lovely form stretched within her light garments. He imagined the arc of her back in the moment of prostration. That was the voyeur's appreciation. More straightforward, more eye-to-eye was his memory of her standing upright, looking to the wall, through the wall, really, toward Mecca. What he had always, if casually, regarded as a ritualistic artifice, a dogmatic compass-fixing upon a place on Eiarth, now seemed, in that small apartment in New Jersey, a freeing of oneself from the immediate locale, the stresses and limits of the moment, a turning of the heart not toward a place but a moment of the beginning of a faith's revelation.

Yet while the murmurings behind the door brought these pleasant (not exactly the word, but close enough) images to his inner vision, The New Man was also of a mind that he intruded on a faith not his, a faith he could hardly—or cared to?— comprehend. He went to the TV, its images and sounds, not so much out of idle curiosity about the latest news, but because he could show, at least to himself, that his attentions were not invading the privacy of mother and son.

There was a program on bin Laden. Snippets of footage The New Man had already seen. Bin Laden crouched and aiming an automatic weapon; bin Laden smiling beatifically like some tripping desert saint; bin Laden with a walkie-talkie, the tail of his head covering away from his face.

The New Man channel surfed. With a sort of horror he was suddenly arrested by a girl talking about her father who was missing at the World Trade Center. The girl was eleven. There was a photograph of the father inserted at a corner of the screen, an ordinary man made extraordinary by the lament of his daughter. "My mommy's too sad to talk to anybody," said the girl, who began to cry quietly herself. And quietly, mirroring her, The New Man also wept, surprising himself. He lost the girl in the blur of his eyes, and her words in the soft body of his sobs.

What came on next struck him violently, like a physical blow. His head dropped and he just looked down at the floor, almost paralyzed by the turmoil and anguish in his heart, emotions greater than those that had drowned the girl's lament. Though he forced himself to look up—with terrified caution; simultaneously, the door of the bedroom opened and Haziz appeared. Her face was cast with the moments she had just spent with her sleepy son; then she was anxious at the battered spectacle of The New Man. Her mouth opened with a question, but his gesture—a motion of his arm fighting against an enormous weight—stayed that. She looked to the screen and understood.

There was The New Man's wife on the screen once more, talking with sadness and control about her missing husband. The New Man's soul was kicked to its guts. Why he was even more stricken seeing her this second time on TV he could not have said. Perhaps the sorrow of the girl had made him more vulnerable. Perhaps the repetition itself was a special horror. And he must have exhibited such a look of horror and helplessness that Haziz had to rush to him, as if trying to help a man who was choking, or who had been shot in the heart. He was suffering some violence, a brute disruption of his psyche. It seemed to him monstrous that this woman who did not love him could speak of him so plaintively—as she had when he had seen on her on TV the first time.

He was terrified that by her very appearance on the air she would expose him to all eyes as a fugitive from his true—at least original—life. And indeed, in another moment, he was exposed. For as he gestured again, both to keep Haziz from touching him (what he would have wanted so much only a moment ago, he now so desperately wanted only the isolation of his secret) and to indicate—or disguise?—the source of his distress, his wife's face was replaced by his own on the screen, one photo, then another, the first photo a full face shot taken a year or so ago, the second a photo with his two grown children. From somewhere behind the photos, welling like a chorus of doom, of judgement, of God pointing a finger at the sinner, a narrator spoke briefly and superficially about the old New Man—about what he had been, his job, his age, where he lived—nonsense, nonsense—

Haziz was looking at the screen with her own sort of horror. At least it seemed so to The New Man. Or perhaps it was just utter astonishment. Then she looked back at him. He thought she seemed betrayed. Or, simply, filled with pity. His hand found repose and a modicum of strength and grasped the remote and clicked off the TV. He stared into the deep, dark, feeling eyes of Haziz. He drew deep painful breaths.

Haziz made as if to speak; no words came. The New Man waited. What could he say? Only the shameful—ridiculous?—truth. Though why was it shameful? He could defend it to himself, but not to her. And yet she allowed him an exit. "You do not have to say anything." But he said, his torso heaving, controlling tears, "It makes it seem something else."

She stepped toward him, tentatively, like the most kindly soul approaching a wounded bird. "What?"

"That we—she and I—*shared*—" He was gasping. There was a trembling, an earthquake of agony ripping across his face. It was a farce, a cruel farce he had inflicted upon himself. There was no escape. No escape from— What? If he had only known just what he had tried to escape.

She said, quietly, not accusing him: "You didn't share." It was a soft statement, meant to make him see. He was both reprieved and condemned. He hung his head. He spoke down into himself. "No. Not for— I wasn't wanted. When it all came down—to—"

"You're not divorced."

"No." He let that word break the protection of any lies he had told Haziz; and it let her sense the truth of what he had not said.

And after another gasp he told her, concisely and roughly, what he had done.

Her expression was unreadable as he told her this truth; as she accepted it. Perhaps in the way she accepted the truth about her husband. And The New Man wanted to add, like a whimpering child, *I'm sorry. Do you forgive me?* But he killed those words, out of shame and, perhaps, some remaining pride.

At any rate, "confession" had not settled his being. Like a curtain that roared down over his eyes, his mind, his flesh, an inner cataract battered him and he felt himself plummeting down through One World Trade Center, and then the buildings themselves came down, with terrible conclusion. He faced the genesis of when he had chosen to be another thing. Here was the implosion of his spirit. He jerked, violently. She grasped him. She spoke something. It was lost in the roar of his— recreation. His transformation. A metamorphosis so profound— and yet so terribly violated. She clutched him with great strength. She was trying to rip him from his inner violence— and the outer violence that had entered him. He shook, trembled slightly. He said—like a man gasping out one last plea not so much for help as for another to see the illumination he had suffered, the illumination he had to bear, the lie he had to make a truth: the soul of a man who desperately did not want any longer to be what he had been—he said something unintelligible. She could only repeat, afraid at his attempts at speech that seemed to bring him to the verge of shattering, could only say, "You don't have to talk." What was any speech now? Unnecessary, even wrong. She pressed her hand against his face as if to still, with the utter simplicity of contact, his anguish. He shuddered, and then subsided a bit, and he clutched her other hand and held it on his lap as if fixing the weight of her at his center, and then, bound to an abrupt gravity, they pressed their bodies together with a fatefulness born of an impossible sorrow each suffered, a plague of secrets, a lament of displacement, a diaspora from a better place from which each had departed through a poor and common choice, a place to which one could not return. The man and woman could only return to the lostness in each other. Abruptly the flesh of each felt shared, palpable and indomitable on either side of the barrier of their clothes. Eyes looked profoundly into other eyes. This was seeing without the disguise of image. In the great silence the TV had left they breathed upon one another's face. It was the rushing of a wind across a desert that needed wind, a warm wind, not a scorching wind. The New Man surrendered to what he wanted and what he feared, and she, of the faith whose name meant submission, surrendered to a betrayal of the most ancient code while at the same time fulfilling a faithfulness to her singular, aching, determined soul. They kissed. It was an awful seal, in the old way of the word: awe-full, a passion bursting with a fear of God and a godly passion and lusts that would have chosen to defy God if God had said, *Choose this or me*. And, once begun, they kissed continuously, timelessly, in the dim end of summer night, two beings fed with each other, and the tragedy that had begun much farther back in the past than two days ago.

In a descent that seemed destined, he lay down with her in the bed she had once shared with her husband. She didn't exactly say that, only "I haven't slept here since—" and left off the date, left off time, leaving The New Man to correctly imagine her, since the departure of her husband (and whenever he had been away on his "work") sleeping with the boy in the child's bed, the abandoned wife and son comforting each other with the immediacy of presence and the oblivion of sleep through the hourless night.

And the sheets seemed cool with the gathering of those days the bed had not been occupied, as if it had for so long been bereft of flesh that it had lost all intimations—even memories—of fleshly warmth, of bodies and the heat of their blood; but, like a deluge upon a dry riverbed, The New Man and Haziz flooded that sleepy place, and it became warm with breathing and words and nakedness. Indeed, her dark darkness overwhelmed him; it was vast and extraordinary. A darkness that seemed to gleam in the room that held no light, only the dim light that seeped in from the rest of the apartment, and the glow of scattered streetlights from outside, the artificialness of a disrupted city, a city that was real only in its distance; and yet, her body, slipping from the light, long garment that had at once so hid her and revealed her, had that special light of dark flesh, the gleam of darkness amidst the darkness, and his eyes as well as his own flesh, paler, and hardly lovely, wept at the sight and the touch of her. A moment ago, for all these past long days, these past long years, he had been stricken with the absence of sexual revelation, the absence of this common and yet unique loveliness, and his hunger was vast (vaster than he could have believed), and grateful. At first he lay upon his back, looking up at her as she leaned on his side, her breasts, larger than he would have thought, full with the weight and roundness of a beauty that raised the hardness of his center even more exquisitely than her kisses; he lay there, as a man receiving the very force of life, something more than food, even more than love, after a near starvation, or a long illness, or a calamity, a man that would be revived by caresses and the vision of her body as she caressed his thigh with her hand, as she murmured something like a cooing, like a child-like private song, until he was lifted up by it, by all of her, and turned to her, so their bodies met on their sides, were poised like that, in a sort of ecstasy of a borderland; and then, with a gentleness that was like a gift, she was upon the sheets and he rested and moved on her and he looked with all the weight of gravity and desire and helplessness into her eyes and her expression was beyond smiles and passion and willfulness; it was an expression like one touched with a religion of acceptance, the bravery of discovery; and he saw, minutely, amazingly, the reflection of his face, turning, turning in those eyes so that he was swallowed into the all-ness of her expression. And he was in her and she was the sea; it was too smooth, too joyous, a body slipping into water, a water that more than flowed over flesh, it embraced flesh.

Her legs bent, the soles of her feet pushing on his calves, her body arched up as he rose on this swell, and he saw the great ocean of the bed below, the billows of her hair, he felt the rise of an earth when all earth was sea. She arched down and then up again, and twisted with an artfulness from side to side, almost formally, as if to a music—while he moved singularly, possessed now beyond himself, and flooded into her as she arched up and down and twisted again and rippled back into him with a shuddering.

Later, when his body was not so filled with the suddenness of that sea, she rode upon him, his hands cupping the haunches that sat firmly upon his exhilarant hardness, her torso bending down toward him so his mouth could reach her breasts. She twisted then too, or more swayed, so that one breast was in his mouth then the other, in a rhythm she orchestrated and he acquiesced to in a pleasure so extraordinary he seemed flushed with great joyful exhaustion and great joyful strength. They did this a long time and she pivoted upon him, his hands going to the great taut softness of her ass to her breasts, and she often bent lower and lower, her hair sweeping across his face, so for a moment all was darkness, an intimate darkness greater and more immediate than the darkness of the night, her breath hissing on his face and then the hair was swept back, her breasts thrust up so he lost them from both mouth and hands, and it made him want them more and she bent down again, in rhythm, and he was at them, though in a moment she pulled away once more; it was the swell of the waters, the ocean again, washing over him and as the hair came down again they shuddered together like vessels thrust through a storm, a violence at the end of which would be the ultimate grace of an extraordinary calm.

He almost cried out for her in the middle of the night when Rasil cried out for her (for an instant it sounded as if the call for prayer out on the street) and she slipped with a word—in Farsi—from the bed and went to her son. He lay there, a man who had been fulfilled trying not to feel lost, thinking thoughtless things in the night that lived apart from time. He slept, awoke to her return, slept again, her weight against him. He dreamed. A bubbling, a roiling of his life: mathematical formulae, Vietnam, marriage, his jobs, the children, the final job, the last year, the Moms Mabley look-a-like on the bus that brought him to this town in New Jersey. She was mumbling something about God's plan and redemption. The New Man awoke in the dimmest dawn, that point in which one sees yes, there is a definite arrival of light, that the promise of the sunrise will again be fulfilled, but its fulfillment seems distant, and he looked at Haziz, and he could see her so clearly now, never mind the dimness (as if that promise of coming light illuminated her from the future of the day), her face in profile and one breast nearly escaped from the sheet and so plumped to even greater fullness by the catch of the fabric. He wanted her again, and yet he did not want to shatter the paradise already passed. There was a little more light now. Could he claim in this world what he had claimed—received—in the dark of another?

His gaze, the psychic strength of it, wakened her. In fact, she seemed to wake with a start and half rose, looked about, seeing everything but him, he thought. She said, "It's late. Time to pray."

He was a little startled—and, to be honest, dismayed at what still claimed her. He said, "The sun isn't up yet."

"Before the sun, before we pray."

"Before dawn even comes?"

"When it's light enough to see the difference between a white thread and a black thread."

This struck him as a profound demarcation. There were no such threads before them, though The New Man accepted it was light enough for the division of passage of night into day.

She began to get out of bed; she realized her nakedness. The New Man saw she did not want to him to see her naked at this moment. He muttered a wordless sound—an apology?—and half turned away. He was confronting the timeless reality that all lovers face; the ardor of only hours ago, the sacred space, must be forced to survive in the callous world.

When he looked back she was half robed. She said, "I don't want to wake him today." The New Man nodded. He understood she would not want her son praying with her at this dawn following a night when she had so unleashed herself from the ethos of those prayers.

Then he thought: But how could she pray at all this morning? Here was the human duality, the two sides of the heart, feeding from lust and piety, desire and— He stopped himself. This was too much of a pat observation. He accepted the mystery.

She went out of the room. In a moment he heard, from the other side of the door, the murmuring of her devotions; then, as if commanded, he returned to sleep.

18. *The Mirror of the Other in the Morning After*

When he awoke again, she was not in the bed. He was anxious with the feeling that the fullness of daylight had found her rejecting the passion night had allowed. In the white thread of holiness she had repented.

He lay on his side at the edge of the bed. He saw a coin on the floor—a quarter. He reached down to it. It must have fallen out of his pants last night. It was one of those quarters whose obverse featured one of the states and its symbols. The coin was new, shiny, minted this year of 2001. On the other side of George Washington's head was the embossed outline of New York State and the Statue of Liberty. "Gateway to Freedom" was the motto. The Hudson River was a line cutting down through the southeastern part of the state—to the city the terrorists had maimed this very year. A benign commemoration had become an omen.

The New Man reflected on this no more than an instant. He heard Haziz speaking to Rasil.

He had the decency to feel extremely awkward at emerging into the rest of the apartment; the stranger appearing from the room where the boy's mother had—so recently—slept with the boy's father. Though surely the boy could not have known what was going on. At only five. Or could he? The New Man was invaded with the possibility that the son of a terrorist might have preternatural perceptions. The father who had perished in the explosion of an airplane and a skyscraper in the carrying out of his faith to an extreme, must surely have passed to the son an instinct of dark things.

Dark things and faith. He found himself wishing for the dimness of night, and the faith of the passion that had welled up in that dark. But here was the day. Three mornings ago he had chosen freedom, but now— That Joplin song: "Freedom's just another word for nothing left to lose—" But he did not feel he had lost things, only turned from them, turned from what he had not possessed in the first place.

Simultaneously hearing Haziz calling out Rasil's name, The New Man saw the Koran across the room. He could not read the script on the binding—was it Arabic or Farsi?—but he knew it was the Koran. He rose (and had the dull instant of a thought that sometime during the night he had put on his underwear, so that his impulse to pick up the Muslim holy book did not find him naked); taking the Koran, he opened it to its foreign script. At that moment, Haziz entered. She wore an astonishing, embroidered robe. Her lovely body in this beautiful garment seemed of a world other than this poor apartment. She looked at him holding the holy book. "I don't think you can understand that." Both she and The New Man had the thought that a remark meant to comment on language had a deeper, more abrupt meaning. He closed the book and put it down.

He said, "I bought one, with English and Arabic, from Mr. Rahman—at the book shop." (As if she wouldn't know there were two Rahmans.) "I've read a little of it."

"The Koran—like the Bible—takes a while, much time, to see the whole picture."

The New Man believed he was seeing at least a portion of the picture. "I want to thank you."

She sighed as if disappointed. "That is a strange thing to say."

"Well…it's almost as if you…did me a favor."

She might have received that as an insult. "I wouldn't do…what I did—that way."

"I guess I'm saying…did I cause you to—?"

"Betray my faith?"

He made a gesture saying, *Yes, but I can't say that.*

She said, "Are there not Jews and Christians, Buddhists, all of them, who believe the big things of their faith and even most of the small things but break the smaller rules for a larger thing?"

"You flatter me that sleeping with me is a large thing. But what you said: couldn't that just be an excuse?"

"Do you want me to say I am sorry?"

"No. Absolutely not." He added, "That would be terrible."

"I am not sorry. That would ruin it. It was…good. Very good." She finally smiled at him again. "Perhaps I should not have. Perhaps a week ago. But since, since—what happened…I feel…pushed past the end of things.'

The New Man thought: *If only there were an end to things. At least some end to reach.*

She said, "There is Allah. And there is my son. My husband isn't here anymore. My body, my self feels lost." She considered him: "Last night I did not feel lost."

She stepped toward him. Involuntarily he stepped back. Perhaps he feared the remembrance of pleasure. Or its continuance. He said, "I think we've both gone to the end of the world, lately."

"Can I ask you to go now? I think it's better that Rasil—"

"Yes." Now his fear wondered if—

"Come tonight."

A relief like nothing he had known or everything he had forgotten flooded him. He smiled softly. "I will."

Rasil was in the livingroom, watching TV. Before leaving, at the door of the apartment, The New Man said (it might have almost sounded sarcastic): "At least I didn't keep you from your prayers."

She seemed to have no anger at that remark—and, no shame. She raised herself a little to kiss him. It was practically a chaste kiss, but it was thunderous with the implication that the sexual furies of last night could be resumed.

"I'll see you tonight," he said. "But the day is so long."

"Not long for me." He looked a little hurt at that. She added, "I have Rasil."

That was true. The New Man had only the labyrinth of his metamorphosis.

"Go." She pushed him gently. With the door of the apartment shut behind him, he heard the voice of Rasil, and Haziz' responding voice.

Out on the street, he raised his eyes to the Friday sun. He walked. He was getting to know this neighborhood. He passed across the street from the honey shop and the bookshop, but was hardly aware of it until he was directly opposite them—and realized that a figure who had been walking from the other direction on the same side of the street as the stores was entering the honey shop. "My God," whispered The New Man. It was The Double.

The New Man crossed the street, not directly to the door of the shop, but positioned himself at the edge of the store's small front window. Through it he saw the tall, thin Double talking with the bespectacled Mr. Rahman. They seemed to be having an argument—or perhaps were debating a point.

Abruptly Mr. Rahman got up from behind the counter and retreated into a doorway that led to the unseen rear of the shop. When he did not return right way, The New Man had the feeling the shopkeeper was visiting his twin next door through a connection between the two stores. The Double looked after the vanished Mr. Rahman as if he expected him back at any moment. Though this was not the case. The Double frowned and, appearing bored, looked about the shop—then directly at the front window. The New Man could not be sure if the Double could see him. He would not appear foolish and dart away; he waved. The Double seemed to stiffen. The New Man took a deep breath and stepped toward the entrance. The Double rushed to the door and met The New Man as he came in, in fact pushed him back a little, so The New Man was kept on the border of the threshold. The Double was staring practically open-mouthed at The New Man, who should have felt uneasy: this image of bin Laden had nearly brought him death two days ago. But The New Man was almost debonair when he said, "I am glad to see you are all right."

The Double's eyes widened even more. He looked hurriedly back to the rear of the shop. "Why are you here?"

The New Man was feeling viciously turned about in the maze. The Double was a creature whose absurdities he had long passed on this strange journey. His new identity had become submerged in Haziz, the reawakening of the flesh; he did not want CIA reports and code and narcotic-stupored impersonators to return him to some more venal hour. But he said, with the lie of confidence, "I'm visiting the neighborhood, remember?" And when the Double looked back to the rear again, The New Man added, "As long as your friends aren't here."

"No," said the Double quickly. "They're not here." He felt compelled to add—to explain?—"I—I have business…."

"With Mr. Rahman?"

The expression on the Double's face said: "How do you know his name?"

The New Man said, flatly, "I bought some honey the other day." Or was it just yesterday?

The Double, peering at The New Man with unfeigned curiosity and anxiety said, "A man likes sweetness."

The New Man almost laughed. The Double had said this as if it were a threat that would drive The New Man back. But it was the Double who stepped back. The New Man stepped into the shop. The Double said, "In my country…." But could not finish this ambiguous lead-in.

"Sweet things in your country?" echoed The New Man vaguely, thinking of the narcotic the Double had shot into his veins. Then, with a concern that surprised himself, he said again, "You are all right?"

"What should that mean?" An American would have said, "What does that mean?" But if the difference came out of the difficulty of language, The New Man sensed this was the more accurate phrase. He began, "Your friends—"

"I said they are not here. It has been settled."

"What has been settled?"

"They were afraid."

"So was I."

The Double said nothing, and nothing could be read on his face. The New Man said, "It would not have mattered to them if they had killed me—or you."

The Double would not side with the infidel at this possibility. "They thought—a secret—" But at that very word, the Double himself seemed to exhibit fear.

"What secret? That it's obvious who you look like? That somebody knows about your drugs? You don't think the government—"

It was good the Double cut him off with a repulsive laugh; The New Man wasn't sure where he had been going. "The government! They think—! They believe—!" And he looked at The New Man as if with these fragments he had explained everything—or, rather, The New Man knew all this, without explanation.

And perhaps it made The New Man feign some sort of knowing. "From what I see on TV, they're tracing everyone down quickly."

The Double snorted. "Everyone?"

"That had anything to do with—" The New Man looked in the direction of the destroyed Towers.

"It is not possible to know of everyone—" The inference was: the government could not possibly know about *him*. But if any eye spotted him now, that observer would think him bin Laden. But perhaps the Double meant his true self: who could know that?

The New Man said, "They know he had a Double."

"Speculation," said the Double, more calmly now, mocking proof of his own existence. "And I know *your* secrets."

The two men regarded each other quietly.

"We will not," said the Double, "betray each other."

So they had a…bond? The New Man felt this as a sort of defeat. He had met another impasse in his new life. A sadness clutched him. Three days ago he had assumed a new identity; already, two individuals knew about his—deception.

"At this point," said The New Man, "what is betrayal?"

The Double looked at him with a sort of pity. Here was the weakness of the West—its sin: ambiguity. "This is what I will tell you about your government," said the Double suddenly; but instead of words he reached into his loose garment and took out a small object: it was an American flag pin. With an ironic gesture he displayed it on the palm of his long hand. It had the bright fresh look of something just made, its colors vivid, even lurid. And then, without another word, the Double stuck the pin on his breast and smiled broadly. It was a mockery that shocked The New Man and made him despise this façade of a human being, this wretch taken out of wretchedness to become the image of a terrorist. And he disliked the Double no less when the man said, "Are we not all brothers?"

After a long beat, The New Man said, "Is that from the Koran?"

The Double seemed almost surprised. But he defended himself with, "All *believers* are brothers."

"And what do you believe?"

Now it was the Double's turn to be shocked (for it was plain to The New Man that the Double had lived a life more of reaction than faith)—but he was saved, in a sense, by the appearance of Mr. Rahman, the Mr. Rahman of the honey shop, with ominous glinting glasses and an anxious expression. The New Man and the Double might have looked back with their own anxiety; they seemed to have forgotten Mr. Rahman would reappear.

The honey seller paused, perhaps calculating whom he should address first, and how. He chose The New Man. "So you are here again." He might have been snidely commenting on the repetitive behavior of an addict. "Everyone tells me—if they buy some of my honey—they cannot come here just once."

In The New Man's state of mind, wrought by being confronted with the twisted surrealness of the Double after having spent a heavenly night with Haziz, he took this comment as a menacing insinuation, as gloating over the "fact" that The New Man was drawn helplessly into a situation he could neither appreciate nor from which he could withdraw—or defend himself. Satan himself might have said as much to the couple in the garden as each took a second bite of the fruit.

"I just happened by here again. Your shop—yes, it's very…interesting."

But Mr. Rahman, having satisfied himself that he had thrown The New Man off balance, now addressed the Double—without naming him: "I have your—honey." Indeed. The word "honey" had been pronounced like the forbidden fruit itself.

"Good," said the Double quietly, as if this simple statement had effaced all of his problems. He followed Mr. Rahman to the counter. The two men now ignored The New Man, who still stood just to this side of the interior of the threshold of the shop. He took two steps forward, despite his better instincts. But he found he could not linger far from the entrance, as if to provide ready exit for himself should any menace he sensed in the shop become tangible. He took in the lovely jars of honey and their varied shades, and the way in which they contained or modified or reflected light and made him think of the flesh of Haziz. The jars of honey had a sensuousness that promised more than the pleasures of taste.

Meanwhile, out of the corner of his eye, he watched Mr. Rahman and the Double. Mr. Rahman was handing the Double a rectangular wooden box, about a foot in length, but not more than a few inches high. Mr. Rahman said something in Arabic, and then, obviously for The New Man's ears, said to The Double, "Your honey."

The Double nodded, said something back in Arabic (The New Man was assuming it was Arabic) and walked back down the narrow aisle of the shop, the flag pin incongruously gleaming on his dark clothed body. He was an impersonator who mocked his own guise. He paused only briefly as he reached the threshold, nodded to The New Man and said, "Goodbye, secret man."

The New Man would ignore that word, "secret": "Will I see you again?" He might have been cautiously addressing a lover.

"If Allah wills it."

The Double had "Allah," The New Man had chance—or that near-paranoid vision of a future beyond the unraveling of his comprehension.

The Double left the shop. The New Man noted that the small box, if it had been filled with the weight of jars of honey, would not have been handled so lightly; in the tall man's hands, the box seemed weightless. The New Man's instinct told him there was no honey inside. The near weightless, supernatural powder of God, perhaps? He looked back down the length of the shop to Mr. Rahman, who regarded him with dark eyes obscured by the black frames and thick lenses of his glasses. The New Man realized how indifferent he had been to Mr. Ragman's presence.

Randomly, The New Man took a jar of honey, walked toward Mr. Rahman, and said, "I'll take this."

He placed it on the counter before Mr. Rahman, who said (as if approving the selection), "Ah, you've had this before?" Though there was a bit of sarcasm, too. As with the honey he had bought previously, the label on the bottle was entirely in Arabic.

"No, I liked the color."

Mr. Rahman regarded The New Man as if he had said something obscene—or again, as if he tread too freely amidst the most obscene possibility of violence. He accepted The New Man's bills and offered change. The New Man was on the verge of joking that he was surprised Mr. Raman did not require Arabic currency; but it was more a "joke" for himself, not to be shared. The two men looked at each other for an awkward moment. The eyes behind the glasses blinked with the slow complacency of a reptile. It was both a summons and a farewell. The New Man went out into the light, with the solid little jar of honey held for a moment to his chest (he did not recall he'd done the same with the jar he'd bought yesterday), as if its weight would press some message into his heart.

He saw the Double nowhere.

It was just ridiculous. How could a man, looking like bin Laden, walk about freely, even in this neighborhood?

The New Man's next impulse was to go into the bookshop of the other Mr. Rahman, but he rejected that course, and walked back to the motel.

19. What the Angel Spoke; or, Infinity

Across the courtyard of the motel he was startled to see a man enter a doorway. There was nothing special about him, nothing distinct or menacing. He was of average height, slim, wearing slacks and a short sleeve shirt. But the simple fact of another at this motel which had been so strangely filled with the New Man alone, struck him with an apprehension he told himself was irrational. He entered his own room, glad this stranger was on the opposite end of the motel from him.

He told himself, aloud, "Everything doesn't have to do with you." But a dull instinct, roused in him since Tuesday, denied this obvious logic.

In the room was the loneliness of the end of the morning, the flash and flicker of the TV: the collage of a damaged Pentagon, grieving families, an earnest President, a stern Rumsfeld, and the imploring face of the UN's Kofi Annan. It was like being confronted with the babbling faces of a dream. The New Man knew what all these individuals were saying, but what he wanted to know was the answer to the mystery of all this, a desire that intensified as he heard, once more, very faintly, the call to prayers. It was Friday noon, the time Muslims would be called to the mosque for their weekly observances. He thought of Haziz and Rasil. And would the Double be facing Mecca— and the stolid outlines of American military bases? He looked across the room at the Koran. He looked down by the bed at Wilson's black bag.

In another moment he was looking again through the pages of his calculations, the infinite progression of the fractal sequence and the outcome of his deciphering. There was the thought: his deciphering had led him to the Double, and then, in a way, Haziz…but suppose there was more than one "solution" to the code? And that solution would have led him—could still lead him—to other paths?

Just as the energy of the atom is released in quanta, with no steady progression of energy but distinct leaps, a jumping from one "level" to the next with no steps in between, it abruptly seemed to The New Man that his deciphering had merely moved the unraveling of the code to one level of a quantum progression: there were other leaps to be made.

But wasn't that a frightening spectre? Wasn't he in deep enough a labyrinth?

But he could not help finding a pen and paper and beginning his mathematical work once more. Only after some timeless moment of the afternoon had returned to him, prompted by some shout or the rumble of a car rising from the street, an awareness outside of the mathematical maze he constructed—or discovered—did he feel uneasy, perplexed, and a little afraid. He went back to the list of numbers, sprung from the template of the first impression of the phone number that had been stripped from the top of the pad. He took the words he had formed from those numbers and distilled them back into numbers, but of another pattern: a simple series, in groups of four: 4719, 4720, 4722, 4725, 4729, 4734. The first two numbers the same, the second two jumping by one, then two, then three, then four, five….

Crude intuition or the flash of perception that fires genius—

or at least its momentary invitation—drew his hand to the Koran. He turned to Surah 47.... Was this any more of a bizarre stretch than the use of that phone number? Any less frightening?

47:19—"Allah knows your place of turmoil and your place of rest."

He heard the Double saying, "If Allah wills it." He frowned and went on. All places seemed of turmoil to him, and none of rest.

47:20—"When a decree is revealed and war is mentioned therein, thou seest those in whose hearts is a disease looking at thee with the look of men faintly unto death."

47:22—"Would ye then, if you were given the command, work corruption in the land and sever your ties of kinship?"

That was something that stabbed him: "...sever ties of kinship—"

47:25—"Lo! Those who turn back after the guidance had been manifested unto them Satan hath seduced them, and he giveth them ruin."

The TV held for many moments the smoking ruins of the Towers, the small figures of men working amidst the infernal rubble, like souls struggling slowly with a damnation they could not comprehend.

47:29—"Or do those in whose hearts is a disease deem that Allah will not bring to light their secret hates?"

He felt again the four men beating him, intent on his death; and he felt, with a great horror, his own pool of violence—that he had not needed to act upon simply because he had not been in certain situations.... But then, the memories of Vietnam, the buck of the rifle as he had fired—he been allowed the *uncertainty* of being, specifically, in his deed, a murderer. And this uncertainly was worse than knowing.

37:34—"Lo! Those who disbelieve and turn from the way of Allah and then die disbelievers. Allah will surely not pardon them."

So these terrorists feared Allah's rejection.

He looked for 47:40, but the surah ended with the thirty-eighth verse ("Allah is free of all wants… If ye turn back from the path, He will substitute in your stead another people."

Am I reading tea leaves? he thought. Am I like those fools who open the Bible at a random page, and at random place a finger on a verse and from such "guidance" are chastened or urged?

But the figures, the math could not be by chance. And yet—"The place of your turmoil and the place of your rest…work corruption in the land and sever your ties…."

This cut too close to him. He wished himself with Haziz again. His deep pleasure had been a sort of corruption—as much as it had been a genuine freedom. Perhaps freedom was corruption—in a surprising way, a sort of disguised way, that few perceive. And, yes, he had severed ties…. Through his own will or another's?

"To turn back after guidance…bring to light their secret hates…die disbelievers—"

He had been almost killed (twice) by Muslim fanatics. Now their holy book spoke to him. It was—diabolical. Or, as the saying goes, God working in the most mysterious way?

And what if he went on to another quantum level of calculation, and another and another? *There* was a terrorism; that perhaps this "revelation" was so complex and continuing he could not gain a simple—a final—truth from it. He could not be Saul at Damascus or Mohammed receiving Gabriel. As his body held him tense and helpless and confused in the stupor of the afternoon light, he considered the infinite vanishing point of his passage through a mystery.

Infinity. When very young, he had been astounded—and, equally, delighted—to learn that mathematics is based on infinity: the idea that there is always another number: there is no final number. And that one can always add, subtract, divide, multiply—one can always manipulate any numbers or numbers infinitely. If in the real world one could not divide an atom and then its interior particles infinitely, because there would be a point at which the quarks and gluons would not be that original composition, the freedom of numbers was not attached to such things. (It was interesting to note that the ancient Greeks saw atoms as that which could not be divided; though they did not seem to say this was where infinity stopped.)

The freedom of infinity. It struck at him like a wave at once drowning and refreshing him. He had mused upon this decades ago, before the human limits of the flesh he'd encountered in Vietnam had stripped genius from him by making its powers useless in the brutal world. If mathematics was infinite, if numbers were infinite, and mathematics was the true language of the mind, of the mind that conceived language, then the mind was infinite—*and what is infinite could not end.* Now, in the room of Ahmed's motel, the survivor of the Twin Towers, The New Man, Haziz' lover, considered that man might exist within infinity, that the mind itself might be infinite, but yet this did not make the human at one with infinity. To be *in* it, but not *of* it. And so he looked at his calculations with great despair, and prayed (if it could be called that) not for infinity, but its opposite: an endpoint, a destination—a release.

For there was the infinity of meanings to consider: his escape, Wilson, the intelligence reports, the Double, Haziz and her husband, and what was most immediate: whatever would happen next. The maze was exponential in its corridors. He felt that by joining his flesh to Haziz he had bound himself to a certain course, whose most immediate route he could not see. He was suddenly stricken with the recollection of a certain look the bespectacled Mr. Rahman had given him that morning, a light from an uncertain source glinting off his glasses, a look that might have said: "We are uneasy that you are here, it is not good, but the woman will keep you in place until we decide what to do…."

Yes: "we." But who was the "we" he himself had posited?

He dozed. Or almost slept. In that half sleep, when often the power of the mind strangely possesses a preternatural wakefulness, his long submerged mathematical acumen surfaced once more and roamed over the facets of infinity and absorbed his own surreal circumstances within it.

It was a simply illogical curiosity that the set of all numbers, apparently infinite, was equivalent to the set of all even numbers or the set of all odd numbers. Everyday logic would say that the set of all even numbers or the set of all odd numbers must comprise half of all numbers, and so could not be equivalent to that grand, infinite set. But the set of all numbers, the set of all even numbers, the set of all odd numbers—they were each infinite. They could be nothing less. Could infinity in one case be "less" than infinity in another case?

In his mind's eye, The New Man saw a large scrolling white

sheet of paper. On top were 1, 2, 3, 4, 5, 6, etc.; below, 2, 4, 6, 8, 10, 12, etc.; below that, 1, 3, 5, 7, 9, 11, etc. In theory—and, indeed, in practice—one could "match" the first or the third or the thirtieth or one thousandth or one millionth number in any of the sets to the corresponding first or third or millionth number of another set. No set ended before the other. The odds and evens went on, just as the set of all numbers went on—and The New Man, recalling, and recalling viscerally, this tenet of basic mathematics, saw the "odds" and "evens" of his own life, its events, matched with the apparently grand Set of Reality, of life itself. He was stricken in his poignant half sleep by the revelation that his life was *equivalent* to life itself, and as infinite.

But wait, wait. Were there not a finite number of moments in a man's life, and thus a finite time—seventy years, a hundred, less or more—to act in, to have things happen to oneself? Ah— but life, reality, was not merely *outward* things, acts, whether the choice of picking up the telephone one minute or surviving the attacks on the Towers. The outward was lived within; and this inward life was not bound by time. Everyone knows dreams seem to escape hours by "seeming" hours—days—long, but "exist" only in minutes when measured by the clock. In his lucid half sleep, The New Man's eyes did perceive the small alarm clock by the bed, noting the progress of time, and felt himself verge closer and closer to the event horizon of some overwhelming understanding of the infinite and the spiritual experience one derives from the everyday and the common. At least for the moment an Einstein of the inner world, the metamorphosed New Man also considered that one could derive the spiritual *only* from the physical life—and the press of Haziz' body against his returned, the murmurs of her prayers, her son's prayers, that man on the street who had prayed on the dirty pavement; and his wife's plaintive words on television. This was infinite; he was of infinity. And the burden of this was overwhelming. He looked at the clock in the room as if he were a vast thing looking upon something very limited. The clock told him, with each instant, that another marker of time, each second had gone to those already passed and irretrievable, but the clock could not tell him how many instants of time would be left in existence, if the life of the universe was still young or middleaged or in its autumn.

For that matter, was the universe all of existence or only *within* it?

And the clock could not tell him, whether of those instants to come or those instants that had passed, of the *within-ness* of this instant, the infinity apart from time.

He watched the clock. With each full sweep of the second hand, the minute hand moved a notch. He thought of Zeno's Paradox, which could be taken as a rigorous mathematical argument, but which did not work in the real world. A runner starts out from Point A and heads to Point B. To reach B he first has to travel half the distance between A and B. Logical enough. To reach to that halfway mark he has to travel half of that half—then half of that, half of that, etc., on and on, in a progression that appears to negate all motion and assures the runner will never reach B. In real life, the runner—or pedestrian—completes the course. And yet, in minds such as The New Man's, Zeno's mathematics nagged at the heart, suggesting a reality in which motion was indeed stymied but the math was true.

Perhaps he felt something of this. Three days ago—God, *only* three days ago—he had begun to race from Point A, with the instinctual belief, without thinking about it, that a Point B was before him and he would reach it: a destination in whose realm his "New Man-ship" would be complete and achieved. But as the hours, the days and nights had come on, the many events, it seemed now that to get to Point B he had to travel half the distance, and then half of that half, etc. Everything that had happened to him, the code, the Double, Haziz, and on and on, had increasingly halved and halved the distance he had traveled, until he now felt rooted in the maze. Perhaps it was not exactly Zeno's Paradox; motion had not ceased; but it had fixed him in a certain orbit. Not that, in this bed, he felt orbiting with any speed around any center. He felt immobile. He felt— He heard faintly, very faintly, the call to prayer. Disparate callings like the gathering of a flock of birds. He wondered…he almost rose up; there was the sensation in him to do so, the odd desire to rise and stand in the light of the window, the light of the end of summer and perform some sort of —what? Some sort of prayer to some sort of God? But he continued to lie in bed. He dozed more deeply, he lost the half sleep, though the vestiges of the nagging of infinity remained, and so did a perceptible lucidity, if it became more and more dreamlike. His mind recalled that vast sheet of unscrolling paper, but it was devoid of numbers now; instead, there was a thin, vibrant, continuing, infinite line. The set of the points on this line could not be "matched" with the set of numbers, or any equivalent set. The set of numbers, whether all of them, odd or even, were quanta. You went from one to two, to three and so forth. But the set of the points on a line were of a *continuum*, not quanta. In fact, such sets were called a continuum.

The New Man mused and brooded. Was life of the quanta or of the continuum? And was this knowable or not?

And then he considered that on this afternoon he had for some reason been applying mathematics to *things*, when in the past he had loved mathematics because it could exist apart from things.

At the end of the afternoon, The New Man, filled with the paradox of Zeno (and perhaps the infinity of Blake), left his room. He was going to see Haziz. Neither he nor she had agreed to another meeting— But no, no: She had said, "Come tonight." It was almost as if he had slipped into a parallel world where she had not. Why? But this new life was like that, a forking from each event so that one might take either path....

20. Another Country; Moving Day

Though before that he stopped in to see Ahmed, who was watching the ubiquitous "America Under Attack" coverage.

"I owe you another day, I think—"

Ahmed accepted payment quietly, a little uneasily, The New Man thought, as if the motelkeeper were resigned to a role in a play whose theme was too mysterious to consider. Though looking somewhat cautiously at The New Man, he said, "So how do you like the neighborhood?"

It was a twofold query. Within it was folded, "What are you doing when you go out?" The other facet was, "You're staying here longer than would be expected."

There was truth to The New Man's reply: "It's like another country."

Ahmed nodded. "Every new place can be like that. When I

first came here—" But he broke off at the interruption of some event and voice and image on the screen, and The New Man was left unsure if Ahmed referred to arriving in this specific neighborhood or America itself. When the motelkeeper looked back at The New Man he finished with: " But you—adjust." And then said quickly, "You are very fortunate. All those people—" On the screen were the small figures working away at the rubble of Ground Zero. "Just to have life—" he said, with emphasis, looking full upon The New Man as if to catch his odd visitor not appreciating this boon.

"Yes, yes," The New Man muttered. He knew he should feel more grateful, but could not. Abruptly he said: "I see you have another guest."

Ahmed's eyes widened a bit in concert with a soft "Ah…. Yes. He stays here occasionally when he visits relatives here. He is from Dearborn—Michigan."

"Michigan?"

"There is a large Arab community there."

"Why there?"

"The automobile industry."

"Why that industry?"

"Mr. Newman, I can't answer everything." Ahmed was smiling, but perhaps he was also a little puzzled at Mr. Newman's trying to pursue a random fact into an explicable one.

While The New Man had the paranoid vision of cars being sabotaged by Arab extremists, though of course he did not share this with Ahmed.

He left, thinking he could not stay in the motel much longer.

He sensed something had to happen: another fork in the road. He had no idea what. The New Man did not believe Ahmed would instigate anything unpleasant, but the single fact that he was staying on in an unlikely place called attention to himself.

When Haziz opened the door her face seemed resigned to his reappearance and yet was also pleased he had returned.

He felt awkward, even foolish. "Hello."

"Come in."

Those plain words gave him relief. He looked about for Rasil.

"He's playing in his room." She gave him a look that said, If you have something important to say to me, say it.

He tried. "Haziz…" This was the first time in fact he had uttered her name aloud.

She smiled, as if this were as satisfying to her as the lovemaking of last night. "Yes?"

"Are we… to continue?"

There was no hesitation. "I would like that." Contrary to the stereotype of the Islamic woman demure before a man, she looked him straight in the eye.

"This is too strange—too frightening," he said.

"But, somehow, necessary."

So: there was no doubt. Or there was no doubt they would continue, despite any doubts. They reached for each other's hand. He felt the weight of her arm travel into the warmth of her hand, and felt the sensual fulcrum of the body that moved that arm.

Surely the greatest doubt was of the future they faced.

"Are you hungry?" Perhaps this was the stereotype, of the woman offering food.

"I—I'm not sure." As if, sensing her body, he was unsure of his own. "Not right now." Then he said quickly, "I can't stay in the motel much longer…." At her look he added, "No, I wasn't going to suggest—here."

"Yes, that would not be good for Rasil."

"No, of course." Yet he was almost disappointed.

"But in this building," she said, "there are apartments."

This was as almost as fantastic to him as the proposition of moving in with her. Or, somehow, more fantastic: his own bachelor pad in the Arab quarter.

"Well, I guess the rent isn't much."

"It is nothing. There is no landlord—anymore."

"I don't understand."

"I will explain it—another time. That's how you say it? Most of the apartments are no good, but there are a few…with lights, water—and heat this winter."

He wondered, her husband being who he was, or had been, if Al-Qaeda were the landlord that was no more, but he did not speak this thought. He considered if he took this step…was it a further bondage—or freedom? Zeno's Paradox?

"Haziz…." He needed to say her name again. "Are you sure your husband—"

"He's gone."

That didn't—to The New Man—mean he was dead. "But you can't know for sure."

"Mohammed—he believed in Allah's will. Though he destroyed himself because of his own will."

"I question my will all the time. *Is* it mine?"

"That is for all of us to do. All the time, as you say."

He raised their still clasped hands. "And is this Allah's will?"

"It is for us to find out what is Allah's will and what is ours—and to meet both, join them, properly."

"But for you to...sleep with me—" Her eyes raised. He recalled vaguely they had discussed this last night. "If I cause you to go in any way that you begin to resent—"

"It is *my* sense *you* might resent."

He did not want to look at this. "If you...pull back—"

"Yes? If I do?"

"That's what I don't want."

"Things begin. Things end."

"You sound cynical."

But she had spoken without defiance or resignation, offering this wisdom calmly. She said, "You are afraid."

"Yes, I am." How strange it was so easy—in this moment—for him to admit this.

"You went through a catastrophe, you survived."

"With nothing left. I'm walking around the world with another name."

"You chose that."

"And choosing that should have been choice enough. That was big choice. More enormous than I could have known. Now—it seems I'm in something larger."

"You have the chance—to leave what you did. And me."

"I don't want to."

"Then choose me like you chose your new life."

"The problem is I feel it's chosen me."

"Allah's will."

"If I believe in a God, that God has no name."

"Then how do you call your God?"

For a moment, The New Man was, literally, stunned. With

the somberness of a tapestry, the light of the end of the day lay broadly in the belly of the room. He did want to call to something, but what? He had the vague memory of his half sleep enthrallment to the avenues of Infinity, of wanting to beseech something greater than either himself or that. He sighed and said to Haziz, "I don't know. I guess I don't…call."

If he could have stepped outside of himself, The New Man might have described himself as a neo-existentialist, traveling on the edge of this precarious millennium's angst. From the half opened windows he smelled the scent of burning. His nostrils lifted, like an animal's. This scent was always in the air now. One became unaware of it out of habit (even though a habit of brief standing, embraced out of a sort of defense), then aware of it when a stir of consciousness broke through this habit, or the wind blew a certain way.

She noted what his senses—and psyche—scented. She said, "It comes and goes today…across the river."

He almost said he had crossed that river, too, to come here, to all this and to her. Then he remembered her husband's use of the river of history. He heard himself dimly saying, almost cruelly, "Does it make you think of him?"

She looked to the window. "The…destruction?"

"Yes."

"No. He is so much gone he is not even in that rubble." She gestured in the direction of the city. In that instant The New Man realized this was also the direction in which she prayed: to the destroyed Towers and Mecca, beyond. She looked at him, but surely did not see the appreciation of this irony on his face. "He was gone from my heart long before."

Sincerity makes any cliché profound, and honest. The New

Man moved to embrace her. She placed a palm between them. She was psychic to the moment. Rasil opened the door of his room, holding wooden toy figures in one hands and looked at his mother and The New Man—who thought: *What can he possibly think of me?*

Haziz smiled and said, a little too loudly, in the way adults do in front of children in order to hide a reality: "Rasil has been very quiet, very good, playing today. I think Monday he'll be ready to go back to school."

"I don't want to go back." His blank look disguised his knowing of some great sea change.

She went to him, saying, "You were only there a few days." She held him to her legs and said to The New Man, "That morning I went to get him. I had to bring him home." She ruffled her son's thick hair. "You wanted to come home, didn't you?"

"I don't like school."

"You can't know that right at the beginning of it."

The boy said again, flatly, " I know it. I don't...like it." But that weak protest was mask of a profound distrust. The New Man thought Rasil had perceived the essence of some horror, some duplicity, some moral numbing in the structure of public education.

To The New Man, Haziz said, "He was worried—I thought. The heart knows." The New Man anticipated she had been about to add the word "father" in some way. Was Rasil more worried about the disappearance of his father or the great uneasiness—and hysteria—in the world since the attacks? Did he connect the two? He must, in some way; how could he not?

Haziz was saying to Rasil, "These are very interesting,"

pointing to the wooden figures.

The figures were perhaps four inches high. They were of men in traditional Middle Eastern dress. The New Man asked, in a hopeful, cautious manner, "Can I see them?"

Tentatively, out of politeness to an adult, and a little out of fear, Rasil handed one figure to The New Man, while holding on to the others. In his larger hands, the figure was small. That perspective diminution in size, the lightness of the wood, and the surprising indefinable delicacy of the carving gave The New Man the sensation he held a piece of fine folk art—even creative art—that was somewhat out of place in this neighborhood. And yet, also, somehow fitting, as this was the son of Haziz.

And also the son of Mohammed. "It is from Saudi Arabia. His father gave them to him." Haziz said this in a low voice, as if trying to keep Rasil from hearing, but of course he could.

And so the hijacker, the terrorist, had left this remembrance: a portion of an artistic soul. The small figure, which looked to The New Man like a desert chieftain out of *Lawrence of Arabia*, had such a distinctly carved face; in that minute area the carver had somehow wrought such an arresting expression, one of— of— The New Man couldn't quite say of what. An expression pained and resolute, proud but anxious, an expression of the gentler things lost in life. An expression of…preparation.

The New Man, a little unnerved at the vividness of the carving and the depth of feeling it conveyed, gave it back to Rasil, who took it from this stranger quickly, with a sudden grasp—as if he might not have another chance to recover his plaything. When he had repossessed the carving he said something to his mother, who answered almost curtly, in resignation. In this quick exchange of foreign words, The New

Man intuited: *When is my father coming back?* The answer: *I'm not sure yet.* The vagueness and dishonesty of the response caused the boy to withdraw and return to his room, frowning.

When Haziz turned back to face The New Man he saw her eyes were holding tears she tried to keep from falling across the strained disguise of her expression. "Mohammed was always gone somewhere, but he and Rasil had a closeness. I am so worried—"

He wanted to wrest her from the subject of Mohammed. "Are you staying here?"

"For a while." She seemed just as unhappy saying that as dwelling on her husband. She was sensing he might draw from her something that might expose her too much; she placed matters back on him. "We will look at the apartments."

The New Man suddenly recalled something." Is there anyone else living in this building?"

"Why do you ask that?"

"When I came last night I saw a light above yours."

"There is a retired professor, Egyptian, a very…smart man."

"Smart?"

"He is a psychiatrist."

"From Egypt?"

"Yes, they're even in Egypt."

The New Man smiled at himself. Perhaps he pictured the psyche of that part of the world as being so close to the surface of things no one there had a need to search for the depths. "Is he…an associate of your husband?"

"They did not get along very well. Mohammed and Mafouz are different people." Then, as if explaining this difference, she said, "Mafouz has a telescope he brings out onto the roof."

"So he looks into the psyche and he looks into the stars." She seemed puzzled at his flippant connection. He said, "Not very good skies for stargazing here, I would think."

"I have looked through his telescope. It is very interesting. I saw the rings of Saturn. Do you know that many stars were named by Muslims? Arabs," she added, with a bit of resignation.

"No, I didn't know that," he said slowly. "With what's happened the government might think Muslims looking through telescopes to be suspicious activity."

She shrugged. "I don't think anyone sees him doing it—here."

"How do you think he would react to my living in this building?"

"I think…you would find him interesting."

"But how would he find me?"

"Do you worry how people find you?"

"No. I only had to worry on Long Island."

"Why?"

"I couldn't explain it now."

She accepted that. "Yes, this is not…Long Island." She pronounced it as if this were not a real place at all.

He smiled. "Maybe that wasn't my turf after all."

"Turf?"

"Where I belong."

"What—where—is it then?"

"I'm looking for it."

There was a pause. She said, "I will show you an apartment downstairs."

Moment later, after having commanded Rasil with sharp

cautionary words, she quickly led The New Man downstairs. "I should take him—but I think it would bother him—if he sees—I have to go right back up."

During the brief descent to the floor below, The New Man felt he had caused Haziz to abandon Rasil in order to take care of him, her sudden strange lover—an exchange he felt Haziz bore only out of immediate (and perhaps even unpleasant) necessity.

In another moment, The New Man and Haziz stood inside an apartment, much like Haziz'. The apartment contained some furniture. It had the sense of having been exited from in a hurry. There was the feeling that some things had been taken, others not. The items in the latter category had only been abandoned out of a lack of time to gather them, nothing more.

"No one will bother you here."

The New Man had two simultaneous questions. "Someone just left—?"

"Yes."

"Not another—of your husband's friends?"

"No." He looked as if he did not believe her. "I am telling the truth."

"But you knew who lived here."

"I knew, but did not know why—the leaving. He—kept to his business."

The New Man wondered about that business, but instead asked, "So who is the landlord here? Oh, but you said no landlord. How do the water and lights stay on?"

"A friend of Mohammed's took care of that."

"So the landlord is Al-Qaeda."

"No. Mohammed just knew him."

"And he lets people live here for free."

"Mohammed saved his life, years ago, in a protest in Saudi Arabia. He was being beaten. Mohammed…got him away from the police."

"That must have been difficult to do."

She sensed he had wanted to add something to that, but had restrained himself. "You do not need all these questions. Just accept things now."

"You're asking a man who chose a new life to accept things?"

"You said—it chose you."

He was silent. "Did you choose me, Haziz?" The New Man had the sensation Haziz might abandon him here, even though she would be right above him.

She sighed. "As much as I can choose." Then, abruptly, "I have to get back to Rasil."

The New Man was left in the apartment. Its half emptiness was uncomfortable and too resonant with the sound of his step. The light that came in from the windows seemed blunt and indifferent to human eyes. Of course he knew all this was his mood, the circumstance…. Perhaps there *would* be some sort of privacy here.

The apartment had one bedroom, a living room and kitchen. It was enough for him. He grinned wryly at that. Yes, to pare down his life. He contrasted these few—and small—rooms to his sizable home on Long Island. But what *is* enough for me—now? He asked himself.

Being on the second floor, the view of the street below and also his view of the lot was not as ascendant as from Haziz' third floor apartment. Like a typical apartment hunter he had the common thought that it was too bad he could not have gotten something above Haziz, on the fourth floor. But he supposed the Egyptian shrink had the only good apartment there— convenient, in its height, for his telescope. Wasn't that incongruous, in this neighborhood, some academic looking at the stars? He considered that academics are often revolutionaries, enemies of the state....

Whether this doctor of the mind was of such ilk or not, whether the unnamed landlord was more than a friend of Haziz' terrorist husband, The New Man ceased to care for the moment.

He lingered in the apartment a long time.

He looked out on the rubble outside; it was too close; the shadows in the lot made him think it was about this time he had struggled with the Double—and the four men—two long days ago.

He stepped quietly, even carefully from room to room—as if someone might be listening, from below, or the other side of a wall. He realized he was often beset by the sensation—the paranoia—that the life he was escaping was trying to find him out, suck him back in. He was contemplative, anxious, and a little confused. He felt a little trapped. The infinity he had been pondering such a short time ago, the sense of being in an endless maze—it was too much the truth. This was another "place" to which his new identity had taken him—through, once again, chance. Chance and his new identity seemed to go hand in hand. But hadn't that been the case with his old self? Vietnam, his marriage, his job—hadn't they all come out of the bubbling chaotic pot of chance to take hold of his life?

He left the apartment. Did one need a key here? The door had been unlocked when he had entered with Haziz; he left it unlocked behind him. He was about to go back upstairs to

Haziz, but instead went downstairs, outside, and returned to the motel. He decided he would effect the move quickly.

He settled his bill with Ahmed, who said, "So you'll be with your family soon, Mr. Newman." Ahmed was testing The New Man, who replied, "Yes, yes, it's good." And to Ahmed's inquisitive "Is someone coming for you?" The New Man said, "I'm taking a taxi—" and let the further expected words, "to such and such a place," be lost in the brevity and abruptness of his departure.

In the motel room he gathered the black bag, the clothes he had just bought (folded neatly in their plastic bag from the store) and was just about to leave the room for the last time (the first interior in which he had been The New Man) when he realized he had almost forgotten the Koran. He stuffed it into Wilson's bag, Allah's word among U.S. intelligence reports. It seemed a final act of departure.

He imagined, absurdly, surreally, that Wilson had been the occupant of the apartment he would now occupy. Hadn't stranger things happened? Wilson the link between CIA reports, the Double, and who knows what, having some hideaway beneath Mohammed the hijacker.

He shook Ahmed's hand firmly and with apparent goodwill. He had come to like the motelkeeper and understood the man's unease and curiosity at this stranger's presence here. The New Man was actually sad to be leaving this first sanctuary of his new life. He felt a pang of guilt that he had somewhat deceived this kindly man. Then again, why should he have to relate the upheaval of his life to anyone if he did not want to? Sufficient unto the crowd the common catastrophe of the day—which the "news" explained…. At any rate, The New Man was touched when Ahmed said, with sincerity, "Allah saved you from death. He has given you more of life."

What could The New Man say to that? "Yes, yes—I've got a lot of life left. I'm blessed." And was a little wondering at himself at that last statement as he got into the taxi with his few worldly goods. While he thought: *Have I gathered too much in such a short time?*

It was just after sunset. The warm day was vivid with the beauty of a sky that somehow seemed cold.

The taxi driver was Middle Eastern. He treated his fare with mundane indifference. The New Man could see no surprise or curiosity in those dark eyes. The New Man was grateful—and then, inevitably, suspicious. But it was a brief ride, to a subway stop where trains ran into the city. The taxi had been for Ahmed's benefit. The New Man did not want the driver to take him to an even more unlikely neighborhood.

He went down the subway steps, paused in that semi-descent as the taxi pulled away; he listened to the sound of a train somewhere in the caverns to which the dark turn of the dirty steps led. A bearded man with a tightly woven turban came up the steps. The New Man pretended to be checking something in Wilson's bag. The man gave the briefest look of curiosity and ascended to the street. The New Man felt no apprehension; he was used to casual duplicities by now. After a pause, he went back up the stairs and walked to his new home. In the twilight and then the evening's new dark, it took about half an hour. With the slightest expression he acknowledged the glances of those who noted him. He had no concern about walking through this neighborhood where he was still a stranger. Perhaps he felt less strange in regard to that strangeness. Perhaps strangeness had become a sort of comfort—his one true home, in fact.

21. A Dream of Cities

He went to the apartment and deposited his clothing and Wilson's black bag.

He stood by the bed, as light rested upon it. He squinted tiredly at the window. He felt himself in a place either newly desecrated or consecrated.

Then, just to make sure, he went to the sink, and turned on the faucets. For a few moments, he watched the clockwise spiral of water circle down the drain. It seemed a beautiful symmetry. In fact, a mystery.

He shut off the water and touched the sheen of wetness left on the hard curve of the sink; as if he needed to touch the remnant of something elusive and indifferent against his hand.

He went upstairs to Haziz. "Well, I've moved in," he said as she opened the door.

Her face, lovely and tired, leaned against the half opened door. "That is good." It was as if her face were partially framed.

With the smile of a man who accepts a situation, he said, "I hope so."

He looked at her with desire and an odd surge of peacefulness. He felt for a moment his flight had ceased—at least gained a sort of respite. "I guess this is the next place I had to go."

She drew open the door. "Allah knows our paths; we follow."

Ahmed's recent invoking of Allah and now Haziz gave The New Man the sense of a further irony of passage. The labyrinth. Infinity. On and on. But this was a place to stay. For now. Haziz, this woman, did seem a destination. (Like the apartment below?) He allowed himself the comforting illusion of this unexpected...love?

She had come to bed in the act of sewing a ripped seam in Rasil's pants, as if she had to hold this sign of her maternal duties even as she began the fulfillment of her desires with her lover.

Their loving was swift and short and so in the sense of time less intense than on their first night, and yet this second time was a powerful brevity that sealed their bodies into the fact that they had created a genuine beginning—of something.

In the quiet of the deep night, when The New Man could believe himself and Haziz the only two people in the world (yet the thought of Rasil was hardly far-off), for it seemed that no sound at all came from anywhere, he said, as if in allegory, "It's a quiet neighborhood." She murmured, perhaps not in agreement, but simply to utter an answer, an echo, the response of recognition; and, as if it were a natural segue, he asked when was the last time she'd seen Mohammed.

The silence that followed that question was longer than it should have been—had the question not sought something less than an emotional milestone in her life. "You want the precise date?" she asked, offering a question for question, letting a little sarcasm and defiance linger in the air. He made his own cautious offering: "A month? A week...? I think you told me—" She sighed, and surrendered to interrogation. "The second week of

August…." Her voice was drifting, as if there could be nothing precise about that time, as if even the month of August were a vague realm. After letting further silence gather, after he too felt the drift of uncertain things and sad things (he had the abrupt image of a figure in a small boat on a bright sea drifting slowly from the shore, and looking upon the land of departure), The New Man asked, "And did he—say—?"

Her face turned accusingly to him in the dark. Her eyes were of another dark, one that flickered. "What should he say? That he would—would—?" Her face turned away abruptly, making a distinct noise in the bed. In a moment she turned back, just slightly, looking upward, the dark waves of her hair like barriers around her head.

But he had to go on. "Do you think he knew all of it then?"

Her answer was quick. "I don't know."

"I heard—they were speculating—all the hijackers might not have known…they were going to crash into buildings."

"I don't excuse him." This was as final as a woman could make it. From her breathing he sensed she wanted now only a long silence.

He allowed her that silence for but a moment. "That last day—" She had turned her back to him. It was a mark of the familiarity he felt with her, one that had grown up so quickly, that he continued. "I mean, did he say in the morning, 'I have something special—important—to do,' and walk out the door?" What he wanted to say more than that was: "Had you had, had he given you, a day of—farewell?"

Her back still turned from him, she said abruptly, "It wasn't like in your movies." He waited. Almost longingly she said: "It wasn't—clear."

Clear. Clarity. What we all want. We suffocate without it. The New Man waited again. Her back spoke to him again. "There were phone calls. Mohammed was always leaving, always coming back. That day in the afternoon he said he'd be away a little while—"

"Not forever?"

"No." She turned, on her back, and looked up at the ceiling again. He listened to her breathe.

"Did you think it would be a little while, or…?"

"I didn't think." Pause.

The New Man said, "Orl forever."

"Who believes in forever?"

"Isn't your God forever?"

She was angered. "I am talking about people. A person."

This silenced him. She said, "He was Mohammed. I had become used to him."

Another pause. He let it gather long enough so she might have thought that would be the end of his questions. But then he said, "Were you—happy?"

Her head moved just the slightest bit, as if she wanted to look at him, whether in reprimand or imploringly, but she kept her gaze on the ceiling. "Not since—a while. I had given up on the future—with him. But…happiness: that is what the young imagine. Happiness is a foolish thing, against life." In the dark, her eyes seemed to glisten. Was she crying?

"How did the two of you live? I mean, what did you live *on*?"

Slowly, as if against her will, she sat up and faced Mecca. Her naked back astonished him—the light from the street gave him enough light to behold it—and he had almost forgotten his question when she answered. "Am I asking you questions about your family?"

"No. But then, no one in my family made history."

"No, you are just alive, but you are dead." Still sitting up, she twisted to face him. He lost her face in dimness; he looked at her breasts.

He said, "You think I'm a coward."

She shrugged. "Men do certain things. It is not being a coward or—"

"Was Mohammed brave—or a coward?"

"What is the difference?"

He had to admit: "I don't know."

"Men do—stupid things." She started to say this with anger; then she was sad.

"Stupid? Destruction? Murder thousands?"

"The stupid thing is your questions." This was more a plea than a reprimand.

He considered. "Maybe my most 'stupid thing' is to…become Mr. Newman."

Her sigh was the acceptance of what she could not know. She laid herself down, stretched out alongside him. He arranged himself to match her. Bodies at length and touching, they breathed quietly together.

She said, "I did not ask you what your other name was."

He was surprised he did not fear this. "No, you didn't. Ask." Then he remembered. "You saw it on TV."

"Yes, they said it. But I didn't hear it. I was—" She looked away, then back to him. "You were so—"

"I suppose my hysteria drowned everything."

She only said, "I don't ask."

But he was about to tell her. She sensed it and cut off the first sound of it. "No. I don't want that now."

A little wounded at her refusal to allow him to be so vulnerable, he fell silent.

To assuage him she said, "I want to know you by the name you have with me."

They rested side by side for some time, bodies warm. He said, "Can I just ask one more question?"

"If I say No…?"

"Then I won't ask."

"If you don't ask it now you'll ask it later. Ask."

"I already did. What did you live on? Did he have a job?"

"At the honey store."

The New Man was struck with an unvoiced Aha! He recalled the Double quickly departing with the lightly weighted box. "So Mr. Rahman is involved."

"Mr. Rahman—and his brother—political, that is all."

"And your husband made enough at the honey store to—"

"Why do you ask obvious questions? Money came from other places, too."

Now The New Man was sure of the contents of the Double's box: money. He said to her, "And you were comfortable with that?"

"What does 'comfortable' have to do with my life?" She said this bitterly. Once more he was struck silent.

When she spoke again she seemed distressed. "When I saw the buildings on fire, saw them fall— How could I think—?"

"Did you say anything to Mr. Rahman? Either of them?"

"I waited for them to say."

"Do you expect them to? So you go in and buy your honey—"

"You're accusing me."

They both stopped, neither knowing where to go. She said, "No more questions. No more—"

But everything to him was a question. He said, "Are you going to stay here?"

"For a while."

"You can move. All this just happened."

"So I should move and you stay here?"

"They'll track down your husband's connections. And you—"

"And you'll be here too when they come."

"Why am I not worried now?"

"Because you're still American. You think you can escape."

"*Still* American. If I stay here I won't be?"

Her voice was tired, wanting to end it. "I don't know what you'll be. What you are now."

The New Man tried to look at all this starkly. He had come into the center of the web. Or was he merely on the periphery, feeling the awful trembling of some beast, the web-spinner, at the slope of midpoint?

She said, "I need time, to think of what is best for Rasil."

"I understand."

"I think you do not."

"I am a father."

"You say it as if—you try to remember being a father. As if it was a long time ago."

He accepted every mark against him. "I guess it was."

He felt immensely close and immensely distant from her. He held her hand. They left off words. She kissed him lightly. He breathed quietly. Perhaps he fell asleep before she did.

$$\bullet \qquad \bullet \qquad \bullet$$

He dreamed a long, complex dream. In the apartment below, in that half empty new home, he was being interrogated by the FBI: two men, with crude, indistinct faces. In the course of questioning they took off their suit jackets, rolled up their sleeves and loosened their ties, grilling him with an incessant intensity: *So you just happened to come to this neighborhood. So you know his double? You've been in and out of the honey shop. You screw the wife of one of the hijackers—* The words battered him, the assumption of a deep guilt on his part, a deep, duplicitous intent ripped at him psychically. His interrogators, his accusers came at him with their questions and condemning statements in an alternation of rapidity and the briefest pauses, so the effect was one of being in an involuntary dance (or trying to do an dance one didn't know) in the midst of pulsating strobe lights. The instant the senses accepted the lights, the lights flicked off; the instant you accepted they were off, they flicked on. The barrage of the continued interrogation drove into him such a pitch of continued yet ungraspable sensation that abruptly something in him shattered, broke, fragmented, and was scattered. There was the inner image of himself, disembodied, intangible, slipping out of every corner of the apartment (as if he had broken into innumerable amoebae) while the voices of the agents still ranted and battered (as if they directed their furies at every existing place in the universe), and the thing, the being, the manifold entity that was himself escaped the apartment, and in disparate pieces fled through the foreign neighborhood— and then, with the force of its flight denying gravity, rose skyward, ascending, expanding.

In this constellation of himself he looked down as if with myriad eyes, some grotesque insect. He was above the town, he was higher, there was the river between New York and New Jersey, and the waterways glinting with their movement between the boroughs—and the Twin Towers stood tall and unscathed in the sunlight. They too, glinted, with calm indomitability. But even as he gasped at this, at this wondrous resurrection, he watched a plane plunge into one tower, and then, in the speeded up time of dreaming, he saw the second plane burst into the other tower. Great and furious smoke billowed upward. In another moment one tower fell. He was conscious of the screams on the street from the unseen and the helpless. In another moment the second tower collapsed, and the lament from the city below was frightful. It was a fearful din of horror that swarmed piercingly inside his flesh. He could see the ant-people running along the streets, souls fleeing for their lives; and he wondered, *Where am I—in that crowd? Where?* Unvoiced, perhaps, was: *Which I was I then?*

But that search for the essential "I," the old New Man on one side, on the other side his new identity—in another instant that was subsumed when suddenly countless planes were slamming into the other skyscrapers of Manhattan, and bodies and debris fell in a great storm down upon the vast ground of the city. The Icaruses of a thousand tall, tall buildings were flung down upon their shadows in the sun. The sky was filled with the roiling black of destruction and the street below spotted with its mangled victims, while the living ran over and across the dead, or were themselves stricken and killed by the plummeting bodies. There seemed no safety at all to which to run.

The New Man was taken higher, higher, until the ravaged island was small and dark and he could see the curve of the Earth with stars glinting beyond that curve and a sort of rationality invaded vision, for he was a single body now, but he could not breathe, he gasped, he struggled, he could not reach the worlds out there and he fell, fell, and returned to the primal nearness of Earth, of descent through the thickening atmosphere, and then he was falling alongside the one hundred stories of the building he had fled only days ago, its bright side glinting in the early morning sun of its death. The building was not burning—then it was. He shot down and down, joined by bits of the great structure, along with other bodies, anonymous shapes, flappings of paper, the shattering disintegrating monitors of computers, like uncountable mirrors being shattered in a fairy tale, and he fell and fell, more than one hundred stories, more than two hundred and he fell faster and faster and the earth grew closer but still he did not reach it, existence was an endless plummeting and he cried out—in another tongue, another language and he did not understand his own cry, and with that cry he no longer plummeted but was abruptly walking, his body had been yanked from freefall, as if his great anguish had yanked him into another plane; he was walking, stumbling, running, his breath sharp in his flesh, his body ripped through a landscape of debris, like the lot outside the building where he now dreamed, where he had struggled with the Double. And he realized that a voice, a child's voice, was calling him. It was Rasil. And he saw the boy ahead, dressed like the wooden figure Rasil's father had given him, and this child of the desert waved to The New Man. And when he reached the child, Rasil turned and The New Man followed him, at a bit of distance, for he could not keep up with Rasil, who seemed to know how to traverse the debris with alacrity, while The New Man kept stumbling, stubbing his toes, banging his legs against chunks of ruin—until the child had gotten so far ahead of him that The New Man cried out, again in another tongue, but the boy had disappeared. The New Man was left in a topographical maze of debris and threw up his hands to the sky from which he had descended, plummeted, a sky bright, unsullied, and he cried out, foreign-voiced once more.

And was raised. Slowly, slowly, then slightly faster, and he cried to himself—in words he knew: "I can't, again—!" But he went up and up so that the debris-land shrunk beneath him but he only gave it one look, for in an instant something burst inside of him and he was wholly blinded or rather he was seeing an intense, immense, all pervading light and in that intensity he felt the body of Haziz. He could not see her, but it was so fully her, and he held her and pressed into her and there seemed a moaning from her and he mocked himself with a laugh: "Is this Heaven?" But that mockery was a lesser understanding of the light and of her body and the thing beyond both their bodies and this light—

He awoke. They were embracing each other. She said, "You screamed."

It took long moments before he could fix her in his vision and speech. "I was dreaming." But he looked at her as if he still were dreaming.

"What? What was the dream?" How palpable her face, yet also ethereal, as if it might escape his vision if he blinked.

"The Towers." He took a deep breath and tried to settle into the concern on her face. He looked into the dark of her eyes as if seeking the peace of nothingness.

She was quiet. Then she tested the question slowly. "When…it happened…?"

"Yes." He looked away, as if shamed.

There was a long pause. She said, "Where you...?"

"Afraid?"

"I was not going to ask that."

"What then?

"I don't know." Another silence. "I just...wanted to know...your dream."

He seemed to shrug so subtly and abjectly; all his memories and his passions had made him helpless.

She said, "Do you want to tell me what happened?"

He sighed. He was resigned to echo himself: "I don't know." Then he did.

22. *The First Day: Atlantis*

When the explosion first shuddered through the building it was so enormous and invasive it surpassed the power of fright and fear to be any proper response to it. He recalled, from somewhere in front of him, behind him, now he couldn't say— a great flash of light. Perhaps the light was from everywhere. "Like some sort of...announcement," he told Haziz. And then said, puzzled, "But shouldn't the sound have come after the light? Light travels faster." She shrugged with a soft rise of her shoulders in the dark. He said, "I'm probably not remembering it in order."

Though for the most part he did. "That sound, the explosion, it was so big and it seemed far beyond me—and at the same time in me. It was like it was living in my body and at the same time it had begun from so far away."

The building had shaken and swayed with abrupt, surreal

fury. "I looked out the window. The city tilted. One way, then the other."

He was standing in the sway of the superstructure. Memory gave him vague images of other bodies standing too, crying out, turning this way and that, as if they had been summoned by the extraordinary eruption—or disruption—of a divinity. These were no longer individuals, but a chorus blasted with one emotion.

He had no distinct memory of his passage from offices to the corridor, into which others speedily emerged, calling out, questioning, making ridiculous statements, as if they had already surrendered to rumors they could not have possibly heard. "It's a drill!" But things like that were a madhouse cry in a situation whose reality drowned any attempt at self deception. An ageing security guard, his gold plated badge like a toy on his shirt, shouted out things that were supposed to calm: "You don't have to leave the building!" But this was rote; he could not have believed himself.

The elevators were not working. The soon-to-be New Man paused by them in a knot of desperate people who pressed the Down button violently, and pounded on doors. The primitive instinct against failed technology is to maul it. But technology is not a weary beast to rise up from the road in order to accept further exhaustion in lieu of pain. The elevator doors remained closed.

Did he decide himself on fleeing to the stairs, or did he follow someone else?

There was the descent. Descending, descending inexorably with a mindless purposefulness, a strength of desperation, the black bag slapping against his thigh. "I didn't feel it at the time," he told Haziz. Though now he looked to his leg as if the bag should have left a mark.

There seemed, just above, also descending (almost as fast as he descended) the scent of smoke, of the world above him being devoured. "That's what made it horrifying. Smoke should have risen. But it came down, it seemed, anyway."

The descent was a hell of sameness. Each floor looked the same. They were numbered on each landing, but the numbers became meaningless. What were these marks? Though two floors became individual by dint of being flooded. His feet slapped swiftly in two inches of water. There was the faint slap-slap of a sprinkler system—or was it the fount of broken plumbing?—hitting walls. He tried to keep track of the numbers attached to those floors, as if they could mark by their difference some sort of progression, but a flight or two below the flooded floors he forgot the meaningless numbers and just continued.

For several floors—or was it thirty?—he helped a man, easily seventy-five, who gasped and stumbled, and kept thanking this stranger for the aid of other arms and legs. The older man had the face of a man completely ensconced in pain. "It's that expression of pain I remember now," he said to Haziz, "not the face. If I met him I wouldn't recognize him. I wonder if he would me. I doubt it."

She understood. "There are different faces for different times."

A woman flew past, tripping on her high heels, catching herself on a railing. She stopped and took off her shoes and continued. The New Man had the briefest thought that there would be some point when she would reinsert dirty feet into those shoes, if she lived.

Whether people ran behind him or alongside him or ahead of him, he knew them only as figures, only as bodies. "Like salmon in reverse," he told Haziz, who frowned. He had to explain.

Fireman, policemen surged upward, past him, going to their deaths in most cases. Two policeman saw the distress of the old man and relieved The New Man of his burden—"I wonder if they did that just to have an excuse to turn back: so they could be saved while they saved a life."

"They are supposed to save lives."

He almost said, "As your husband was supposed to take lives," but, instead: "Well, I was thankful. I could move faster."

Indeed, his descent seemed to accelerate. What had seemed difficult even before the chance burden of charity, was now less so. He felt himself fly down these last flights with a strength that curiously overrode the exhaustion he should have felt.

Outside, he emerged below the flame-engulfed Towers—both were burning now, covered with roiling smoke, licking flames. He had the recollection some time during his descent that there had been a second explosion, another great thundering from somewhere in the near world, but he had been so overcome, so transformed by the first explosion, so inoculated with unnatural power, he'd felt this second explosion dimly. Perhaps he had received the fact of it by the osmosis of disaster: the knowing, without physical means, of the extent of calamity.

Though on the street, the devastation of this second explosion was as powerful as the first. Ash drifted down upon him, stuck to his sweating face, his sweating, stained clothes, his straining hands (which shook a little now, released from the effort of descent). He might have looked like a figure of clay, abruptly molded, features half discerned; while paper and debris, shards of plastic and glass, coffee cups and missiles of pens shot or drifted down from the sky, so that he seemed on the bottom of a rain of artifacts from a civilization that had just suffered a cataclysm in which he still stood, with the black bag, exhausted, but alive.

It was at that moment he had decided to become The New Man.

What he said to Haziz was, "I decided to remain among the dead." She looked at him with a pity that angered him.

Though it could hardly have been a precise thought, arrived and grasped with the clarity of a decision exactly put into words. The world outside the burning Towers was dominated by the scent and sensation of conflagration suspended, increasing, high above the fleeing masses of people. A burning high above, but descending. He heard voices shout, simultaneously, "Run!" and "Look!" He looked—or did he run first, then look? He was already a little distance from the Towers—a little distance: he looked and saw Two World Trade Center begin to collapse in upon itself. He and innumerable others stayed their flight to witness this unbelievable implosion. Something that had always been there, this enormous monolith, disintegrating.... Perhaps, if there was not a precise moment of decision to sever his lived life from future moments, it was then that it coalesced. The destruction that had hit where he had worked for twenty-one years, the destruction that had then hit the companion monolith, had so thoroughly annihilated a place in which he had *been*. Something from out of the sky had done the work of obliteration—that he himself had longed to do with the decades of his life. And he had submitted to the violence of this destruction in order to clutch rebirth.

He rushed on. Firemen, police, medics—the crew of disparate individuals and functions who would be lumped together as rescue workers (he could not have remembered these faces either)—rushed past him in the opposite direction, just as he had passed them in the building, in his descent. They had the roles of their old lives. He fled through and into his new one.

He was reaching the water when he heard, behind him: "It's down! It's down!" One World Trade center had collapsed; but now—and perhaps it was from his vantage point—he could not see that second, terrible implosion, only the increased rising of smoke ravaging the air. He stopped, looking at this violated skyline, more in contemplation now than awe. So abruptly, so thoroughly had the Towers been eradicated. The others who paused with The New Man gasped and cried out with an anguish they themselves would not have believed they had the purity to express.

The river's edge was lined with boats—impromptu ferries, mostly private vessels. Like water through a sieve, the crowd flowed onto this variegated fleet their presence had created. Yes, passage over water would gain a safety. Who knew if more of Manhattan wouldn't fall, building by building? In the jumble of the small boat, the packed together slice of humanity, The New Man (for now he was indeed that) saw only the blurred conglomerate: again, no face distinct. It was in this crossing and over waters and the press of bodies The New Man first heard the word "terrorism" connected to the Towers. Hadn't he realized that two planes hitting both Towers fifteen minutes apart could be nothing but the judgement now being spoken? Only later would he understand he had not been thinking of causes, just effects. Even on that small boat, ferrying him to the New World of his New Man-ism, he was less concerned with the instigators of the act than the aftermath as it now pertained to him. What *he* could do with it. Unlike most of the others in that crammed boat who—now that they believed themselves headed for safety—began to speculate, rationally, irrationally, on further attacks, The New Man might not have cared if all or most of lower Manhattan were strafed and burned. "What have I to do with thee?" might have been his unvoiced pronouncement as he gazed at the burning skyline of the world's most powerful city. Near him on the boat, a young woman leaned over the side, trying to throw up, while a friend steadied her, to keep her from going overboard and risking death by water so soon after she had escaped, upon the water, death by flame. To The New Man this retching young woman seemed to represent an old illness that these other survivors could only superficially expel, while the virulence would continue within them.

Death. It had been death that had given The New Man life. He did think, when someone in the boat, a half bald, half grey-haired man with dirty tie askew moaned out loud with apparent genuine concern and horror, "How many are in there!"—The New Man did consider the bodies caught and murdered in the collapse, flesh and bones interred by this act of God or Godlessness. He might have also whispered to himself, "And I alone am escaped to tell thee," like Ishmael echoing Job in *Moby Dick*; but he had not escaped alone. Then again, he was the lone individual become something other than he had been.

Something other. He looked down at the water passing alongside the vessel, the sunlight glinting off this surface disturbed by the passage of survivors. Glinting as it had immemorially glinted. He saw the frothy wake of the boat. The young woman, who had perhaps vomited into this vast if now tainted element, had withdrawn herself from the railing. The stricken passengers murmured among themselves, grateful, horrified.

When the ferry reached the other side, perhaps The New Man stepped ashore with a calmer purpose (or purposefulness) than the others. For they *were* other. He was, would be, at last, himself. Whatever that was, whatever that would be.

They said little after his story. His tale of escape, flight and transformation—of *creating* a border to cross seemed too enormous to add to for the moment. And he felt he had done it poorly—wretchedly. She only said, as he laid himself back down on the bed, "Allah did guide you—through all that horror."

He might have resented this. But he accepted her words—because they came with her caress? Accepted with a murmur he lost as he returned to sleep. A sleep wonderful, without dreams.

23. Heaven, in Egyptian Eyes

The New Man awoke in the dark. He rested in a tight anxiousness next to Haziz, listening to her regular breathing. He had imbued her with horror preceding his transformation; it seemed to have left her with a deep peace.

He rose slowly and dressed. In the dimness he looked on her body in the bed. The stillness of her flesh belied how passionately she had received his. As if he were committing a surreptitious farewell, he left the apartment. Somehow he was able to exit with total silence. About to descend the flight to his floor, The New Man did just the opposite; he climbed one flight to the top floor. Why he was doing this, he would not have been able to say.

Though when he was on the fourth floor, in the corridor that seemed to have its own sort of silence, The New Man recalled the other inhabitant of the building: the psychiatrist with the telescope. He wondered which of the three doors in the hallway led to the Egyptian's apartment; but the gloomy stolidity of each doorway gave no clue. Then The New Man saw, at the other end of the hallway; stairs that led up to an opened trap door that was lit with the different darkness of the outside.

The New Man's psyche might have returned to the state of his dreaming just before he had related his escape from the Towers to Haziz. He moved to the steps as if compelled. He effected the easy ascent—only a few steps—but now he seemed steeped in a consciousness that made all acts long in time; he might have been ascending in some thick steam of a barely controlled angst.

He was out on the roof and breathing in the coolness of the night that would soon face dawn. It was a quiet dim world to which he had ascended, with only the faintest, far off noises: in some distance was the muted passage of a truck; and then, a sound he couldn't define: soft and unobtrusive, nearby.

He looked to the eastward edge of the roof and there was a man, peering into the eyepiece of a telescope. The New Man's disappointment was sharp and weary; he had sought some solitude above the sleeping streets, but here was another—who apparently was seeking a further height.

There was the impulse to go back down into the building; but it was too soon to re-enter that interior. He simply stood, looking at the man and the telescope, whose silhouettes blended into the dark outline of one odd beast. Beyond the figure and the instrument was the glow of light from the round-the-clock efforts at Ground Zero. It was a hellish mixture of illumination, reaching up and spreading out across a good portion of the sky, obscuring the heavens.

Though one heavenly body was plainly noted, if blurred: the sliver of a waning moon, not long ago risen, was ghostly and sickly in the east, poised above the irregular skyline and the surreal toil below.

Just as The New Man recalled the other's name—Mafouz— the man looked up from the telescope and turned to face this unexpected intruder. Across a distance of twenty feet or so the two looked at each other, with equal—or unequal—foreboding.

"I'm sorry," The New Man said softly, so softly he could not be sure the other heard him. At any rate, Mafouz—was that his first or last name?—stepped in front of the telescope, as if trying to hide it. He also might have been speaking softly; if he said something, The New Man did not hear it.

The New Man halved the distance between them. He was both quick and cautious. He said, a little more loudly, "I'm a friend of Haziz." (Though what "friend" would be there at this hour?) "I just came up for…some air. Couldn't sleep."

This newer proximity allowed him to see Mafouz much better. He was a slight dark man with a goatee. He wore a white shirt and pale tan slacks that seemed bright and crisp in the dark. There was the scent of cigarettes about him.

Mafouz' expression seemed as curious as it was wary. "You know Haziz." Here too was dichotomy; the words bordered on both a question and a statement.

"She told me…you had a telescope." That would be a safe bit of knowledge to admit to having. Before Mafouz could respond, The New Man added, "I escaped from the Towers." As if that would make everything explainable—and acceptable. He gestured to the wan, dominating glow beyond Mafouz, who turned, at least half turned; he had enough wariness to keep him from turning his back fully to The New Man.

Of course, Mafouz was only turning to something that was no longer there. When he looked back at The New Man he said, "You—got out?"

"Yes. I escaped across the river." He might have been reciting the outline of an allegory. "Took a bus, ended up here." How simple these words, condensed and swift, evoking nothing of his descent and the flight to—here.

But perhaps the other was trying to divine a depth to that terse description. He was silent; he seemed to peer more closely at The New Man, who was saying, "Must spoil things—with the telescope—" He gestured again to the light from Ground Zero.

Mafouz gave a glance at that pervasive spread, as if seeing it for the first time. And it seemed he lingered on the blurred, imperceptibly rising sliver of the moon. Now the New Man could see there was a bright, if blurred star near the moon. And then he could pick a scattering of other stars, more towards the periphery of the illumination from Ground Zero. Looking back at The New Man, Mafouz said, "Yes, it's…difficult." His face seemed briefly pained with a resignation he still questioned. He added, "The east is always brighter—the city—" He gestured to the scattered, violated stars. "But Orion's bright enough—"

The New Man, who was hardly an astronomy buff, now saw the great rectangle of Orion. He did know Orion, along with the Big Dipper. That was about it, as he had to admit to Mafouz, who asked him, "Do you know the stars at all?" It seemed a friendly question, presented in the manner of someone prompting another for a password any traveller had to know— or as if the Egyptian were accepting the presence of this stranger who had come from the place that no longer was.

"Not really," said The New Man. "I could never remember all those stars."

The New Man might have just admitted to a deprivation; Mafouz gave an almost sad twist to his head, as if fighting against an expression of pity. He said, "Come here. Look at this."

So The New Man moved to the telescope—a bit cautiously, unsure where this was all going.

"Look at that star," said Mafouz, pointing to one of the stars in Orion's belt, the one on the right (from the perspective of the observer) of the bright trio. "That is Mintaka, 2,300 light years away." He announced this fact as if no one but he knew it.

Looking up at the star, The New Man took in that great measurement of time and distance (and felt vaguely their intrinsic link). The light of this star had begun its journey to his eyes here, tonight, 300 years before the birth of Christ—and 900 years before Mohammed.

Mafouz was aligning the telescope. "Now look." And The New Man, carefully leaning over the reflecting telescope, heard

Mafouz say (as if giving blunt directions), "You can adjust it—"
The New Man did so only the tiniest bit. Within the faint haze
of light spread upward from across the river, he saw the blue
white star and a dimmer star near it.

"A double star," Mafouz said, with an odd sort of pride.

The New Man looked away from the celestial companionship
revealed by human optics. Mafouz appeared charged, excited.
"There are actually three stars. Mintaka is an eclipsing binary.
Another star circles it, it's too small to see with this; it reduces
Mintaka's magnitude—brightness—a little, hardly noticeable—
about every five and a half days."

Before The New Man could express—or feign—interest,
Mafouz was gently, with the slightest touch, pulling him from
the telescope and guiding the black tube elsewhere—while The
New Man took that moment to pause and look down at the
height, if not very great, from this roof to the lot of rubble below.
He had not realized how close to the edge he was. The night
seemed to both amplify the height and disguise it. Well, he had
faced a greater height than this—

Mafouz was saying, "There's Heka. Look. Look."

And then The New Man was looking through the telescope at
the star that was midway and slightly above the line of the two
bright top stars of Orion's rectangle, as the Egyptian said,
"...1400 light years away—" So The New Man had to think:
This light started out in the time of Mohammed. The New Man
did not reflect then that only a few days ago he would not have
been measuring centuries, millennia by the eras of Christ and
Mohammed. The catastrophe that had rent the secular world had
also been invaded by God.

Meanwhile, here again in the lens one blue-white star was

split into two.

The New Man looked back at Mafouz, who spoke with a calm passion that must have been his habit. "I find it fascinating: you see one star with the eye, but there are really two—or more."

He showed The New Man multiple star systems: three stars and four stars—even six, in the heart of the nebula dangling from Orion's belt. The New Man had the feeling he was moving toward an infinity revealed by an incessant series of minutely executed separations of giant worlds. Each time The New Man drew his eye from the lens, Mafouz had the oddest smile: as if he were satisfied with himself for showing another a wonder inarguably marvelous.

And The New Man was taken, in a way. Here were suns, creators of light, far from our concerns, both in distance and nature. He saw stars of different colors, paired in gravity's mysterious arrangement, and the ghostly mysteries of star fields and nebulae while Mafouz sprouted sporadic facts: light years, magnitudes and the mention (like a boast, really) that so many stars had Arabic names— Saiph, Rigel, Betelgeuse, Bellatrix, Ainitak. "Without those names, where would the sky be?"

It was a stupid question, really, thought The New Man. Those stars would simply have other names. Though it did make a point—which The New Man did not want to pursue. Perhaps he was weary of all things Arab, in this hour before dawn. He said to Mafouz, "I don't think I ever saw double stars before…."

Mafouz said, "When I was a psychiatrist—that's what I was—"

"Haziz told me."

Mafouz took that with a little surprise, and a shrug. "I was…intrigued" (he seemed to savor the word) "by double stars, because you are seeing what has been hidden. Hidden…influences. As when one very stable and bright star has a dimmer, erratic companion—that could threaten the stability of another star—or a complex of stars. I saw people were like that; they might seem one type of individual, but after a while, you discover what goes around them and what is not so easy to perceive at first."

In the night, there was a stray glint of light that flickered across Mafouz' eyes. And then another sort of light, as he extracted a pack of cigarettes from his pants and lit one. The flash of the lighter seemed preternaturally vivid. The New Man's nostrils widened at the smell of tobacco.

He felt the Egyptian wanted to fix him too sternly in these considerations. He let his gaze drift over the constellation of the hunter and surrounding stars. The New Man gave an expression of acquiescence to what Mafouz had said; but at any rate, he had to weigh the other's vision. Here, above, was a mirror for the human: the apparent singularity of life broken into disparate parts. Why if he, The New Man, were a star, there would be two stars: one the past, the other—born on September 11, 2001 (born, but not conceived)—of the present. But which was the brighter star others would see first now? Well, Haziz would see the present; his wife, the past. And Wilson might see both; he would cleave the two and know both as one.

And Mafouz showed him Jupiter and Saturn. The two giant worlds were blurred and creamy. Hovering over Jupiter in the eyepiece, Mafouz said, almost scolding, "If it weren't for those lights"—he flicked an arm to the east while remaining focused on the lens—"you'd see the moons."

And when The New Man looked at Saturn, bulging with its rings, Mafouz said, "You can't see the full beauty of that now, either. I am afraid all autumn the sky will be ruined." Here was a man who had accepted the violation of the city's lights; but this, now, was excessive.

And there was Venus, bright, bright Venus, near the sliver of the moon. "A few nights ago they were so close." Mafouz held forefinger and thumb an indiscernible distance apart. He added, "It was the night after the attacks." As if heaven's pairing of the night's brightest worlds had been aftermath to some darkest horror.

Ultimately the Egyptian returned to the constellation of the hunter. "I've missed Orion; so many rich things to see." In the dark, The New Man nodded. "It's gone from the sky by the middle of the spring; only with the end of the summer you see it before dawn." Without the telescope, Mafouz seemed to survey the sky as if this observation were his alone. "I like this hour for the stars. You see what will be coming. In three months the sky as it is now, before dawn, will be the sky you see in the evening after sunset—in December. The stars are this way: the sky before dawn will be the evening sky of the next season." He looked at The New Man as if confessing a deep pleasure.

But the New Man could not respond appreciatively. "I don't want to think of December."

Mafouz smiled—forgivingly? "Of course. Who wants to think of the cold now? Some nights in winter it is too cold to come up here, no matter how I dress. Though usually I manage it. The winter has the best nights for looking at the sky, especially here in the city. So much clearer."

The New Man had an image of Mafouz in the nearing, future cold: his silhouette—a bundled silhouette—joined with the telescope, while to the east the ruins of the World Trade Center would have begun to take on the aspects of history. Would men still be toiling there? Probably, if the accounts he heard were accurate.

And, more importantly, what would the New Man be doing? Where would he be? He feared the unknown of that future, more than the cold.

Or perhaps it was not quite fear, but the knowing—like a runner training for a long distance but only beginning his training—that he could only deal with each immediate day one by one.

As if Mafouz were intuiting The New Man's thoughts not of the future but of the east, he pointed the telescope directly into that vast, sickly glow over lower Manhattan. "Look."

"At what?"

"Even in that you can see stars. Just move the telescope slowly."

And so The New Man saw in his field of view the artificial light that suffused the heavens. It seemed like some primal tension cut through the universe—a dominant energy (the aftermath of another sort of Big Bang) that drowned out everything else. But as he moved the telescope slowly—"More slowly, said Mafouz, "more slowly"—and The New Man's eyes adjusted to these peculiar conditions, he saw, if so faintly, stars here and there.

"You see them?" said Mafouz. "You see them?"

"Yes. But what stars I don't know."

"Doesn't matter. Even through all that, the stars come through."

The New Man kept his eye on this redundant sky as he carefully moved the instrument; and again, as when the Egyptian had enthused about seeing a preview of winter's stars in this end-of-summer predawn, he could not share the other's pleasure. The ubiquity of the stars, their persistence in the sky despite this enormous wash of artificial light, in a sky also filled with smoke and vapors—it made him feel a weariness that nothing in existence could be effaced.

And then there was always the moon. A little higher now, a slip of waning crescent, it was still the brightest thing in the sky and it came into the circle of the lens with enough light to make The New Man squint, not out of need but out of reflex. Under magnification, the dying moon showed a little of its shadows, peaks, valleys and plains. It was a more familiar thing of the heavens than the stars. He drew his eyes from the telescope and looked at it in total, in a more natural way, he thought. Its crescent was like a curved ship of bone, an ancient thing, a vessel with no sailors in an ancient sea now polluted with a modern catastrophe.

Mafouz was also fixed on the object of The New Man's gaze. For a long moment both stared at the waning moon, as if sharing the aspect of a primitive herald—or sign of departure.

The New Man looked at Mafouz. "How long have you been…interested in astronomy?"

"All my life. As a boy I knew the stars like they were a road outside my house. I might have been an astronomer—but I found the mind as interesting. People, I should say." He nodded, as if abruptly coming to a truth. "People are more than the mind."

"Yes," said The New Man, very quietly. Perhaps he would

have had the other pursue that reflection, which seemed behind all this parting of the single lights of double stars and the insistent light where the Towers once stood and the suns of the cosmos that would not be effaced.

But there was another aspect of nature that was inexorable. In the east was the beginning of the next day's light, a light that would drown both the glare of the lights above Ground Zero and the stars above, beyond it. And for The New Man, this as yet faintest of lights put an end to things, that is, this meeting with Mafouz, who had followed The New Man's look and noted dawn's as yet subtle appearance with a bland "Oh—" It was not quite disappointment; it was more the manner of a man who expected such—delays?—in the course of business (or, more precisely, his passions).

It was also the moment for both men to assess the possibility of further meeting. Later the New Man would reflect how easily Mafouz seemed to accept his presence. Perhaps the Egyptian sensed something in this stranger as solitary as himself. The hour, the place, the activity of looking at the stars above a metropolitan area suddenly thinking of apocalypse, made an odd sort of friendliness possible.

"I think I need to sleep a little now," said The New Man. Mafouz nodded, almost as if The New Man had asked for permission to leave. "Thank you for letting me see—all those stars."

"I am up here almost every night…if the sky is clear enough. If you want to look again—"

"Thank you."

It seemed Mafouz would be staying to squeeze the last bit of night from the hour. The New Man left the man and the telescope and the encroaching dawn.

He was thinking that here was another person who knew of his strange presence in the neighborhood. He had intended to lose himself in the anonymous crowd, but felt he stood out— in a crowd becoming less anonymous.

Though as he descended back into the building, The New Man thought: Speaking of strange…what was a retired shrink with a passion for the stars doing in this neighborhood? He would imagine a psychiatrist would have done well enough in Egypt. Why was he not living somewhere…better? Was he connected to Mohammed? To the departed tenant of the apartment? Or was there a more innocent explanation, if one still as mysterious?

When he reached the third floor he hesitated. Should he go to his apartment, or return to Haziz? In another instant he was opening her door. He did not feel "his' apartment enough his to return to it at this sad hour; and then, Haziz might be worried if she awoke and found him gone.

With a silence equal to his leaving her bed not so long ago, he crossed the small dark room and slipped back alongside her and almost immediately—as if with a wave of exhaustion— slept.

He awoke to her flesh in a room that was dark but fully on the edge of light. He had probably slept briefly, but it seemed to him otherwise. He slowly recalled the odd moments up on the roof with Mafouz.

Light crept slowly into the world. He could feel its approach as if it were a large animal, that subtle border of twilight become a creature, short-lived but ever returning. He looked to the closed eyes of Haziz; in that very instant she opened her lids and looked into his eyes. What wordless things, or secrets that could not be shared, swam in both pairs of eyes.

Haziz sighed and said, "It's time to pray."

"It's not dawn yet."

"Soon, soon." They both waited and she said, softly, "Now. Now." It was a little lighter; objects in the room were becoming clear. "The exact time."

"Exact?"

She reached somewhere down on the floor along the bed and brought up Rasil's pants she had been sewing. "Remember, I told you: the white thread. When you can tell it apart from a black thread…it's time for prayer."

He saw the white thread leading from the needle to the awkward form of the little pair of pants.

And she rose from the bed that her faith taught her had been blasphemous and left the room and The New Man, that bed that was still scented with her body, the man that was still scented with her, who had known her weight and her tongue and The New Man heard the murmuring of God's name and the name of God's Prophet and The New Man thought: *Somewhere here is the center of this mystery; the mystery of myself and all things: the destruction of cities and the names we give our hearts.*

24. *Hajji*

He left Haziz' apartment as the dawn took hold, and he took pleasure in the brevity of this trip from bed to bed. Here, going down one floor was simple, peaceful descent. To reach the rooms where he sought sleep again. It seemed for a long time that he had been awake to startling things, then allowed a brief sleep, then had to confront the upended world again, then slept again.

He ignored a hygienic distaste that he was sinking into a bed in which someone else had slept not too long ago, with blankets that another had used. He had the irrational sense that in his new identity he was invulnerable to the past.

Again he slept a little while. He awoke dully. He sat up and looked around him at the apartment. The stark feeling of the sacred or the forlorn was absent. The apartment was even more drab than Haziz', which at least had the grace of her womanly presence. For a moment he considered it was a step up from a prison cell—then laughed mockingly at himself. As if he'd ever been in prison. Perhaps that dream about the FBI had caused him to make that connection; but stretch metaphor all you wanted, this dullness was not Sing Sing.

It was simply that the intensity, the compression of events of the last few days had crashed down upon him. He was exhausted with the struggle of having crossed the most peculiar and bitter of borders. He had escaped the destruction of the Towers and had wound up in the bed of the wife of one of the hijackers...and was now sequestered in a half abandoned building of an Arab quarter in New Jersey.

Come with me to the casaba, he recalled from some old movie.

His sigh was long. A man desperately seeks to...resurrect himself—and only *this* is gained.

He tried to reverse his outlook. *I am alive. I have been given—by chance, what else?—a lovely woman.... I have rediscovered mathematics—*

But was his recent alacrity with the code a true return to an old power? He recalled his youthful ambitions; how he would cleave through the riddle of the Riemann Hypothesis, solve Fermat's Last Theorem—which, after generations, had been solved, in the last decade. Here in his new and strange life he recalled his sudden stab of disappointment when he'd seen the headlines in the *Times* one day. *He* should have done it; it should have been his photograph on that page millions held. Over lunch, he'd lamented—to Wilson, yes, Wilson. The old New Man had gone on for a while, about how he had begun to work out a plan, a course to solve the theorem about a year before going to Vietnam. "Another year or so I would have had it." But then, embarrassed at his youthful, naïve projection of quick success, embarrassed that he had left the game (and perhaps horrified that Vietnam had so defeated him), he'd dropped his sad, self-pitying tale, and Wilson, after a few perfunctory consoling remarks—what was it Wilson had said? Something about—yes: *Like a toss of dice. Life goes one way or another. It's not your fault. You play the role where you are.*

The words came back suddenly, all too clearly to The New Man, and struck him as if they had been said yesterday.

What was that famous remark of Einstein's? God doesn't play dice. Well, something is tossing us about, thought The New Man. And what role was he, The New Man, playing now? Improv?

He opened an eastward facing window. The gentlest wind, a breeze, rather, blew into the apartment the scent of the destroyed Towers. And in the blueness above were streaks of grey: ghosts of that terrible deed. Here was a sky that could present only a sorrow that could not be grasped.

He dressed and left the apartment. His first inclination had been to go up to Haziz, but he had the sense that if he were to be with her too often it would be bad for both of them, at least at this point. He recalled the poignancy of the cries of Rasil in his dream. To love the woman, he had to violate the child's possession of his mother.

Right outside the building he might have stepped into another transformation of his world: he was struck by the extraordinary activity in the debris-strewn lot. There were giant, yellow earth moving machines vivid in their color and which threw rippled shadows over the rubble. They seemed to have just arrived and had swung into the action the moment he had stepped into view, not any sooner—for the racket they made that bright morning would have been heard inside. For The New Man had the feeling—the conviction—that this sudden activity had precisely awaited his entrance, like some furious business in a scene in a play commencing when an actor comes onstage.

Whatever the instigation or reason for what he saw, The New Man gazed upon it with astonishment and a sinking feeling in his stomach. He did not want the busy, obliterating world at his door. Men in hard hats, work clothes, thick work gloves went about their tasks with the strength of those having a precise purpose—and of those who had had a good night's sleep. Unlike The New Man, who felt exhausted—by dreams, memories, double stars, ardor and vast trepidation of the future.

A number of the workmen looked distinctly Middle Eastern. In fact, most did. And it seemed incongruous—though certainly it was the tenor of the times—that the majority of the workers wore American flag decals on their hard hats. As did most of the machinery. It was an emblem that gave further power to the machines.

The lot was certainly being cleared. The New Man did not like it. It seemed that wherever he went, the world followed right upon him. And it was as if something integral to his life were being destroyed. He realized—with ironic amusement—that he had a sort of nostalgia for this area of ruin. In fact, even as he watched, a machine attacked the small valley of debris in which the Double had told The New Man his biography—and in which he, The New Man, had told the Double his.

He forced himself to turn from integral things and pretend this was nothing more than annoying. He had just taken this apartment below Haziz, and now it was obvious there would be a racket here for many days—weeks. It also meant there would be many eyes, to watch him coming and going.

And would there be something built here?

.   .   .

He left the building and the lot. To his surprise he began to notice a number of American flags—in windows, storefronts, on little sticks dangling from stoops and potted plants. Overnight they had appeared, stiff little emblems on everything imaginable. *This* was irony, among these people. Then he thought: isn't that racist, though—"these people"? But you had to grant it was odd.

He walked on, through the flag-strewn streets, as if he were passing through a ceremony.

He found himself outside Mr. Rahman's bookstore. And there, in the corner of the narrow window, was a flag…. It seemed a further challenge to sanity. The New Man had not intended to enter, but he did (what did Wilson say about playing roles?), and saw Mr. Rahman placing a stack of Arabic magazines by the counter.

He appeared to greet The New Man with—was it sympathy? "For some reason I thought you'd come again," said the Iraqi.

The New Man had the quick and quickly discarded thought he might say he was with some publication, assigned to observe a Muslim neighborhood in America after the attacks of Tuesday, but to lie at this point would weary him. And least that sort of lie.

"It's an interesting neighborhood," was what he said.

"Yes, Mr.—?" Mr. Rahman gave a definite pause. He demanded identification.

"Newman. Theodore Newman." The New Man felt uneasy enough with this lie. Though if one chooses a name, is it really a lie?

"Mr. Newman," echoed Mr. Rahman, though with a trace

of—what? Mockery? The New Man thought: He knows—senses—something is wrong.

"So you find it…interesting—here."

"I—"

"And Haziz is interesting, of course."

The New Man felt almost shocked—and, certainly, helpless. Mr. Rahman came to his rescue, in a way. "It is not necessary to say anything. Her husband…he was—difficult. Always vanishing. I don't think she knew where." Thus he might be condescending to Haziz' adultery. Did he know Mohammed was dead? "If you will excuse my curiosity: where did you and she meet?"

The New Man dredged up a sort of suave manner from somewhere inside of his confused, newly created being: "You'll have to asked Haziz." At least he began in a flippant manner, but knew he could not sustain that guise.

Mr. Rahman returned a worldly gesture. "Of course, it is not my—affair, as you say. Or is it the French who say that? Or the English?" And as if dismissing the disparate manner of the disparate West in a way that should leave no disjointed feelings, he shaped the stack of magazines in front of him—The New Man caught the name *Kalifah*—and said, "So…you have been reading your Koran?"

"A little. In a very erratic manner."

"That may be all right at first. Just to get a taste of the waters. If you wish to read it more…intelligently, you may ask my guidance any time you wish."

"Thank you."

"That is a sincere offer." Mr. Rahman gave an expression that said The New Man should be grateful of any such aid.

"I may take you up on it." The New Man fully took in the face before him for perhaps the first time. It did seem sincere, with its calm expression and calm dark eyes. But what did that sincerity disguise? For these long condensed days now, The New Man unconsciously sought meanings behind the apparent.

He considered he might want to ask Mr. Rahman about the Koran not so much for "guidance" but in the manner of an anthropologist who studies a cultural perspective in a native—a displaced native. (Though wasn't The New Man the one truly displaced here?)

Mr. Rahman was saying, "After you know a little more…what you might find interesting is to attend prayers at a mosque. That is the Koran made truly alive. By next year at this time—or sooner—there will be a new mosque only a few blocks from here. Perhaps by then you will be—"

"There's no mosque in this neighborhood?"

"No—Muslim people came fast to this neighborhood. We haven't had time. But of course one does not need a mosque to pray."

The New Man thought of Haziz and Rasil, of the man prostrating himself on the dirty street. "Yes," he said, "I know."

Mr. Rahman went on: "Even your own Bible, I believe it was Paul, the one struck and blinded by God on the road to Damascus, Paul said a place of worship is not made by human hands."

For some reason The New Man did not want Mr. Rahman to know he had little knowledge of what Paul had said. To divert this theological path, he said, "So there's going to be a mosque here soon?"

"Yes. A few blocks away."

Suddenly The New Man had more than a frightening premonition; it verged on a conviction. "Where, exactly?"

Mr. Rahman told him—exactly: so The New Man knew the location of this new Islamic house of worship was the lot right next to The New Man's new home. His face must have conveyed how this hit him. Mr. Rahman asked, "Is there something wrong, Mr. Newman?"

"No, No." After a pause he said, "It's the smell of that burning from the city. Sometimes I can't breathe."

Mr. Rahman wasn't sure if he should believe this. "Yes, yes, it's bad. Though inside here it's usually…. But it will clear."

As quickly and as naturally as he could, The New Man withdrew from the bookshop with this sudden, incredible knowledge. And then was halted in his tracks by the apparition of the Double, right outside the honey shop, setting up a display of small American flags that stiffly stuck out from wooden sticks. The Double gave The New Man a mocking smile and held out one of the flags to him. "For America."

Stunned, The New Man took the flag. It was the size of his hand, of cheap material. The wood was thin and nearly weightless.

"People want these now," he heard the Double say with a laugh.

The New Man noted a larger American flag in the window of the honey shop—and, through the etherealness that glass gives, from inside the shop, as if just across the border of different world, the other Mr. Rahman waved at The New Man, who returned no greeting at all, but simply stared.

"You can have that," said the Double. "No price."

It was too bizarre. The spitting image of Osama bin Laden selling American flags. The New Man had to jolt himself. He returned to something a little less surreal. "Have you seen Wilson?" he asked. And was astounded with himself he'd actually said that.

This actually gave the Double pause. The mocking smile vanished; the mirror-terrorist frowned. "You told me he was dead." And when The New Man didn't answer, said, "But people believe you are dead."

"He should be dead…I don't know," said The New Man, as if in numb apology. (*Yes, just as Haziz' husband should be dead,* he thought.) Now he was indeed smelling the scent of destruction from across the river.

The Double spoke with cautious anger. "If he is not…we will see him."

The New Man could at least fake irony. "We?"

"You—me." The smile returned to the Double—though it was tenuous and wary: the presentation of a disguise. He said, "So you are staying here."

Why deny it? "Until—"

"You are here. That is enough for the future."

Those two statements hit The New Man like a blow of truth. The two men stared at each other. They were quiet for a long moment as an old couple passed by, giving squinting, suspicious glances at the display of flags. The man wore a turban, the woman was in a long flowing garment, her head covered. Had they uprooted themselves at this advanced time in their lives to come here, half way around the world? At any rate, this plain vision of age made The New Man uneasy. He was not young. What *was* his future?

The New Man said to the Double, "What will you get—from anything?"

"Get?" Perhaps the Double could not conceive of himself as possessing anything.

So The New Man offered: "Dope, I guess."

"Dope?"

"You know what I mean."

"You are American: you make things narrow."

"What else, then?"

"That cannot be said to you."

"You'll be arrested—for just being what you look."

"Not here."

"Is 'here' that safe?"

"I am safer than you."

Again there was silence as both looked at each other with the honesty of enemies—enemies by something no more profound than chance, bearing an enmity that could disguise an involuntary comradeship each man might be afraid to consider.

The New Man said, "This is not the end."

The Double shrugged. "Whenever that comes, it comes."

The New Man blinked, turned from the Double and walked on. The Double called out, but the word or words were foreign.

As he crossed the street, The New Man wondered why he did not feel it, well, monumental to have met the double of UBL?

He continued down the block; but in another moment he ran into Mafouz.

The New Man was surprised. Perhaps he had already regulated the Egyptian to the realm of the building, the rooftop—and, also, dark hours. And Mafouz did seem out of place. He appeared uneasy to be moving about at street level; he had the pained look of a weariness he abruptly explained. After a bland "Hello," he said, "I almost did not recognize you. I am tired. Could not sleep." His eyes crouched painfully in the light. It was a sort of déjà vu, with Mafouz taking The New Man's introduction from only a few hours ago on the predawn roof. It was then The New Man thought they had not asked each other's name during that time at the telescope, below the redundant heavens and the violation of light from the destruction of the Towers. And so The New Man began to say, awkwardly still, his "new" name, but Mafouz spoke over him— almost sharply with an odd energy that overrode weariness: "You know him?"

The New Man was bewildered a moment. Then he realized. He turned—it was a rhetorical movement. He did not need to see the Double again, through some distance and on the other side of the street, to say, "You mean the one who looks like—?" He paused before speaking the name, which Mafouz too perhaps did not want to hear.

"He may be crazy," said the Egyptian, flatly. He implied this was a warning The New Man would be foolish to ignore.

And if the Egyptian had said "may," this sounded more ominous than if Mafouz had given a judgement without qualification. "What do you mean?" asked The New Man.

Mafouz did not answer right away. The two men saw the Double rearranging the little stand with its small American flags. Mafouz indicated the flag in The New Man's hand. "One of his gifts?"

The New Man raised the flag before his own eyes, as if only now aware he held it. Mafouz said. "What has he told you?"

The New Man looked back into the dark eyes—yes, they did look tired. The eyes that had easily located and discerned so much of the heavens seemed powerless in the nature of this opposite hour. And the Egyptian's clothes, which had appeared crisp and clean in the dim, warm air of the roof, now seemed burdened with a vague dirt in this light of day. "Told me…?" The New Man began, cautiously.

"Yes. You seem friendly with him." The Egyptian might have been urging The New Man into an idiot's simple comprehension. The insinuation was hissed with a proximity that carried on the breath the aftermath of a cigarette.

The New Man found himself resenting the other's manner. "He's from Afghanistan." Mafouz blinked, mockingly it seemed, at this statement of geography. More pertinently, The New Man added, "He's…a double."

With that, Mafouz widened his eyes and gave a scornful gesture. "And he walks around here?"

The New Man took the Egyptian's tact, avoiding the absurdity the other had presented and which he himself had thought. He said, "You've talked to him?"

Mafouz ran a hand slowly down one side of his face: a sleepy man forcing himself to face a fact. "A little—he's in the neighborhood." He wanted to explain any guilt by association. "A little…enough to—doubt." He added quickly: "Everything he says can't be trusted."

"But some things can?"

There was an expression in Mafouz' eyes and a wave of his hand that said, "Yes, I suppose *some* things…." He reached into his pocket and extracted a flattened pack of Camel cigarettes. There was the one-humped beast backdropped by pyramids and desert trees. "Empty," said Mafouz to himself with dissatisfaction, and made as if to toss the pack on the street—but, perhaps simply because another looked on, thrust it back into his pocket.

Then both men were again diverted by the Double at his little stand. Another couple had paused before the small display of flags: a dark haired man in a loose flowing shirt and a woman, again with a head covering. The man gave the Double a broad smile and fished about his garments for money. Through the distance The New Man caught the glint of a coin passing from buyer to the seller. It was a swift, jarring signal from the sun. The New Man found himself saying, "There can't be much profit in that."

"What?" said Mafouz.

The New Man twisted his flag in the air. "This." But then he looked at the object as if dumbfounded, as if he had stated there was something intrinsically worthless in the substance for which this symbol stood.

Mafouz was saying, "What if he is mad. I have seen it before."

"What before?" The New Man looked at the tired face, which paused before speaking and blinked once more.

"Delusions," said Mafouz earnestly.

"So bin Laden didn't pick him as his mirror?"

The name of the Islamic avenger seemed to warn Mafouz that he should proceed carefully. He peered intensely into the New Man's own cautious eyes. "People take some truth; they make their own story."

"Yes, that's true," said The New Man, perhaps thinking of his own "story."

Mafouz didn't seem to regard The New Man's comment—which, after all, had been half mumbled. "He could be like a person looking like your Elvis. So he becomes—"

The New Man had to smile. "Not Elvis but a double."

Mafouz was not smiling, but quite serious. "Every man pursues fantasies his own way." Though there was the question: was the psychiatrist transferring the method of his own passage to another?

Meanwhile, once more since he had escaped from the Towers, The New Man felt himself in a fantasy. He said, "He knows things, though."

"What things?"

"I can't say now."

Mafouz looked at The New Man as if the latter were indeed laboring in his own fantasy. "And there will be a time when you can say?"

The New Man couldn't quite answer. And there was the distraction of further activity at the flag stand. A group of boys had stopped before the Double. They were smiling and laughing, jabbering and reaching out. Their bobbing faces appeared linked to the impetus of one organism. The Double was returning his own smile. He handed out a small flag to each reaching hand and waved away the offerings of coins from some of those hands. The organism of boys bolted off, randomly decorated by repetitions of the tri-colored flag. The Double beamed at their eagerness and, perhaps, his own generosity.

Mafouz and The New Man were silent for several seconds. It hit The New Man as if he had forgotten: the Double knew that "Newman" had been someone else. Why, Oh God, had he told him that? Of course, it had been the circumstance. Caught in the surreality of the meeting, this first entry into the maze via the cipher, the situation in the lot of ruin had given The New Man the illusion of the forced freedom of a dream. So he had told the Double his "truth"; while after a dream he had told Haziz, with sudden anguish—an anguish that had been released by his wife's reappearance on TV, not the weirdness of the dream.

Did Mafouz threaten to become a third confidante? The New Man stared at this slim, tired Egyptian. And resented that he had run into him twice in the space of a few hours.

In answer to the Egyptian's question concerning time and revelations, The New Man finally said, "I don't know." Mafouz blinked as if he could not recall just what the other was responding to; then he gave a long breath that showed he understood. The New Man was going on: "Anyway, for now, I believe him. At least, the large picture, if not all of the details." He might have been declaring himself for a faith.

"Ah, the large picture." It was a phrase that seemed to give Mafouz a sort of peace. Or at least something with which he could empathize. His face relaxed into a peculiar irony. The astronomer was a man who viewed "the large picture" night after night; and the shrink was someone who saw something both large and petty in every psyche.

Such as the Double's—who, if he had not already noted The New Man and Mafouz gathered in chance conversation, now did. Across the distance of the street he smiled and waved. The New Man gave a helpless gesture; the Egyptian seemed to bite his lip. He said, "I need to get some sleep. I've been walking to get tired." He involuntarily crunched the depleted pack of cigarettes in his pants. The Double waved a flag. Mafouz winced. "I think I'm tired now."

But if he sought sleep in his own bed, he abruptly he walked on, going in the opposite direction of the building. Perhaps he knew some shortcut.

As he watched Mafouz depart, The New Man thought of `those scattered stars, drowned in the violation of the lights from Ground Zero. But, speaking of fantasy, in this harsh light of day, those lights of heaven seemed of some inner, dreamwork invention.

Mafouz was out of sight. The New Man thought of more immediate beings. W*as* the Double crazy? But the image of the terrorist had come to the lot because of Wilson's message; it wasn't the Double's imagination. Still, the man could be mad to a large degree.... A caravaner of poppy, a double of bin Laden—wasn't there madness in that life alone? Yes, what if the Double were truthful *and* also mad? A sort of freaked out, renegade mirror of UBL?

Simultaneously, as if intuitively cued, The New Man and the Double waved to each other; they were free of the unbalancing presence of the Egyptian. Through the distance of the street, the two were somehow connected. There was a resigned smile from The New Man.

And Mr. Newman walked on. He had to conclude that on this edge they all skirted—the Double, the Rahmans, Mafouz, Haziz and the departed husband and, of course, himself—on this edge, a sort of madness may be absolutely necessary to continue, to keep balanced on the sharp border, a madness that was an extraordinary complementarity of self-deception and brutal assessment.

For on either side of that border, should balance fail, lay a further, more terrible madness.

No, he said to himself as he walked on, *I can't be that mad. I am seeing some things clearly. At least some.*

.   .   .

The sun rose higher; the day was brighter, harsher. It was a brightness that would hide nothing of this horrible new world.

The flag of the United States of America had sprouted up everywhere. The red, white and blue rectangles were in windows, on vehicles and in the waving hands of children, an emblem whose meaning they could not understand. It seemed, in fact, the first day since that awe-filled Tuesday that The New Man saw many children at play outside. In one small group, a boy—about ten—darted about with a flag, while another darting boy, his hands flung out like a cross, made zooming airplane noises and chased after the other with the flag. His dark eyes were gleaming with the confidence of success. The New Man had the pang of unpleasant recollection: those children the other day in the park.... After a few moments of swift, agile darting, executed with the spontaneous energy of the young, the "airplane" boy grasped the "flag" boy—who laughed, mocked a stagger, and let the flag fall to the ground, as he made the exaggerated sounds of an explosion and fluttered upward and downward with his hands, apparently mimicking flame. Or, more unconsciously, the very psyche of destruction. There was a cruel grace to his movements; a grace that came from cruelty.

As if encircling a victim they had bullied, the children stood about the fallen flag, laughing.

If children mocked a real tragedy with the symbol of its victim, perhaps that was not so odd. But what was the truth of these adults who sported and displayed Old Glory? Perhaps, The New Man had the sudden thought, they were like a people who needed to bear this emblem on their artifacts and dwellings and person as a visceral rite. They needed these renderings of the flag the way primitive people wore the masks of an animal or painted that animal on cave walls, shields and masks: to ensure they'd capture their prey.

Had the prey been captured? Had it been devoured?

The New Man almost stopped short. There was reality here, with this difference: if "primitives" used their prey for sustenance, the "prey" of the people here certainly wasn't sustenance. Though some might have said America had to be hunted down in order that they, the hungry hunters, could live as they were supposed to live—

The New Man drew his hands across his forehead. He was giving too much meaning to all of this. Here, simply, was human madness, mockery, and nastiness: the glee of kicking the fallen.

And, perhaps, a surreal empathy? He stopped by a vendor of flags of various sizes spread out on a blanketed table. The vendor appeared to be Indian. Squinting and smiling in the warm light, he said something to The New Man and held out a flag on a thin stick. He nodded quickly in the manner of someone sharing a thing necessary and good with a stranger whose people had been wounded. As if reacting to a stimulus, The New Man fished in his pocket for money, and came up with a collection of coins. He could return to the vendor nothing of the manner he had been extended. The New Man paid the vendor a dollar for this cheap flag and heard the plunk of coins (with the jumbled faces of Jefferson, FDR and Washington) being secreted away as he walked on—carrying and continuing to see the proliferation of the symbol he had perhaps never considered so vividly, and which had never impressed him with the potency it did now. An old thing had been made desirable with the disaster of Tuesday; and it was making money. The

New Man thought of the Double and the flag, of drugs and terrorists.

There was a little rise at the corner of one street, and as he looked down the long avenue, the scattering of bright new American flags was like the evidence of a new flesh, or a new, interior heart that marked both The New Man and the people of this neighborhood. And the people that moved here were evidence of a changed life; an old life that had awaited this change, this metamorphosis. It was a transformation that was not limited to the vista here. *We have entered them and they have entered us,* he thought. But could he really consider himself part of any "us"?

At any rate, his brief time since the disaster of the Towers had brought him into another country, another world.

I can't go back now, he thought. *I can't return to where I've been.* And abruptly there was the pain of the familiar, the longing of the refugee—for his distant wife, his college age children; for the monotony of that other life, the job, the suburbs—the role. Yes, as Wilson had said....

He was thinking about the summer sky settled over the swimming pool in his yard. In early June he had taken a helicopter ride across Long Island into the city—on a day off, his employer had called him about the necessity of attending a sudden meeting. He had been surprised—though he should not have been—at the many swimming pools the copter passed over: circles, ovals and rectangles of water reflecting their safe and bordered mirrors of the sky up to the casual study of his eyes. Those pools were still there—if a number had been drained between Labor Day and now, but their *continuance* remained; though those reflecting mirrors of water now seemed to The New Man as lovely—and naive?—remnants of a long ago world.

Reaching Manhattan, the copter had circled the southern end of the island. The New Man recalled, with enormous nostalgia, the Statue of Liberty, the shining Towers—that seemed to grow even taller as the copter descended to the heliport by the water.

But had he now "returned" to something he had been before all that—before, even Vietnam? Though he could not simply consider himself the mathematical prodigy anymore. If in those pre-apocalypse days he had been adept at the purity of mathematics, now he had used number to upend his very life. To be more accurate it had seemed numbers had used *him*, not the other way around—and yet.... Perhaps one does create one's destiny, was his stray and weary thought.

He noted, in the distance, in between buildings, a flag flying at half-staff, flapping languorously in semi-silhouette against a sky that would soon have the cast of autumn. There must be some official building there, he thought—an outpost in an uneasy frontier. Probably just a post office. Against the bright blue the flag might have been the sign of an indomitable spirit, the ineffable spirit of a nation, an ideal—or some signal of farewell, an acknowledgement of passage, leave-taking—or failure.

Farewell. The New Man had made his unvoiced farewells. But did he know exactly what he had bid farewell to? He understood its essence was a greater—and even more mysterious—thing than his longing for the habit of family and the reflection of a suburban sky in a swimming pool.

He stopped somewhat down the block, watching from a distance the machinery and its operators clear the lot. So here at the address he had arrived at using the mirroring infinity of fractals to pierce a cipher, with the surreal help of the imprint of a phone number, this address where he had met the Double and where Haziz had rescued him, was to be the address of the God of the men who had brought the catastrophe that had given him his new and inexplicable life. The New Man considered he was a slave in a drama of divine destiny (or simply a destiny of belief), and that his spirit was being wrung through by a terrifying surreality into a purity that might possibly destroy him.

Four workers seemed to be incongruously clearing an area of rubble by hand. In their hardhats, work clothes and gloves, they appeared oddly banished from the efficacy of their machines. Abruptly The New Man was struck with a creeping remembrance: the four men who had attacked him (and the Double) in this very lot. But with distance and the covering of their heads, The New Man could not be sure. Though his gut was sure, pronged by the pang of instinct.

The men were forming a large pile of debris, roughly triangular in shape, with a crude apex—and forming it with great effort; the chunks they were lifting were large and certainly heavy; often two of them were needed to move one. It seemed ridiculous they were doing this without mechanical help. The triangle of debris grew as tall as a man. It seemed some primitive structure of worship, perhaps foreshadowing the mosque soon to be built here.

One of the four climbed up the small pile and stood on its irregular apex, as if enacting a statement of some achievement. He turned his body slowly, carefully, seeming to survey the lot. The next moment he stretched out his arms to the side, in the manner of a man welcoming some unseen gift—or as if imitating wings. But this expansiveness threw him off balance; he staggered and, rather than fall, stumbled down the rough, small hillside. The body language of his companions suggested laughter.

In another instant, one of the great machines rumbled over; with a loud noise, it scooped the pile of debris up into the air. The four men darted back—they seemed surprised, even afraid. The New Man watched that abrupt ascent effected by machine; the robotic arm swiveled and deposited its load into a dump truck that had backed into the lot. There appeared—or did The New Man imagine it?—some sort of cries of satisfaction from the four men, a triumphant gesturing; their fears seemed to have been transformed.

"Erasing evidence," The New Man said to himself.

The four men then drifted separately into the larger group of workers, whose concentrations and patterns of placement changed like a swarm. The New Man tried to follow two of the workers (his mathematical mind telling him two would be easier than four) in this swift school of almost identical fish, but soon he could not pick out which of the workers had been among the four.

But *were* they the four? Perhaps he had been drawn to them only by their grouping of number. Fantasy through mathematics. Yet the presence of the four fit perfectly in all this. Once his attackers, and, now, the builders of a mosque. Well, how many sinners of equal venality and brutality had been among the builders of the Old World's reverential, monumental, God-fearing cathedrals?

The New Man tried to imagine the geometrical solemnity of a mosque in this space—where, just as across the river, men worked in rubble. Of course, here the rubble had not come from violence, but time and neglect. Though those forces may be the more thorough violence: inexorable if subtle.

He wondered, when the shadow of that house of worship would be cast upon the building in which he had sought refuge, if he would still be here.

He climbed the two flights of stairs to his apartment. There was a quiet inside the building, a silence that somehow kept its hold despite the noise of the machinery that came in from outside—as if it were a silence that could not be invaded, a silence that could exist alongside noise, apart from it.

In a dingy room he looked out the window that looked out upon the lot, the window that looked toward Mecca and the smoking remnants of the Towers. If this were a new vista, it was itself undergoing change.

Desultorily he took up the Koran. Neither afraid of nor steeled against its piety and warnings, he read here and there, without any verse catching his attention. Again, he may have been looking for the tea leaves of prophecy.

And then he read: "It is not the purpose of Allah to leave you in your present state till He shall separate the wicked from the good. And it is not the purpose of Allah to let you know the unseen. But Allah chooseth his messengers when he will…." Surah III, verse 179.

The New Man put down the Koran. He was thoughtless for a while. The muffled noise outside occurred in another world. When his consciousness returned to something nameable, his eyes rested on a phone he had not noticed before. It was somewhat of an antique: an old, black, rotary dial. Would he get a phone bill here? Would it be addressed to Theodore Newman?

He leaned over the phone, peered at it closely. Just above the dull metal of the dial was a strip of plastic, yellowed with time. It obscured but did not efface a faded number. The New Man squinted at these seven figures; it took a moment to realize they comprised the number he had found on the impress of the pad in Ahmed's motel.

He hissed out a helpless, anguished "Oh, God—" This soft, exhaling despair was further passage into the labyrinth. He had reached another impossible corner of the maze. So in this very room the phone had rung when he had dialed it from the motel. As if—as if The New Man of the past had been trying (no matter how unknowingly) to reach The New Man of the future, the very near future. Had Haziz, upstairs, heard its faint ring, and uneasily intuited it as a summons? Involuntarily, The New Man picked up the phone and pressed the receiver to his ear. But there was only the dial tone, like the low roar of a seashell, cast ashore from a speechless sea, denying him any message to himself. Slowly—as if to do it swiftly would result in something terrible—he returned the receiver to its cradle.

How could so many impossible things be true?

He rubbed his eyes. Once more he experienced defeat by reality. When his vision was freed of his hands, his eyes again took in the activity of the lot. He raised the window; not only did the sounds of that activity increase, but the spectacle of it, uninterrupted by dirty glass, became more vivid. The bright sun glinted off the machines that moved with rough purpose over the area. The men with their flag-decaled hard hats seemed a tribe bearing the mark of their totem. But did they believe in it? Though they called out and gestured with the confidence of some sort of faith. It was like the call to prayer he heard on the streets. But *was* God at the center of this? He thought of the bookseller's remark, about Paul being blinded on the road to Damascus and in that dark hearing only the word of the divine. The New Man thought himself blinded, but receiving no clear word. He wondered if there were indeed a God behind the God we think we know, the God Haziz imagined; and he tried to call it to him (or at least to spy it), in the recollection of the warmth and weight and movement of her flesh. He said to that God—or the bright, hot end of summer air: "I'm here—what's the deal?" Only the wordless roar spreading outward from the lot, of machinery laced with the calls of the workers, was returned to him. This was the immemorial din of humanity and its artifacts. A cacophony that sustained the species and deafened it. Against that wordlessness was the weight of the Book of the Prophet and the promise of the body of the woman above him.

—Autumn, 2001

The face in the mirror won't stop

—Jim Morrison

www.ingramcontent.com/pod-product-compliance
Lightning Source LLC
Chambersburg PA
CBHW061128200626
46817CB00016B/384

* 9 7 8 0 9 9 9 9 0 3 8 0 3 *